SMALL SILENT THINGS

SMALL

SILENT

THINGS

a novel

ROBIN PAGE

HARPER PERENNIAL

NEW YORK • LONDON • TORONTO • SYDNEY • NEW DELHI • AUCKLAND

HARPER ⬤ PERENNIAL

This is a work of fiction. Names, characters, places, and incidents are products of the author's imagination or are used fictitiously and are not to be construed as real. Any resemblance to actual events, locales, organizations, or persons, living or dead, is entirely coincidental.

P.S.™ is a trademark of HarperCollins Publishers.

HarperCollins books may be purchased for educational, business, or sales promotional use. For information, please email the Special Markets Department at SPsales@harpercollins.com.

FIRST EDITION

Designed by Jamie Lynn Kerner

Library of Congress Cataloging-in-Publication Data has been applied for.

ISBN 978-0-06-287923-3 (pbk.)

19 20 21 22 23   LSC   10 9 8 7 6 5 4 3 2 1

For, my love, John Beran, and also in memory of my brother, Rick Page

PART I

What is the source of our first suffering? It lies in the fact that we hesitated to speak . . . It was born in the moments when we accumulated silent things within us.

—GASTON BACHELARD

JOCELYN

AND SO, GLADYS IS DEAD.

Wishes in bunk beds or on the number 17 bus, a prayer at church unanswered. As a girl, she blows out the candles, tries so hard, but in the morning, the menthol Newports are still burning. Her sister, Ycidra, is making breakfast. An extension cord lays limp as a dead snake on a chair back, just waiting to come to life. Jocelyn's mother is still alive.

Palm a kiss on the roof of a car then, racing through a tunnel, eyes closed tight, hands held—a chain of sister, sister, brother, for good luck: *We wish that Gladys was dead.* But nothing.

And now, all these years later (and yet all of a sudden), she *is* dead—her head in an oven, the inevitable snore. The policeman speaks of minutes too late, of next of kin, of only she.

"I see," Jocelyn says, and grief, surprising and heavy, fills her.

"It happened," the policeman says, "just this morning."

Jocelyn is silent, picturing the scene. Even from the coast of California, after more than twenty years, it comes clear: the Winton Terrace government housing, the mustard-colored stove, mice feces in the cereal cupboards. Cirrhosis makes the stomach bloat.

"Are you there?" the policeman's voice asks, coming through the receiver, but how to answer that?

She places the phone down. She walks into her vast living room. She sits and runs a flat hand along the white suede of the couch. She tells the girl she is, to begin now, to see the death for what it is: clemency, light. She speaks her sister's name and then her brother's. The names of the dead like a prayer for strength. *Begin*, she says. *It is safe to begin.*

She looks at the ocean from her living room, wonders as she often does, *How did I get here, from there? How can I fit in a place like this?*

When her husband comes into the room, he asks her what is wrong. *My mother is dead*, she wants to say, but she is unable to speak. *It's something I've always wanted.*

HER MOTHER'S DEATH DOES NOT CAPSIZE HER. INSTEAD, IT CREATES A subtle seeping. She is like a rowboat with a tiny hole. She is able to get dressed most days, to make herself clean, but an opening, no matter how small, lets things in. There are glimpses, blurred pictures of history, images she does not want to see, hasn't seen in such a long time. The death is not the thing, but instead the narrow window.

Her husband catches her taking a toothbrush to the minute stains in the Waterworks tile of their brand-new bathroom. While he is away at work, she hires men to paint freshly painted walls. He notices. He worries. He tells her it can't happen again. She has to keep it together. *We have a child now*, he reminds her. *Lucy.*

"Yes," she says. "I'm okay." But a sound, her child voice, a beg, fills a slit. She tries to shake it away.

"Do you want to go to the funeral?" he asks her. "Will that make it better?"

She stands beside him blinking. The visions that abide around her mother's casket are not good. They are unruly. They are fingers in decomposing flesh, a body lifted out of the earth and stomped on.

"No," she says. "No."

At school drop-off, her daughter, Lucy, stares at her as she cries, as if she is some strange creature on exhibition, a fetus in the murky waters of a pickling jar. Jocelyn's face is hot with tears. She avoids her friend Maud. She has a headache from not sleeping. When the car comes to a complete stop, Lucy undoes her seat belt and hops out of her booster seat. She reaches into the front seat and retrieves a tissue from the luxury car's glove box. She blots both of Jocelyn's eyes gently. She is a little adult, ministering to her, although only six years old.

Lucy turns to get her unicorn backpack from the car's back seat, and then kisses Jocelyn's cheek.

"Don't be sad, Mama. Papa says everything always gets better. Why are you sad?"

"I don't know," Jocelyn says, because she doesn't. Gladys dead is a good thing. She reaches back to hold her lovely daughter. "It is something I've wanted for a long time, but now I just feel sad about it." She does not say, *It is making me remember. It is making me hear her again.*

"Would you like my Goo Bear?" Lucy asks, pointing to a bedraggled-looking stuffed polar bear that she has managed to strap into the seat beside her. "He'll be lonely today without me, Mama. He'll help."

Lucy hands the bear to Jocelyn.

"Thank you," Jocelyn says, and runs her fingers through her daughter's wonderful hair, making it neat. "I'll pick you up, sweetheart. I would never forget you. Don't you worry. I'll do better."

Lucy giggles. "I'm not worried, Mama. Worried about what?"

CHAPTER ONE

JOCELYN

1

SHE REMEMBERS HER PAJAMAS. YELLOW WITH THE FEET CUT OUT. HER family was poor. They were all poor. She didn't know how poor at the time, but she knows it now when she sees her daughter's pajamas. The feet are intact. The pajamas are stacked high in Lucy's walk-in closet.

"We'll just cut them out then," Gladys would say. "They'll last ya another year."

She tries not to think about it. The voices. The cold floors. His leather shoes. Sometimes she worries that she might not be remembering correctly. Her memory isn't exactly complete. It's as if the girl she used to be is really a different girl with separate memories. She remembers, for example, taking a boy's virginity, but not his name. She remembers having sex with an ecstasy dealer, but not what he looked like. Is that something normal people forget?

It was a small room. She knows her own responsibility. She hasn't forgotten that.

"I am a criminal," she says to the therapist—a Dr. Bruce.

Her husband, Conrad, has made the appointment. *Your mother is dead*, he reminds her, *you have to deal with this*, a fishhook snagging her back to the past. And inside, she wonders, Will he be arrested if she tells the therapist? Is there a legal obligation? Is there a statute of limitations? He is an old man now, but something in her is still afraid to put him in jail.

"I should have said something," she says.

"Maybe," the therapist says.

"I should have done something," she repeats, adamant.

Her whole body is erect with rage on the plush couch. There is a kind of peace in the hatred she feels for herself.

"You shouldn't have been put in the position," the therapist says. "You were a child."

There is a shift in the room like the movement of clouds. The sudden silence is a presence she can feel. She is stunned. It is as if someone has slapped her flat and hard across the face. Without meaning to, she begins to weep. She is afraid that she will not be able to stop in time to pick Lucy up from school. *You shouldn't have been put in the position.* The thought has never crossed her mind.

"I can prescribe something," the therapist says, handing her a box of tissues. "Your mother's death will take some time to work through."

"No," Jocelyn says. She will force the window shut. No drugs. "I don't believe in antidepressants."

"It's going to get worse before it gets better. You'll have to do *something*. Do you exercise? Do you run? Yoga's good. Church?"

Yoga. Running. She can't imagine it. Church is laughable. *When I was a kid, the minister tried to fuck me*, she wants to say, but this woman is such a stranger.

"I used to play tennis," she says. "I mean before my daughter Lucy was born."

The therapist writes something in her book. "Why not go back to it? Just try it. You need an outlet, a healthy one. You'll have to come back here once a week, maybe more. Do you understand?"

"I do," Jocelyn says, wiping away her tears. *You must go*, her husband says. *You cannot fall apart. Lucy.*

"Call me if you need to talk." The therapist looks at the clock.

Jocelyn stands up, goes to the door. She tries to open it, but it is locked. Panic moves through her. She pulls and pulls on the doorknob. She is in her childhood closet again. The lock clicks, a smoky coat with shoulder pads, the floor that smells like cat pee. The starved cat. All life a thin reed. Her mother had gold platform shoes.

The therapist touches her shoulder gently, unlocks the door, quieting her. "It's to keep us safe," she says. "I don't want anyone coming in here."

"Keep the crazies out," Jocelyn says, forcing a smile.

"Exactly."

FROM AFAR THEY LOOK LIKE TEENAGERS, NOT WOMEN IN THEIR FORTIES—firm breasts, tight tank tops, short skirts that are as white as wedding cake icing. The tennis shoes they wear are rainbow colored, grape purple, fuchsia pink, lime green. The colors are emphatic against the private school's lush lawn. Many of them have high blonde ponytails. Six-year-olds play tag at their feet, and nannies chase them. The mothers in their new outfits look on. Lucy drops Jocelyn's hand and runs to play with her school friends.

Jocelyn feels relieved when she sees Maud standing just at the front fountain. She is among the group of women. She is stylish in a navy-blue lace shirt with a matching pleated skirt. Jocelyn is grateful to Maud for inviting her to play with them. She compares herself with Maud briefly, because women do that. She knows that she is pretty and being pretty always helps. It is a way to get things, to make friends, a family. But as she moves closer to the crowd of women in front of her, she sees that she has never had this level of competition. Every woman is like a model out of an ad. White, tall, slim. She is not tall. She is not white. She is black, but not obviously so. Where are you from? people ask her, meaning, What color are you? Even other black women aren't always sure. Maud is the only other brunette besides her.

"Jocelyn!" Maud shrieks when she sees her, excitement in her voice. "You look great. You look fantastic. God, I'm so glad you're coming."

Jocelyn smiles. Forces a confident expression, hugs Maud. She looks intently for Lucy. *I have to keep an eye,* she thinks. *I will protect you.*

"Let me introduce you," Maud says, and then the introductions, all around.

The faces are older up close. Lines present. Unlifted jowls. Botoxed foreheads unmoving.

The women seem nice, but she can tell they are sizing her up: How old is she? Has she had work done? What about her clothes?

"Let's get the kids into school and then carpool," Maud says. "I'll tell Kate that we're partners. I mean just to begin with, so you won't be nervous."

Jocelyn has had her hair straightened, her racquet restrung. A new bag from Stella McCartney for her gear. She decides to be all in. Maud is so nice.

"I'm not nervous," she says, smiling her best smile. She is very nervous. "I'm ready to kick butt."

The women like this and titter.

"You'll love our coach," Erica says, looking her up and down.

"I bet," Jocelyn says. "She seemed really nice on the phone."

"Live Ball," Theresa says. "It's the best."

LIVE BALL GOES VERY WELL, ALTHOUGH TENNIS ISN'T EXACTLY LIKE RIDING a bicycle. She is okay, but out of practice. The pro welcomes her with feeds that are easier. They have a higher bounce. It's discreet. Jocelyn knows enough to make sure to put some good shots away, to move a few of the women around. Being in a group of women is always about subtle power.

She isn't the best there, but she isn't the worst either. Some of the women seem already to be vying to partner with her, assessing her skills, asking her availability. The coach is excellent. Her name is Kate. She is a blonde beauty with green eyes. Jocelyn tries not to stare.

When it is over, Jocelyn bends from the waist to pick up her bag. She feels infinitely flexible. She is aware of her skirt, the length, just cresting below her rear, how young she feels after the drill, how alive. Nothing negative enters her brain: not Gladys dying, not Winton Terrace. There is just the black sheen of an un-lit window.

"Let's get lunch," Maud says. "You were great."

"Let's," Jocelyn says.

They have reached the gate when the coach calls to her. She turns. Kate is smiling—white, wonderful teeth. The blonde hair is in a braided bun. It is as thick as a man's fist. "You're a lot better than you said you were on the phone," she says.

Jocelyn feels herself blushing. "Thanks," she says.

"Are you coming back again?" the coach asks. "Did you have a good time?"

Jocelyn feels as if she is being asked on a date.

"She'll be back," Maud says. "Don't worry."

"I wasn't worried," Kate says, and a little thrill goes down Jocelyn's spine.

CHAPTER TWO

SIMON

1

HE IS IN HIS NEW PENTHOUSE CONDO BY THE SEA. BUT AT FIRST, UPON waking, he does not know this. There is the pygmy, as there always is—his image. Simon knows he is not real. A squat black body. His penis much larger than Simon would have guessed. Hutu, Tutsi, Twa—these are the ethnic categories to fit into. There is his dead wife too. Vestine. Serious Vestine. *My one*, he thinks. *My only.*

He knows better than to stand too quickly. He is used to this—the hallucinations, the living dreams—all consequences of trauma. He is usually not unnerved by it, but today something is different, some element is off. There is a voice in the room today, a new one, and because he cannot locate it, he is alarmed by it. He reaches up to tap his pocket, trying to ground himself. The letter is there.

Papa? Papa? the voice says, and he thinks in a dizzying way, Could it be her come to see me? Impossible, he reminds himself. "She is gone," he says out loud. The muddy swamp is gone. The terraced mountain down which they fled is gone too. He is the thing left.

He sits up when the voice calls *Papa* again, because suddenly he is certain it *is* her. It *must* be her. Who else would call him Papa?

The room is dark except the sun-lit edge of the shade. It is difficult to see, but he is trying. He has to locate the source of the voice: *Papa, Papa*, now more like a song. Less determined, dreamy even. He waits. So still. Be still, they said to her, but how do you keep a child still? He blinks, searching.

He is almost over his grogginess, almost stabilized. Focusing on the small things in the room helps. He can tell now that the voice is not in the room at all, but instead is coming from the exterior hallway. But could she be? Is it because of the letter? Too old to say Papa, and of course not possible, but possible. Not likely though. Would she come without invitation? It *is* because of the letter, but that doesn't make sense. He has not answered her yet.

He does not stand up, but stays, sitting on the edge of the bed, waiting and listening. His feet are like two heavy weights on the floor. The trembling starts. He closes his eyes. Covers them with his large hands. His thighs shake as a woman's thighs do after childbirth. Not a woman's, the memory says—Vestine.

He can hear little feet now. A scampering. She had remained on the toilet, her teeth chattering, her legs moving up and down at a blistering pace. It was his job to hold the baby. He nuzzled her small round head. She was in a pink onesie, the diaper the size of his right hand. He had taken pictures of her ugly little feet. Claudette, they called her, after a favorite auntie.

He stands quickly, an electric shock of remembrance lifting him off of the bed—frantic glee at the memory. *Could she be? How, though?* For a moment, it is wonder, possibility, not fear. *If the pygmy is here*, some part of him concludes, *why can't she be?*

He moves to the front door of his condo—the sound of the footsteps still there. The voice is real: *Papa, Papa*, it says. Elation. Anticipation. He lurches the door open. He blinks. And as if by some miracle, she *is* there, in his exterior hallway, three and a half feet tall, six years old—unaged, even though a lifetime has passed. He bends at the knees, feels the force of love.

He hears a little gasp when he opens his arms to the girl. The sound snaps his head up like a bullet to the brain. His eyes find the place where the sound came from.

"I'm so sorry," a voice says, and his vision clears. "Please do excuse us."

In front of him he sees a woman, a stranger, slim in tennis clothes. She looks nervous, maybe even afraid. He looks back to the child—the girl who was just his daughter, the child calling *Papa*, but she is not his daughter after all.

"No, I am sorry," he says, feeling embarrassed. "I apologize," he says again, in the sanest voice he can muster. He can see the woman relax, but only a tinge.

"I told her to be quiet," the woman says. "But see. Oh, gosh." She looks him up and down. "We've woken you up, haven't we?"

The little girl stares at him, as he stares at her. "Mama," she says, and reaches for her mother, wraps her arm around her mother's thigh.

I must look a sight, he thinks. *Thank God, I am dressed.*

"No," he says, unable to move his eyes away from the slim child body, the regal carriage. A Tutsi birthright, he thinks, but says, "Don't worry about it. I thought you were someone else."

He studies the child with clearer vision. There is just a pencil point of Africa in her, but it exerts itself—more in the child than in the mother. He sees his own blood in both of them. The full mouth, the burnt golden skin. The child's hair is brown with specks of blonde like fallen glitter. She is not really like his own girl at all.

"I needed to get up anyway," he says, remembering the sweet voice saying *Papa*. The word is in his head now. He holds it as carefully as he once held his baby girl. *Remember the tinkling of it*, he says to himself. The diaper the size of a handkerchief.

"Bye," the woman in tennis clothes says. "Sorry we disturbed you."

He watches the girl and the mother return to their own unit. It is just there, at the other end of the hall. The child is being carried now. She is glaring at him over her mother's shoulder. She is confident and openly offended. Encircled in her mother's safety, she sticks her tongue out at him. He smiles. The name Papa is not for him, but he pretends it is. Papa is a small fire. The memory warmth.

HE LEAVES A BARBIE DOLL FOR HER THE NEXT DAY—A BLACK ONE, although in no way is the doll truly black except for her skin tone. She has the thin nose and the straight hair of a white woman. An exact replica of the blonde Barbie, but with brown skin and brown hair. It is as if the white Barbie has been dipped in some factory vat of latte-colored ink. There must be a Barbie factory somewhere, he realizes. Probably China.

He puts the doll in a bag on their doorknob. They are the only two residences on this floor. Penthouse units. Private. Expensive. Exclusive. He writes a note. He lies:

THIS BELONGED TO MY DAUGHTER. I HAD IT HERE. SHE IS TOO OLD FOR IT NOW. I THOUGHT YOU MIGHT LIKE IT. I DIDN'T WANT TO THROW IT AWAY. DO YOU LIKE DOLLS?

He doesn't know why he lies exactly. He bought the Barbie at CVS, just this morning on the way to the bank.

In America, men who give gifts to children are always met with a kind of suspicious fearfulness. He does not want that. He does not want to ruin something that he hasn't yet had a chance to begin.

CHAPTER THREE

JOCELYN

1

She sits in the parking lot of the Miramar Club, reluctant. The club is on the west side of PCH, on the sand. The location is beautiful, but it does nothing to cheer her.

There is the phone call today from Winton Terrace. A bill is all—a headstone, a plot, the cemetery, the day. There is the finality of the closed coffin, decisions too late, embalming not an option, and she hangs up, feels the sail tilt, decides to schedule the lesson on the spur of the moment, wants to get out of the house.

She is due on court 3 in thirty minutes but feels anxiety at the rash decision. She has purchased a new Lululemon skirt. The shirt she wears is collared, sedate—an alligator stitched on the front. More for the mood of mourning. She feels serious today after the phone call, after her mother goes into the ground.

She carries her large tennis bag like a backpack even though there is almost nothing in it: a racquet, a water bottle, a sleeve of new balls, a slim notepad to take notes. She feels the pull of a core muscle—a welcome ache in her body, and yet it makes her feel old.

She walks into the club's main lobby, her new tennis shoes squeak. The woman behind the desk says, "Mrs. Morrow," nods a welcome, and offers a soft white towel. Jocelyn smiles, says hello, but feels a sway. A calling out. *How does she know my name?* she wonders. She is startled and accused.

"Thank you, Shelly," she says, reading a name tag, trying to get her bearings. She grips the towel, the plushness of it helps stabilize her, but then Gladys is there too: a graying robe, threadbare, towels on the Winton Terrace floor, and then a memory of Conrad's mother—the two of them staring at registry brochures. The wedding twelve months away. *One hundred and eighty-nine dollars for a bath towel?* she'd asked. Her mother-in-law's Chanel glasses magnified her eyes. A hand on her wrist, stopping her from turning the pages. *I'll do the registry, dear.* Jocelyn would never know what to ask for.

She leaves the desk, follows the signs to the locker room. There is the smell of sweat as she enters. A hair dryer blows. She remembers roaches climbing out of a light socket. Her mother's smell, days without a bath when Gladys was binging, body odor, mint gum, and cigarette smoke. A lesson to take with her into the After, never, ever to smell. She breathes deeply. She slides onto a dry wooden bench, looks up at the clock there—fifteen minutes to go. Should she go?

She watches the tick of the clock. When there is enough time to exit the building, or enough time to get on court, she stands, decides to leave. She walks out a different way, not through the door she entered, but instead through the outdoor pool area. Strong in the air is the biting smell of chlorine. In front of her is the sweet little lagoon, the blue of it like sky. She smiles, remembering Lucy learning to swim there, the soft roll of flesh, a tiny bikini. She is too old to use the lagoon now.

Jocelyn feels a familiar longing, a sadness, her child growing, life continuing forward. She wants to go to Lucy's school, pick her up, and hold her. It wouldn't be hard.

Just as she is deciding—here or there, my child or me—the

space around her minutely shifts. She is aware of the whispering sigh of cotton, the sense of another person close behind her, the least noise that bodies make.

"You're going the wrong way," she hears, feels a pair of hands on her shoulders, the flash of nail polish, a turning, guidance. "Court three. Come on. I've got a plan for you."

Jocelyn is too shy to look, a child caught skipping school, but she recognizes the voice. She peeks. She does not know why she feels this way, but she must look away. At one point as they walk, Kate leans close, nudges her with her shoulder blade, and then laughs. There hasn't been a joke between them, but Jocelyn giggles. The seriousness inside her dissolves, a cube of sugar in hot water.

Kate waves to women playing friendlies as they pass, to men practicing serves.

"I'm glad you made it," she says. "We're going to have lots of fun. I promise."

And Jocelyn believes her, believes she is glad she made it, believes it will be fun. There is a sureness to the coach. It is a space to enter into, and then to be led forward. Relief. There is a bit in the mouth, a short rein, but a gentle hand. No need to turn back.

The Miramar Club was once a family home. She reads this one day in the *Palisades Register*. The paper is stacked in piles in the seating area of the club's entrance foyer. It is left for the perusal of the members. The house and the land were purchased by G. W. Clair in 1986 with the intention of turning it into a private club. The twenty-two original bedrooms have been converted, the old ballroom is a restaurant. Besides the Olympic-size pool, there is a high diving board, which is a rarity, almost extinct in these times of too much litigation. It is the thing about the Miramar Club that she and Lucy love best. In spring and summer, they jump off it, over and over again, hands held and then released, shrieks of joy and terror.

In 1989, the Miramar Club admitted its first black member—a man. It was a negotiation really, public beach access given in trade. The article means to imply how forward-thinking the Miramar Club is, but Jocelyn has never seen another black person using the club. Maud swears there are at least two other black women, besides the "supposed" man. One, like Jocelyn, is married to a white man. The other is a washed-up R&B star.

Jocelyn has never seen either woman or the man, but of course, she knows that it is not always possible to tell someone's race by looking at them. Either way, she always feels as if she and Lucy are the only black people there. Secretly, she thinks the others might just be rumors.

THE PRIVATE GOES WELL, AND FROM THEN ON, SHE'S ALL IN. THERE IS drill on Monday, Live Ball on Tuesday, team workout on Wednesday, cardio drill on Thursday, a friendly on Friday. Therapy is twice a week.

She's five weeks into tennis and totally addicted. There is something about the sport that is instantly healing. It's anonymous and separate from her everyday life. She finds herself wanting to go back and back and back. When she expects to play and doesn't, she is surprised at how utterly disappointed she feels.

Maud captains a USTA team, and of course she joins that. She is making friends, winning. She is almost popular. As a child, she was too poor for sports, but now she finds she likes it. It feels tribal. All the women gossip. She can't help but gossip too. There are stories about who cheats, who is fat, who does and who doesn't get Botox. Maud tells Jocelyn, a whisper in her ear, that Kate is gay, that she has a "partner," maybe a wife. They shriek with laughter like two high school girls. Jocelyn would not have guessed.

HER HUSBAND, CONRAD, LIKES ALL THE TENNIS. ON A SCHOOL DAY, while she fills her daughter's lunchbox, he comes up behind her in the kitchen and puts his hands up her short tennis skirt.

"You look great," he says. "Get those shorts off."

She laughs. "They're attached, bozo," she says, and he turns her around and kisses her neck.

"You look amazing," he says. "Lately, you're like you were when we were younger."

"I'm the same," she says.

"I told you the therapy would work," he says, letting her go. He plucks a banana out of the fruit bowl, confident and sure.

"Go to work," she says, but thinks, *Is he right? Is it working? Am I better?*

She finishes the lunch, and then stands, surveying her favorite room, the living room: a wall of windows and high ceilings. Room enough to do three cartwheels. It is a clear day—the sea a blue sheet as far as the eye can see.

She is startled when Conrad grabs Lucy suddenly. He kisses her once, and then sets her down on the gleaming hardwood floor. Their daughter takes off running as soon as her feet hit the ground. Lucy knows the game. She knows what she is supposed to do. It is something they do every morning. Six spitty kisses, because she is six.

Jocelyn smiles as Conrad chases Lucy around the vast condominium, pursuing the remaining five. Lucy runs, wanting him to catch her. He pretends she is too fast for him. She teases him from across the room.

"You can't get me, Papa," she says. "I'm a speed demon."

At the word *papa*, Jocelyn remembers the neighbor. They must go and say thank you for the Barbie doll. She is embarrassed to have put it off so long.

Conrad runs, in pursuit of their daughter. Lucy screams, but she is not really scared. Jocelyn has a flash of herself as a child, screaming—a *please*, a *don't*. The memory drops into the room like a shot bird from the sky; her stepfather, her mother's boyfriends, her mother—the belts, the extension cords, the chase. She feels herself deflating. She tries to stop the memories, to focus on the now, as Dr. Bruce tells her. She listens closely to Lucy. Her daughter's scream is different. She owns her body. It is not negotiable. She taunts Conrad and wields her power, which she knows, even at this young age, is his love for her. *I am here*, she reminds herself. *It is now*, she says. *I am here with my own family. I am safe.*

LATER, WHEN HE AND LUCY FINISH THEIR GAME, CONRAD FINDS JOCELYN in the kitchen and kisses her hard.

"Let's have a date tonight," he says.

"I know what that means," she says. "No point calling it a date. Are we going somewhere?"

He smirks. "I'm going somewhere."

He's tugging on her skirt. He puts his hand inside her shorts, grabs her ass. When they were twenty-five they would have done it on the floor. He would have pressed her down and fucked her hard. Now there is Lucy. He lingers in the kitchen, holds her close.

Jocelyn looks over her husband's shoulder at the restaurant-grade Thermador oven. Without meaning to, she thinks that Gladys would fit inside.

"I'll be back early," he says. A final squeeze. And then says goodbye.

SHE PARTNERS WITH KATE ONE DAY AT DRILL. THEY PLAY AGAINST MAUD and Erica because Theresa is a no-show. Jocelyn has never played with a pro, and she is impressed with how little effort Kate seems to require to hit the ball well—an effortless slice, a drop shot close to the net that instantly dies. It's magic.

They play for almost an hour before they arrive at a particularly long point—10–9 in the tiebreak, their advantage. There are volleys back and forth, a lob over their heads. Jocelyn runs as fast as she can with Kate right beside her.

"Mine," she says, and Kate goes back to the baseline, smiling, trusting her to have it. Jocelyn manages to lob the ball back, over Erica's head, but just barely.

The point continues—rally after rally until Jocelyn grows tired. There are ground strokes with topspin, slices and angles that force her out of position. It seems as if the point will never end. She is anxious and alert, not wanting to be the one to mess it up, but she also feels confident, even powerful. Two more drives come crosscourt, just barely out of Jocelyn's reach. She is breathing heavily. Kate is too. *I'll go on the third*, she says in her mind. *I'll go on the third.*

Erica hits a stinging crosscourt return, but Jocelyn is ready. She intercepts it, poaches. Racquet meets ball, and she puts the winning shot away. All four of them cheer. Maud bends over on the other side of the net, breathing hard. Erica throws her racquet down. They laugh, give compliments to each other—*Great point, Really fun, Nice poach.* Kate high-fives Jocelyn and then hugs her.

Jocelyn doesn't really think about the hug until later when she is alone in her car, and then she cannot understand why she is still thinking about it. The small waist, the tight stomach, deceptive in tennis clothes. The breath between them, their bodies in sync, lungs filling and emptying at the same time. A laugh at the bottom of the throat.

The breasts were small, but still, somehow, Kate was curvy, lush even. *It is her legs,* she thinks. *Her hips.* She replays the moment as she drives along the beach, past the club, past her own condo. She gives herself more time. Did she blush? Did Kate? Did they even look at one another? There was the snap and the crack of heat when they pulled apart. Jocelyn had not expected it, but she knew for sure that Kate had felt it too. Afterwards they stood silent and apart like two trees born out of fire. And then Maud said, without the least bit of venom:

"We'll beat you bitches next time."

A hand out to shake—something to startle Jocelyn out of a dream.

So many days of sunshine in Southern California, but today the meteorologists have predicted rain. Jocelyn arrives at the Miramar Club ten minutes early. The parking lot is almost empty. She walks to court 3, sits hidden, and watches Kate finish up a lesson. She tells herself she is learning, but she is not listening that much. She is thinking about the heat from the day before, remembering the high five, the hug. She returns to the memory as if to another place. She studies Kate, her shape, the bright almost-white of her restrained hair.

Without understanding why, Jocelyn wonders what it would feel like to hold Kate down, to watch the hands with their short, painted nails struggle to get free. She thinks about kissing her, making her come, but without reciprocation. She enjoys the fantasy. It is animal and intense. Chemical, even. Its immediacy is scary as a heart attack and as impossible to stop. In college, she kissed a girl, but this is different. This is bewildering. Outside herself. This is more adult.

There is the squeak of a shoe on the court suddenly, and Jocelyn looks up. She snaps out of the fantasy. In seconds, she is back in the apartment in Winton Terrace, the hot, stuffy room of her mother. She tries to slide the window shut, block the view, breathe as Dr. Bruce has taught her, but it is there, clear and detailed. She can see everything.

It's from sinning, Gladys said, telling her about her brother, William. *That's why he got it.*

Newport ash was wet and gray on the carpet. The air was stagnant from smoke and closed windows. Her mother had a waterbed. Sitting on it made Jocelyn seasick, as if on a boat.

An abomination. Nasty. Gladys's voice, self-righteous as a nun. She was drunk on boxed wine. *That boy is no son of mine.*

You are no mother, Jocelyn thinks, pulling herself back to the bench that she sits on, back to the Miramar Club, to Kate—back to the determined Palisades sun. It will never rain, she thinks. *You were no mother. Were.*

Kate tosses a tennis ball into her cart, laughing with her client. Jocelyn thinks of Kate's mouth, her tongue, the slick wet of her saliva.

Maybe she's unclean, she thinks. *Maybe she's sick with the sick that my brother had.* Jocelyn turns away, looks for Maud. She covers her ears like a child does when she doesn't want to hear something. The voice of Gladys, even in death, slurring in her ear.

"SHE IS MIXED," CONRAD SAYS, POUTING. "BIRACIAL."

They are filling in beginning-of-the-school-year paperwork. Conrad is home early. Lucy is in bed. Jocelyn has made small stacks on the living room coffee table. They are necessary for admission statistics, the principal of Lucy's private school explains. Important for demographics.

"Do not write 'black' on that form," Conrad demands.

"She's not mixed," Jocelyn says. "She's black."

"How do you figure?" he says. "How do you figure that?"

"Period," Jocelyn says, as if it's an answer.

"She's more white than black," he says assertively. "Your father was white. My parents are both white. I'm white, for God's sake. That makes her like three-quarters white."

"Not in America," Jocelyn says, marking the "African American" box with a strange sort of satisfaction.

She looks up at her husband. He has a sour face. She laughs, almost hysterically. "The three-quarters-white category," she says with more sass than she means. "What the hell is that?"

Conrad walks out of the room. He is angry.

Jocelyn does not understand her need to hold on to it, her loyalty, her urge to pass this inheritance along. What has it given her, after all?

"DO YOU HAVE ANY FAMILY LEFT?" DR. BRUCE ASKS. "NOW THAT YOUR mother has died?"

It is their ninth session together. She goes and she goes, but there is always the feeling of being on display, a need to lower the eyes. She keeps things hidden.

"Yes," Jocelyn says quietly. "Well, no. I guess not really. Not anymore."

"Not anymore?" the therapist asks.

A pen, a pad. Hot-pink reading glasses. Eyes waiting.

"My brother died in 1994. My sister in 1990."

The therapist writes something in her notepad. Jocelyn watches her pen move and then looks away. There is a botanical print on the wall—"Native California Flowers." Jocelyn reads: California Poppy, *Eschscholzia californica*.

"Any family besides?"

"Uncle Al is still alive. Bad people seem to never die," Jocelyn says, focusing hard on the print. "My mother is finally dead, but you know that. My grandfather is ninety. They've never been family to me."

Jocelyn looks at the poster again, and the therapist looks where Jocelyn looks. She is on to golden yarrow, or *Eriophyllum confertiflorum*. The impossible pronunciation is distracting.

"Can we speak of something specific?" the therapist asks.

"Like what?" Jocelyn says, feeling as petulant as a teenager.

"Like anything," the therapist says. "We could start with your brother. How did he die?"

"AIDS," Jocelyn says simply.

When she doesn't continue, the therapist asks, "What was he like?"

"Nice," she says. "He was a musician. A pianist."

"What about your sister? What was she like?" the therapist asks, and Jocelyn hesitates.

In truth, Jocelyn barely remembers what either of them was like, what she herself was like. They are both ideas now, not really people. She remembers parts of them, mostly parts from the apartment in Winton Terrace. She remembers the beatings, the degradation, the hopelessness, but who would want to remember that? She doesn't want to say that though. She doesn't want to seem cold. She still has a plaid Ralph Lauren shirt that her brother had saved for. It's in an airtight bag in her closet. In the early years after his death, she would take it out and smell it. She has her sister's watch—a Timex. Conrad would die if she wore it.

"How did your sister die?" Dr. Bruce asks, pushing, interrupting.

"Drugs," she says. "An overdose. We were all pretty miserable."

"Did you do drugs?"

Jocelyn thinks of the ecstasy dealer. Her boyfriend from Florida who dealt cocaine.

High-strung sex that felt as if they would never reach orgasm. Doing it again and again. There were endless lines on a Formica table at the house on Mulberry Street. *And to Think That I Saw It on Mulberry Street*, she thinks, and then there is Lucy and Dr. Seuss— one memory switched for something new. Two girls and yet somehow one girl too.

"Jocelyn?" her therapist says.

Jocelyn feels brought out of a daze. "It seemed like everybody did drugs," she says, simply.

"Were you with your sister when she died? Were you using together?"

She looks out the window, rubs a nail. A eucalyptus tree taps its branch on the pane. *Using* makes it sound more serious than Jocelyn remembers. She wasn't like Ycidra. For Ycidra everything was always extreme.

"No. No. She was with her boyfriend. He didn't call 911. She'd be alive if he had called 911, but well . . ."

"How does that make you feel?" the therapist asks.

"Awful," Jocelyn says. "Just awful." And then she starts laughing, because it seems like the dumbest question in the world.

The therapist waits, neutral as Switzerland. Jocelyn assumes it's a part of the job.

"I don't think about it," she says, continuing. "I just sort of leave it back there."

"Back where?" the therapist asks. She doesn't mention the laughter.

"I don't know," Jocelyn says, and realizes she doesn't know. "It's just not here."

They sit in silence for a few moments. She thinks she should tell the therapist about Kate: the thoughts she has. About wanting to hold her down. Wanting to possess her. She talks herself out of it though. It is nothing, she tells herself. *If it's something next week, I will tell her.*

"Were you close to your sister? Let's not talk about the abuse right now. I'm not asking you to talk about that. When you're ready, you can talk about that."

"She was always *for* me, you know? She was like my running mate."

The office is suddenly cold. The sun has fallen behind a cloud. One of her mother's boyfriends would take them to UDF, after, for ice cream. It was a bribe, so the two of them wouldn't tell.

There are tissues on a television tray in front of her. She looks out to the new gray sky, but she does not cry.

CHAPTER FOUR

SIMON

1

THE DOORBELL RINGS AT DINNERTIME. THE PYGMY IS SITTING IN THE recliner. He often sits there in the evening. His legs are crossed, this time with webbed feet. When the doorbell sounds, the pygmy gets up and walks to the door. Simon is aware of the *slap, slap* sound of his steps. The doorbell rings again. He wonders who it is. No one visits him. No family is left. Then the one comes to mind, and he hushes the possibility, not wanting to repeat the hallway scene from weeks before, not wanting to think of his "maybe" daughter and her letter. *I would like to meet you*, she writes. *I believe I am your daughter.* Are you my daughter? He wonders this, and the Twa disappears.

He makes his way to the door, just as the bell sounds again. This time over and over. He hears a woman's voice admonishing: *Stop it, honey. Stop that.* He hears giggling. He smiles, looks out the peephole. It is the little girl from down the hall—Lucy. He remembers the wonderful name! The Barbie doll has done the trick.

He opens the door.

"Hello," he says. "What a pleasure! Come in please."

"No, that's all right," his neighbor says. She is not dressed in tennis clothes this time, but is casual in a cashmere sweater and jeans. "We're just here to thank you for . . ." but then Lucy runs past her, and past him, and is in his living room, and neither of them can grab her.

"I'm so sorry," the mother says, all exasperation.

"Don't worry," he says, gently. He waves her inside. "Come in. I am happy you are here."

She steps into the light of the entry. He shuts the door and looks at her closely. There is a glow to her skin. She has softly highlighted hair; the color is like the color of caramels he ate once in Brussels, in a small café. Two on a silver plate. It matches her daughter's hair. Their eyes are different though. Hers are almost green. The child's are dark brown, as his own daughter's were.

He watches to see if the mother likes his home. She glances about, stopping at the view. She turns to see the kitchen, the white marble island. The child makes her way to his worktable, looks with interest at the architectural model of the huge city park he is planning for the Natural History Museum.

"Is it the same floor plan as yours?" he asks.

"Yes. The setup is the same, but you have much better taste. This is like a retreat."

He smiles at that, and she smiles too. He sees her white teeth. Her lips are the color of crushed berries. The contrast between the two is dramatic.

"It's so spare," she says. "I love it. I . . . well . . . we have so much stuff."

"I'm glad you like it," he says. "Sit. Please. Anywhere."

But she doesn't. They both stand, as if permanently affixed to the floor, eyes on the child, who is intrigued by the contents of his table—the tiny oranges on the tiny orange trees, miniature aluminum slides, pearl-size soccer balls. The little fingers lift and feel and then follow the turning path of a man-made creek he's decided on.

"Is she okay over there?" the mother asks.

"Yes."

"She can't break it, can she?"

"I won't, Mama."

"She won't," he says, loving the child's voice.

"I'm Jocelyn Morrow," the mother says, extending her hand. Her fingernails are painted a deep red, almost black. "I noticed when you bought the place, but we've never really formally introduced ourselves."

"I'm Simon," he says. "Bonaventure."

"That's Lucy," the mother says, pointing at the child.

"I remember," he says. "From when we met in the hall."

"Oh God." A grin lights up her face. "I apologize for that and thank you for the Barbie. She loves it. I should have come by sooner. I've lost my manners living in Los Angeles."

"Where are you from?" he asks.

"Cincinnati," she says.

"Where is that?"

"Ohio," she says. "The Midwest. It's on the river. There's a beautiful bridge. The landscape is very green. There's nothing much to tell besides that. Just a Midwest city."

She walks to the sliding glass doors. He walks with her. They both look out. The surf is rough today. The sea is dark blue.

"I grew up near a river too," he says. "In Rwanda. The Nyaba-rongo." *They belong to Ethiopia*, he remembers. The memory is like a camera flash in a dark room. "A bit green too," he says. "A brown river." *With bodies*, he almost says.

"How nice," she says. She turns back into the room, takes a large breath as if she's finishing a workout. "We didn't want to disturb you. We—Lucy—just wanted to thank you for the Barbie. *Right*, Lucy?"

"Thanks," the child says, without looking up.

"You are welcome for the doll," he says. "You have a lovely name, Lucy."

"It's short for Lucinda," the mother says, but the child says nothing. It is as if she can't hear anything they say. She is intent on the details of the miniature park. She pushes the swing sets into the middle of the green synthetic lawn. She moves the water fountains to the left edge. He watches her infiltrate his space like a mad architect, not thinking twice. Just moving and then looking, changing what doesn't please her, and then changing it again.

"What do you do?" the mother asks. "I mean, what is all of that?"

"I am an architect. I design open spaces for public consumption. City parks or state parks. This is a project I'm doing for the Natural History Museum, but I work all over the world. That's my most recent version. Your daughter seems to like it. Although she is editing it a bit."

"She thinks she knows everything."

"Yes," he says. "Girls do."

Sadness pokes him like a strong finger in his chest. *My girl knew everything*, he wants to say.

"And where is your daughter today?" Jocelyn asks, as if she has read his thoughts. "Is she home?" she asks, looking around the room as if his daughter might be hiding somewhere. "It was nice of her to give us the doll. Lucy ought to thank her too."

"Oh," he says. "She doesn't live with me."

"Is she still in Rwanda?"

He feels the question, what it provokes. He worries that he has gone red. He does not know how to answer. He never knows. *Lie*, he thinks. *Always lie.*

"Well," he says.

She waits. His neighbor is patient. He watches her watch him.

"I lost her twenty years ago. Twenty-two years ago, actually. In the genocide," he says.

"Oh, my God. I'm so sorry."

"She isn't dead," he says. "Well, she might be." *Never to me*, he wants to say. He feels unable to stop his blathering. "Some of the children were taken."

"Oh my gosh," she says. "I can't imagine."

"*She* was taken from me." The words come from outside him. *The truth*, he realizes. *Why have I told the truth?*

"I didn't mean to pry," she says. She reaches to touch him, but he does not allow it. "I didn't know. I wouldn't have . . . the doll then . . . Lucy, we have to return the doll."

"No," he says. "It's nothing. It's nothing but a doll."

He has raised his voice without meaning to. She steps away from him. He watches her move from foot to foot. It is a small gesture. He has made her uncomfortable. He is angry at himself. He wants them to stay.

"May I make you some coffee?" he tries. "Please?"

"I wouldn't want to bother you," she says. She looks at her daughter again. This time very anxiously. "Don't be so rough with that, honey."

"She is okay," he says. "I want to see what works. What doesn't." And then to the child: "I'd be honored if you'd help me with it, Lucy. Can you figure out the best setup for me? If you were playing at a park—a *dream* park. How would you want it to look?"

The girl says nothing.

"If you help me figure it out, I will hide your name at the finished site. We will hunt for Lucy's name at the Natural History Museum. I could do many different versions—Lucinda, Cinda, Lucy, Lulu. I could put it on a brick, or a stone, or at the bottom of a clear pond. How does that sound?"

A devilish grin settles over the girl's face, then seriousness. She reaches her hand toward a slide, she changes her mind and then moves a climbing wall. She looks up at him. He feels pricked, as if her eyes are darts.

"The pond," she says.

"I won't tell where it is," he says, being very serious. "You must spy it. Hot chocolate for her?" he asks the mother.

"I'll never get her out of here," Jocelyn says, but he can tell she is pleased.

"Well then, you must stay for a very long time."

She seems to relax at this, and he is happy. He has fixed it. Through the child.

He watches her set her purse down. The purse is beautiful. It is a python bag. He has never seen one before. He lifts his eyes from the bag to her face. He sees that she is blushing.

"My husband bought it for me," she says, as if apologizing. "It's absurd."

"It's lovely," he says. "I don't like snakes. They are best on bags."

She laughs. "May I sit anywhere?"

"Anywhere," he says. "Make yourself at home. We should get to know one another. I believe that's what neighbors do."

He watches her make herself comfortable on the couch.

"I am very sorry about your daughter," she says. "I would die if something happened to Lucy. I really couldn't go on."

"Thank you," he says, simply.

There is quiet after that. It is not uncomfortable though. She is the kind of woman who makes silence easy. He can already tell. She is someone to be stared at, to be sat with.

The smell of coffee is in the room. The sweet, thick scent of Lucy's hot chocolate. The sun is setting over the sea now. A blinding disk showing through his window. It will be dark in moments, he knows. He prays the pygmy will not come back while she is here. It seems a fragile space to keep intact. It's been a long time since he's had a friend, and he knows he must contain the illusions, lasso them in. Trust, he thinks, but the meaning of the word eludes him. The tail of Habyarimana's python flicks prescient from the purse, taunting him. He ignores it.

"Tell me about you," he says, placing the coffee service out on the light wood table.

"There's not much to tell about me. I'm a housewife. I used to be a librarian, but now I'm just a full-time mother."

"Don't say 'just,'" he says, starting to pour. "That's a big deal."

He sees Vestine pregnant, toddling around. "What else do you do or like?"

"I like to read," she says. And then as if it is an afterthought, "I recently started playing tennis again," she says.

"Oh, that sounds fun," he says. "I used to play as a boy."

She smiles at him, and through the decades, instead of the pygmy, Abrahm's wooden racquet clatters to the floor. The sound startles him and he flinches, spilling a bit of coffee. He looks at her to see if she has noticed, or if little Lucy has heard, but the sound is for him alone.

"Yeah?" she says. "I really sort of love it."

2

WHEN SHE LEAVES, HE WONDERS WHY HE HAS TOLD HER ABOUT HIS daughter: *She was taken from me.* Why did he say that?

He does not like to say or think the words *kidnapped* or *stolen*, although that is what it was. He has never shared the story. Why didn't he lie? The comfort of strangers, he thinks, but there have been so many strangers before.

Maybe it is because of Lucy. Lucinda. He would rather call her that.

The name, he thinks, is like a soft whisper, a hush. A little girl—a girl with eyes like his own girl's. She is in his house again. Lucy has made him feel reborn.

WHEN IT IS TIME FOR BED, HE CLOSES HIS EYES TO SLEEP, BUT THE LETTER from his "maybe" daughter is in the way. He pats his pajama top, the pocket. He grazes the rumpled paper with a dry fingertip, checking. He unfolds the letter, looks at it in the quiet dark, and then puts it away again. In the morning, he will place it in the pocket of his suit. When he returns from work for dinner, it will go out onto the table. When he reaches for it, the wrong pocket, the wrong room, the wrong drawer, and finds it missing, his heart will go—*beat, beat, beat*, a staccato drum of panic until it is found.

He has read it and reread it too many times to count. He has looked at her written name, tried to find answers in the shape and swerve of the letters themselves. Is the writing like his? Like Vestine's? Is her articulation as theirs was? It is useless. It was an entirely different language. There is nothing. He must wait.

He is restless in his bed. He tosses and turns and thinks of his neighbor asleep in the unit beside his. What wall do they share? Lucy is asleep too. Safe. Sound. At the thought of the girl, he rises. He goes to do her work.

BEFORE SHE LEAVES HIS APARTMENT, LUCY GIVES HIM AN ASSIGNMENT. IT is as if she knows she already owns him: *Put some swans in the park, Mr. Simon. Ducks too.* A smile alights on her face as she waves goodbye to him. *My mama is afraid of swans, but I love them. I want them in my park.*

"Swans," he says to the dark room, embracing his insomnia. "Ponds and ducks and all the rest too!"

The night unfolds as he paints. In the waves of her pond, he hides Lucy's name. *She is with me*, he thinks. *I will not be lonely.*

IN THE EARLY-MORNING HOURS, HE DRIFTS OFF TO SLEEP AT HIS TABLE, and a dream, a recurring one, comes to him again and brings back his own daughter. In the dream, he is in Kigali. He holds his daughter's tiny hand. She leads him. He follows. She, pulling with pretty little fingers, drawing him into his old bedroom, so that he can safely tuck her in. On the way, she chatters on and on about a girl in school, a not-so-nice one, and somewhere between the front room and her cot, she disappears. There is a smudge of gray on the floor where she was standing, and he kneels to touch it, to pat it. He panics. He stands. He races around the small room. When he turns again, back to the tiny cot, she is somehow there. It is magic. She is sleeping. At the sight of her small breathing body, relief sweeps through him like something fatal. She has not disappeared after all. She has not been taken from him.

"Baby girl?" he says. "Baby girl?" wanting to wake her gently, wanting to be reassured. There is deep joy as he watches her turn toward him. Alive, blood through the body, his daughter, his house. The world is right again.

The turn of her head is slow in the dream, like a fan's oscillation. And although he has dreamed this dream a thousand times, he is never prepared for it: the child becomes the pygmy; Claudette's baby teeth replaced by a solid piece of ivory, a penis as long and as thick as the python at the president's palace, between her small legs. It unrolls as a fire hose might. There are three hundred pounds of it, filling up the room.

His head jerks up from his worktable. He gasps, a drowning man emerging for breath. He tries to shake off the dream. A paint smear, the name lost, a finger to his chest. He taps the pocket where his heart lies. The letter is still there. *I would like to meet you*, the words say. *I believe I am your daughter. I do not know. Will you know?* He doesn't know if he will know. His breath settles, his heart slows. *My parents are dead now*, she writes. *You will remember my parents.*

"Your parents?" he says to the dark room. "I am your parent. Vestine is your parent." He reaches up again to the pocket, a folded corner, a pricking. The letter is a knife. It cuts a wound open. Something that will never heal.

WHAT IS THE DEFINITION OF GENOCIDE? THIS HE KNOWS BY HEART. HE knows it as well as his social security number or his own middle name. Once she was taken from him, none of the rest mattered. Only that last one. That final atrocity.

> In the present Convention, genocide means any of the following acts committed with intent to destroy, in whole or in part, a national, ethnical, racial or religious group, as such:
>
> a. Killing members of the group;
> b. Causing serious bodily or mental harm to members of the group;
> c. Deliberately inflicting on the group conditions of life calculated to bring about its physical destruction in whole or in part;
> d. Imposing measures intended to prevent births within the group;
> e. Forcibly transferring children of the group to another group.

Forcibly transferring children of the group to another group.
Forcibly transferring children of the group to another group.

CHAPTER FIVE

JOCELYN

1

She is always aware of being appropriate. To not let on. The name is inside her: Kate. Kate. Kate. She comes up with ways to communicate with her, texts to send, privates to take. She arrives early to drill, and they spend a few minutes together alone. Gladys is dead in her presence, no one is grieving, Jocelyn's past stays in the past. Now is now, before is before. She doesn't care about after.

"How was your week?" Kate asks.

She wonders how to answer. "Great," is all she says, not missing a beat.

"We kicked butt against Maud and Erica," Kate says, putting on her sunglasses. There isn't any sun.

"You're an optimist," Jocelyn says. "We *barely* won."

Kate is wearing a pleated skirt today—a rarity. The skirt is designed by a company that is very popular. The sizes go up to 10. Women who are larger than size 10 don't exist for this company. The clothes are made for tall, skinny women. White women without asses. Kate definitely has an ass, but somehow still looks good in the skirt. Jocelyn is very distracted.

"Winning is winning," Kate says.

Jocelyn grabs her racquet. She moves a step closer to Kate. She wants to touch her, the blonde fuzz on her thighs. The skin would be chilled there. A cool day. She is aware that she is experiencing a kind of obsession, but that's as much as she understands.

I can keep a secret, she wants to say. *No one will know.*

She is good at secrets. She has practiced keeping secrets her whole life.

"Let's hit some balls while we wait for the others," Kate says, eyeing the opposite end of the court. A smattering of freckles on her cheek, blonde lashes.

"Yes," Jocelyn says. "Let's."

AFTER THE DRILL CLASS, SHE PLAYS A FRIENDLY WITH MAUD AND Theresa and another girl, Missy, whom none of them can stand. She's unattractive and intense and talks too much during drill classes. She's the type of woman who thinks she's wealthy but has no idea what real wealth is. The only good thing about her is she is always around if they need a fourth. Maud secretly calls her "No Life" and has identified her as Kate's "stalker." They all laugh. The irony is not lost on Jocelyn.

The friendly is won easily by Jocelyn and Maud. There's a little edge to the losers after—they explain that they were practicing new shots. Missy says she is on her period. Maud and Jocelyn look at each other and pretend to throw up. Jocelyn keeps looking for Kate. Is she gone for the day? When will she see her again? A blonde streak by court 4, but is it her? It isn't clear. She says goodbye to the other women.

"See you at pickup," Maud says.

"I'm driving through," Jocelyn says and is off to Lucy's school.

On the way there, the coast road curves, and Kate is in every turn. The fact that Jocelyn didn't see her after the drill is more distracting, she realizes, than if she had. *Where did she go? Who is she with?*

Jocelyn drives up Sunset, past the Temple of Absolution, past the polo fields and the golf course and then onto the campus. The security guard tips his hat, sits up in his chair, sets his mobile phone down. He allows her to pass. She belongs there. The ride has been brief and beautiful, but Jocelyn still feels intense and distracted by thoughts of Kate. It is as if Kate were in the seat beside her.

She slows, searching the small pool of children's faces until

she sees Lucy waiting by the curb. She and Ali Feinstein are holding hands. Her daughter hugs her friend goodbye and walks carefully over to the loading zone—the legs like matchsticks under
the dark plaid of the skirt. Jocelyn pulls forward, so slowly. She
unclicks the lock on the door, welcomes her daughter inside. She
forces herself to engage, to talk. She tries to push Kate out of her
mind. Seat belts fastened, booster checked, and then she guides
the car away from the school.

"How was your day, lovey?" she asks, and Lucy says that she
has a new teacher.

"What do you mean a new teacher?" Jocelyn asks. There is
the sway, the imbalance.

"His name is Mr. Baird," her daughter says, as if reporting the
weather. "He's taller than a basketball player."

Jocelyn feels her emotions spread. She doesn't like the fact
that the new teacher is a man. She doesn't like that she hasn't
been told. She is suddenly panicked. She remembers the men
who were her teachers when she was growing up. The heavy
hands that touched her when she didn't want to be touched. Lucy
goes to a private school, so she thinks she should feel better about
things. She is certain that there are background checks and fin-
gerprints, but still she is uncertain.

She adjusts her hands on the wheel, looks in the rearview
mirror. Her daughter is pretending to read a book. Her expression
is serious, almost angry. The book is about a magical tree house
and time travel. They have read it many times. Jocelyn studies
her daughter, looking for the thing that might let the men in the
world—the Mr. Bairds—know that they can have her: Is there a
mark?

Gladys's voice is in her head instantly. She searches and
searches Lucy's reflection, but there is nothing there. Nothing
damaged or unclean. Jocelyn makes a mental note to ask Maud if
she should have Lucy moved out of the class. Maud knows everything about children. She has three boys and two girls, and a
house off El Medio North on four acres.

From the back seat, Lucy interrupts Jocelyn's thoughts by telling her that Mr. Baird is married. The traffic light changes, and they move on to PCH.

"How do you know?" Jocelyn asks, lightly, but wonders why the conversation would ever come up.

"He told us. Duh!"

"Lucy!" Jocelyn says, but then doesn't really scold her. She thinks it's sort of funny—adolescent annoyance in a six-year-old.

When they get to their building and take the elevator up, Lucy won't stop asking for Conrad. There must be something in her new teacher that makes her miss her father. She walks along the hall, skipping aimlessly.

"I want to see my papa. Where's my papa?" Lucy asks.

"At work," Jocelyn says. "As always."

The annoyance Jocelyn hears in her own voice surprises her. She has promised never to be impatient with her child. Never to lose her temper. It will be different than it was with Gladys. Fear is something that will never exist between them. "Your father has to work so Mama can be home with you."

She gives the second answer more calmly, trying to make up for the impatient tone of before. She wants to say, *So I can keep you safe*, but doesn't.

"Let's go see Mr. Simon, then," Lucy says, stopping at his door. There is the threat that she will knock without permission. "I want to see the pond. I want to see my swans and ducks. I want to see my name."

Jocelyn finds it hard to focus on what her daughter is saying. *Mr. Baird is married*, she thinks. *Is that better?*

She watches Lucy doing a little dance in front of Simon's door, her slight body. She is a beauty. It is a truth. It's not just because she's her daughter. Jocelyn will have to keep an eye out. She will have to stay vigilant. The conversation in the car has reminded her. Friends, family, teachers—synonyms for *perpetrator*. She should be careful even of Simon, right?

Blood will out, Gladys would say to them, when she and Ycidra had the audacity to see themselves as good, as having even the smallest light within them. *Trash will stay trash.*

"Can we? Can we go and see Mr. Simon?"

Lucy is taking tiny little jumps in place now. She turns her head and Jocelyn sees a shadow, just the edge of something blooming, like a bruise on the cheek.

Jocelyn feels her forehead crease. An eye squint. Is it there after all? Has it come through the blood? But then, as soon as she thinks this, the shadow is gone.

You are me, she hears, and feels herself tremble. It is her mother's voice, right here, right now, in this hallway, in this luxury condominium complex on PCH. It is as if she's risen from her grave.

You are dead, Jocelyn says to Gladys's voice. *You are dead. My birthday wish come true.*

You're always going to be me, her mother's voice says. *Ain't nothing to be done about it.*

"Not today, sweetheart," Jocelyn manages to say to her daughter. She pulls the small arm, the small body, gently away from the door and down the hall.

She better not get close to the man, she realizes. A man is a man. A thought delivered. By Gladys? A warning. "A different day maybe, but we can't visit Mr. Simon now."

WHEN LUCY IS THREE, ALMOST FOUR, SHE ASKS ABOUT JOCELYN'S SCARS. They are visible only in a certain light. A Beverly Hills dermatologist has been at them with a laser, but the sheen of the skin there, where the leash came down, where the extension cord snapped, where the belt buckle beat her, is glossy as floor varnish. There is a crisscross pattern on her upper back. On her buttocks and thighs too, and on this day, as Jocelyn sits putting makeup on, lost in the luxury and care that her husband has provided for her, she feels her daughter's tiny fingers tracing the scars, and this startles Jocelyn. She hasn't realized until just then that she is in her bra and underwear—that she is exposed. She has forgotten her scars as those who are scarred do.

"What are these, Mama?" Lucy says. "Why is your skin so weird?"

The fingertips are almost weightless. Feathers. A cartographer going over a raised map. Jocelyn feels her heart cinch. She sits unmoving.

"It's like a net, Mama," her daughter says. "It's like the net the fishermen use at the pier."

Jocelyn recalls the pain, the burning laser, checking weekly after the treatments, the focused pinpricks of tiny needles—an experimental study. Happiness at the progress, feeling almost free of it.

"Your pigment," the dermatologist said in her sterile office, "makes the treatment less effective. It's never going to be perfect."

She lifts her little girl. She sets her on her lap. What to say about a mother who beat you? A mother who let her boyfriends beat you. The weight of her child is reassuring. Lucy is alive. She is loved, untouched. *I love her. She is mine.* It is always a wonder to Jocelyn that she is the mother of this child.

"Well," she says, making up the story. "I never told you this, but . . . I was born a mermaid."

The dark brown eyes of her girl grow big. Jocelyn touches one little shoulder, cups it, to pull her girl in.

"And a fisherman caught me in his net."

"Really?" Lucy says. "Really?"

"Really," Jocelyn says and pauses, building the story. "I struggled, and the net cut me, burned me. The scars are what's left behind."

She waits, looking to see if her daughter believes her.

"Like a rope burn?" Lucy asks. "Eddie Banks got a rope burn when he went sailing with his papa."

"Exactly. From the rope."

"Wow," Lucy says.

"I didn't know I was coming out of the sea to be your mother. I thought I'd always be a mermaid. I was afraid, so I struggled. Maybe I shouldn't have struggled."

Lucy's eyes fill with wonder. "Am I a mermaid too?" she asks. "Since I'm your daughter."

"It's a secret," Jocelyn says to her child. She whispers low and intense in the small seashell ear. "You can't tell a soul."

"Am I?" the child asks again. "Tell me."

"A mermaid," Jocelyn says. She points one finger into her daughter's chest, identifying her. "A mermaid, just not in a net."

She pinpoints the moment that it seems possible. The second it moves from fantasy to reality. The obsession requires constant accounting: *Is there progress? Does she like me? Is she looking at me? Can I try?* Jocelyn is exhausted by it.

There is a friendly foursome: Jocelyn, Erica, Theresa, Maud. A match like any other day. Kate is walking, returning the ball cart to the shed. Like a moth disoriented by light, Jocelyn turns to watch her, wants to look away but can't. Kate sees her looking, stumbles, and the cart turns over. The neon yellow tennis balls roll, bright and harsh against the forest-green artificial grass.

"Let's help," Jocelyn says.

"Let's not," Maud says. "We're *playing.*"

"Oh, come on!"

They do—four of them picking up balls for Kate, putting them back into the cart.

"You need a cabana boy, a slave boy," Erica says.

"A cabana girl," Theresa says.

"In a bikini," Kate says, and they all laugh.

They speak about girls in bikinis, about them in bikinis. Their ages. It feels like flirting, like they are talking about something else. She looks up, and Kate is watching her. Her body warms. She is instantly wet.

"Go finish your match," Kate says to all of them, but she is looking at Jocelyn. "I've got this."

The other women go, but Jocelyn holds fast to the cart. She walks beside it, acting as if she is necessary to push it along. Kate rebukes her, tries to peel her fingers from the cart, but Jocelyn holds fast. Their fingers open and then close, an easily deniable touch. Jocelyn is pleased, an evil satisfaction fills her. A click of power. Kate's intense insistence that she go away makes Jocelyn certain that she feels and fears the attraction too. Jocelyn pushes on, afraid the opportunity might not come again. It might be lost in the wind.

They get closer and closer to the shed, and in a millisecond, Jocelyn imagines the two of them putting the balls away, alone, the pull of panties, her finger inside Kate. Want. She feels tied to the cart. Maud is yelling from the court, telling her to come on already.

When Kate speaks again her voice is forceful, knowing, a red blush like liquid spreading from her chest to her neck, to her face.

"Go back to the court," Kate says. And then with desperation, "Please."

"MY BROTHER HAD A BIG HEAD," JOCELYN SAYS. "THAT'S ONE OF THE things I remember."

The therapist has been pushing her to talk all session. She is trying to get her to retrieve smaller parts of her past in a controlled environment, but all Jocelyn wants to do is think about Kate. She wants to wallow in her, follow her through a door and be somewhere else.

Dr. Bruce adjusts her glasses up along the ridge of her nose. "What else?" she says. "Don't worry if the memory isn't perfect."

Jocelyn looks around the office. She picks at her thumbnail. "It was heavy. You know, like when they say that in novels it doesn't make sense, but it made sense with him. All the time, kids at school made those stupid comments about how big his brain was, what a music nerd he was."

Jocelyn notices that the therapist has moved the botanical poster. It is harder to see. *Has she done that because of me?* There is a new white shabby chic shelf to the left of it, blocking half the view. She is tired of this, the dipping into the past, pulling it out of her. It pecks at her. She wishes she could be like the other women she knows. She would like to have one pure space, one room to live inside that is unblemished by the past. A place of anonymity. Kate's lips come to mind.

"Go on," the therapist says.

Jocelyn sighs, trying to control it. "He was sick. He was tired. He just wanted to put his head down."

She sees the metal desk. The ugly woman behind it. The woman's belly spilled over the edge of her tight blue jeans. Her breasts were large, like overfilled water balloons. Jocelyn felt repulsed by her.

"I thought I'd lose my mind," Jocelyn says. "She told him to get his head off her desk. You know, like he would infect it."

The therapist says nothing but writes something down.

"It was a different time. Not like now. People were afraid. Everyone died who had AIDS back then. There wasn't any living with it. Living with AIDS. Hah!"

She reaches in her purse for her cell. She checks the time. She has ten more minutes. Conrad has texted her.

CONRAD: Call me.

Maud has texted her too.

MAUD: Wanna play a friendly?

Will Kate be there? Will she be teaching at the club? She realizes she needs to figure out Kate's schedule. The thought is sudden and unintentional.

She looks at Dr. Bruce, who is waiting patiently for something from her. The room is like a vacuum—all the oxygen going out of it.

"I used to make a point of kissing him on the mouth, you know. I wanted him to know I wasn't afraid of him."

The memory is in the room with her now, as dangerous as a blade, and she remembers lifting his head up off the desk, the curly hair in her hands—fine as a child's eyelashes. Inanition, is what the death certificate said. She had had to look the word up. She is not going to say that now.

After that, she and the therapist sit without talking, until the session is over. Jocelyn feels as if she has won some sort of protest by not speaking again.

"Next week, right?" the therapist says.

"Yes," Jocelyn says, but doesn't think she'll return. Why come? What's the point of languishing back there? Conrad would never know.

"Are you sure you're okay?" Dr. Bruce asks. "You seem distant today. You can call me anytime. I know this is very, very hard."

"Good. I'm fine," Jocelyn says. A bit of a hum in it.

"Are you certain there is nothing else? I don't have another client after you today."

Jocelyn thinks of Mr. Baird, but what will she say, what is it really, and where will it lead once she speaks his name? She thinks of bringing up Kate, but that belongs to her. She doesn't want to give it away.

"Nope."

The therapist looks at her watch. "Next time we'll use the headphones. You seem a bit anxious. They will calm you. It's a part of your therapy. Don't forget to do your tapping. The EMDR treatment is vital. You'll want to begin at your eyebrows, both hands, make your way down to your armpits. Tap your way down."

"Good," Jocelyn says again. "That sounds good."

CHAPTER SIX

SIMON

1

HE BUYS A MAGAZINE AT THE AIRPORT STORE, AND HEADS TO A JET HE charters through his company. He is afraid of flying. The luxury makes it easier, but still his heart pounds. He sees the Cessna Citation through the plate glass window, the men working on it, making sure it is safe. He pushes through the heavy metal doors, walks onto the tarmac. The dry air embraces him and he finds himself wondering what Jocelyn is doing while Lucy is at school. Does she sit at home alone? Should he have asked her to come, to break up the middle of her day? How weird that would have been. How wonderful. She would have thought him a lunatic. Tennis probably, he thinks. She is probably playing tennis.

He makes a shade of his hand. The sun is bright at noon. It hurts his eyes to look at the gleaming plane, which looks like a large white bird—a seagull or a swan. A swan makes him think of Lucy and her second visit to him—her little hands, shaped like sea stars, the dirty nails—semicircles that topped her fingertips. Jocelyn had resisted his invitation at first, but then had given in. Lucy brought miniature animals with her, citizens for his architectural project—koalas with ties on, hamsters with dresses and aprons. She explained to him that all the girls at school liked them. He liked them too. Maybe he could buy her a set. Maybe he could buy himself a set.

The evening had gone well, but Lucy was too serious—angry when her feathers weren't just so, pissed if the swings were a millimeter out of position. He tried to talk her out of this. He lectured her on the importance of imperfection.

"Why would you want to do it poorly?" she'd asked.

"Not poorly," he had said. "But you shouldn't worry about being perfect."

"I'm not worried," she said, matter-of-factly, as if he were a Neanderthal.

Jocelyn told him to give it up. "I haven't won an argument in six years," she said.

They both smiled in the way indulgent parents do, and he felt as if he *were* Lucy's father, as if Jocelyn were his wife. It was good to imagine, made it seem more possible to father his own daughter. If, in fact, she was his daughter.

As he thinks of that evening, he feels a rush of love for the little girl. He feels hope that the "maybe" daughter is really his own. He looks up to the blue sky again. Planes sing above him. He hears the grind of the wheels of the luggage being dollied along the public end of the airport. So high, he thinks, watching the line of planes waiting, levitating. How do they stay? But he knows they don't all stay. His fear is great, but his urge to get the information about his daughter compels him forward. Is she his? Will she be as she used to be? The detective waits for him in Cambridge with facts and pictures.

He looks at his phone, but there are no messages. He checks the weather—clear. Radio RTLMC comes to him. He wonders if it still exists. He hears the voice of the commentator, the static even, although he is at LAX, twenty-plus years later: *The airplane carrying Rwandan president Juvenal Habyarimana and Burundian president Cyprien Ntaryamira was shot down today as it prepared to land in Kigali.* He breathes, looks at his watch. Five minutes until he boards. *Block the thoughts,* he tells himself. *Count your breaths. Flying is safer than driving.*

He walks toward the plane. The white of it hurts his eyes. He puts his sunglasses on. He wishes he could make a stop at Jocelyn's Midwestern city, see the river she described, the bridge. He has the idea that it might settle him. No bodies in the Ohio River. No tied wrists. He wants her to like him. He wants to know the things she knows, so they will always have something to talk about.

His legs carry him forward, even as his mind resists, and then there is the passing scent of oranges in the air as he gets closer to the plane. It stops him where he stands. He breathes in, wanting it. It is not the first time.

The ghosts of the razed California orange groves, or maybe the trees that are miles away, or even the wind that is strong, brings the scent of his wife, Vestine, to him. The oils she made— papaya, mango, but mostly orange. The drops he placed on her neck, her earlobes, the backs of her knees. Bright citrus. He inhales deeply, feels his heart grow heavy. *I am going to find our daughter,* he says internally, and in this way, he says it to Vestine. *Are you in the trees, my love? Are you here with me?*

He wants to forget. He wants to remember. "I have found our daughter," he says out loud, wanting the thought to create reality. *Her name is Lucy,* a voice inside him says, and that thought comes without understanding. A thought full of need. Lucy is a certainty. The door to the plane opens. There is a woman standing there at the top of the stairs—Veronica, his preferred and requested flight attendant. They know each other well. She is there welcoming him. He walks to her. She waves.

INSIDE THE CESSNA, THERE IS A FULL BAR AND PREMADE FOOD THAT IS served by Veronica. She is dressed in green, and calls him sir, which somehow makes his dick hard. He watches her, assessing her value. He feels powerful looking at her. She comes with the plane in the same way that the food and the menu and the open bar does.

Simon considers the possibility of sex with her as she leans over him, making sure his seat belt is buckled correctly.

"Don't be nervous, sir," she says. "We have a very experienced crew."

He has traveled with her often, but he doesn't like that she has implied his fear. She works for him. He wants her to behave a certain way.

She is white with strawberry-blonde hair. She is large breasted, very tall, very thin. Everything he doesn't like. Still, he thinks he would like to have sex with her. He is not picky. Men aren't. He could make it a story to recount. Sex in a private plane, sex with a white woman. He has slept with white women before. Some for free. Some for money. They are not really his thing.

He is comfortably settled in the plane as it lifts to the sky. The captain welcomes him over the intercom. Because of his fear of flying, he is meditating on peaceful things. The seat is roomy and plush. He can smell the leather. He looks out the window and sees the Pacific Ocean. It is turquoise blue and as still as pavement. The plane thrusts forward and up, and they leave LA behind.

He tries to settle down but takeoff is the scariest part. He squeezes his armrest. The plane pulls to the left, curving, apparently heading back to where it came from. He looks at Veronica. He worries that something has happened. She shakes her head and hands him a gin and tonic in a real glass.

He closes his eyes, sips the drink. There is just a touch of turbulence as they rise, the ice in the glass rocks, and then the plane drops like a ride at a theme park. Gin spills. He opens his eyes. The plane rights itself. He tries to be steady, but the lever has clicked. The mind will not turn. He resists the urge to stand, to run. His breath picks up. Narrow nipples, he thinks. Veronica's will be pink and small as beads. He tries to go there but can't. The radio comes next. Always the fucking radio. *This is Radio RTLMC.* Twenty-six years old, already married six years. A smart boy. His father had cattle, a hat, a staff. *The president's plane has been shot down!*

Veronica comes over to him, takes his drink. She kneels down. She puts her hands flat on his forearms. He is trembling. In the seconds that follow, there is his little daughter, Claudette, in his arms again, her heat—thrashing, fighting, screaming, *Papa, Papa!* No one could fathom how quickly it all would change.

He looks at Veronica, but she is not enough. Would she be enough naked? Small fingers hanging on to clothes, pinching material. Then begging, "Please don't take her. Please." He covers his face with his hands. Veronica stands. The squirm of Claudette's body as they pull her up, up, up into the military jeep. Here now as it was that day. Vestine is offering herself. "Take me. Take me. I will do anything," and then, like a miracle, the little body slides back down into his arms, like a rush of water. They have given his daughter back. He doesn't think. He just turns and runs. He leaves his wife on her own.

Veronica slides into the foreground again, offering him a warm cloth. He cannot move. She is pushing his head between his knees. Love, clear in a way that it hasn't been before, is in him like blood. He, as fast as an Olympic runner with Claudette. Ready, set, go. He is off with her, a hero, earning the awe in her eyes, he is the father, the pursuer cannot overtake him, and then the tire iron across the back of his head. He thinks at first a machete. Over and over again. He can feel her falling away, even as he worries about her fall. A man is there picking her up. He feels hands going through his pockets. By the time he regains consciousness,

Claudette is back in the jeep, and the pygmy has sprayed semen on his wife's face. The sperm, like parasites, like sticky bits of rice, on the edge of Vestine's chin. The Twa inside her—an indignity she will not recover from. He pats and pats his pockets, but the identity cards are gone. The thought of losing them is almost as frightening as the thought of losing his daughter.

Veronica is lifting him now, loosening his tie, telling him he will be okay. Cold fingers feel his pulse. Still, there in front of him is the Rwandan sky, the sound of cattle, and the rumble of the jeep. Simon hears his own breathing. Hears the word *hyperventilating.* The young driver turns to him before he drives off—a ski mask, a machete, a fly zipped up, but the eyes are known over a lifetime. Kites held in the windy, boring days of summer. *They are taking the children*, someone says in the early days. *Hotel, motel, Holiday Inn.*

"Abrahm," he mouths and then screams. "Please don't take her!"

But nothing happens even as he says the name. Did he say the name? The jeep rolls slowly forward across the treacherous landscape, and yet far faster than his own legs can carry him. He tries. He runs, blood in his ears, his eyes, but they are always just ahead of him. His daughter sits with flat, shocked eyes, soundlessly looking over the empty cab of the jeep, at the place where her mother has been raped. The old man in the back is stroking his daughter's shoulder. *Such a little girl. Such a little girl*, he says, or does he say? Is this part of the memory or a part of his fear? The distance has grown between, but none of it stops.

"Sir, I need you to slow your breathing," he hears, as Veronica wipes his forehead. He wants to push her away. "Sir." And then a slap across his face. "Sir. I'm sorry. You've got to calm down."

He comes out of it as if he's been inside the terror of a nightmare. The other world is still in him. The world he wakes to is suspicious and strange. The vague static of the radio, sparking and then out.

If the radio hadn't happened, or the plane hadn't crashed, or the men hadn't come for his daughter and raped his wife, he would have lived to be a good man. A man.

He takes hold of Veronica's wrist. Two handed. Tight. An Indian burn is what the American children call it. She shrieks, but he holds on.

"You're okay, sir. Please, sir. You're having a panic attack. Let me help you."

He cannot let go. Blood beneath the surface of her skin makes her forearm pink as a pig's belly.

"We will have to land the plane, sir. Please, let me help you."

He longs for the twitch in his pants again, but she is too thin, too pale. She reminds him of soft white cabbage in soup. He wants her to call him sir again. Make her say it. He feels his fingers being pulled away. She places something over his nose and mouth. It seems to have fallen from the sky.

"There now," she says. He breathes, a rush of oxygen, stars that twinkle and shine, and then shame.

THEY DO NOT SPEAK OF WHAT HAS HAPPENED WHEN HE REACHES EQUI-librium. Veronica works for him. He is the customer. The one that is always right. He does not owe her an explanation. He thanks her for caring for him. It was nothing, she says. A driver is waiting. A shiny black car. They are in Boston. Cambridge is just on the other side of the river. Rain falls steadily. He knows it will eventually be behind him. He will forget it and Veronica will pretend to forget it too. There is traffic in the tunnel. It takes them an hour to reach the hotel. He is glad when the driver speaks.

"Here we are, sir," he says. "The Royal Sonesta. I think you will enjoy your stay."

"Thank you," Simon says, stunned still, trying to come back from the fear of the flight.

"The river is just there on the other side. Lechmere Canal."

"Thank you for the information," he says. His manners come to the rescue and make him sound sane.

A river city, he thinks, looking out the window. Abrahm would have picked a river city—water, as much a part of the two of them as the hair on their heads. He remembers baited hooks. Massive bullfrogs lured with mice, the mangrove trees. The detective says to meet at six o'clock. He says he has solid information.

Simon is grateful that the pictures stopped on the plane when they did. He is relieved that it didn't go farther. Farther would mean that he'd see the thing that she saw. Farther would show Vestine's despair. It was too much for her and for him when he came back empty handed. He wanted to think it was grief, already missing her child. He wanted to think that grief leaves, but it was deeper than that. It was a complete undoing of all that he and she had thought was true. His ineptitude magnified through her tears. *You didn't get her? You didn't get her? Get her!* He could not live with that. Neither could she.

He sees her back, ahead of him. She is running in the swamp. Running away from him. *I cannot be a father*, he realizes. *I have never been able to be that*, and in that realization, he sees that he has never been a husband either. Has he ever even been a man?

Witness, he thinks, as he steps out of the big car, the car that says to everyone that he is important.

He watches the driver retrieve his bags. There is a bellhop. He is black, in a uniform that is strangely militaristic. There are epaulets. Simon's servants were Hutu in Kigali. He could not know himself or his ineffectualness then, but his wife, Vestine, saw it. Knew it. She saw how deeply he had failed. *What is it to be a man?* The answer in her eyes, unwavering.

BEFORE HE LEAVES BOSTON, HE VISITS THE COMMON AND RIDES IN THE swan boats on the only sunny day. He buys a book for Lucy: *Make Way for Ducklings.*

When he gets back to Los Angeles, he knocks on Jocelyn's door. Lucy's eyes dance when he hands the book to her.

"Come on in," Lucy says, before her mother gives her permission. "I'll read it to you."

"May I?" he asks.

"Of course," Jocelyn says.

"Come on. Come on," Lucy says, patting the space on the couch that is right next to her.

"Are you sure you can read?" he asks. "You seem so young. You must be a genius."

"I'm really smart. Right, Mama? Right? Aren't I like a genius?"

"Right," Jocelyn says, smiling at him. "A very modest genius."

CHAPTER SEVEN

JOCELYN

1

WINTER HAS FINALLY COME TO LOS ANGELES, AND TWO TENNIS DRILLS are rained out. Jocelyn sits at home, thinking about Kate's mouth, her tanned legs, her thighs. What would her skin feel like? Jocelyn would like to see her squirm with need, beg. She is aware of all of these feelings, but she cannot reconstruct the cause. Even the cart overturning is unconvincing as an origin. The effect of her imaginings is the erasing of everything else.

During her days at home without tennis, she tries to figure out what's happening. She reads and rereads the texts between them, but they deal with workout times, practices, money owed. Nothing is inappropriate or flirtatious. On occasion the words seem sly and sexual.

JOCELYN: Is it too wet to play today?
KATE: Maybe.
JOCELYN: Very wet over here . . .

Jocelyn writes the words intentionally, and then, to make them less odd, she adds:

JOCELYN: . . . by my condo.

She tries to stay calm. It is nothing. It is everything. It has to do with aging, she thinks. It has to do with feeling better physically from tennis or her mother dying. Maybe therapy is having a strange effect on her. It is making her too open. She has started to hate therapy, but Conrad insists. He tells her she needs to stay ahead of it. He still finds her crying sometimes, before she can hide. She can't help but brush the tile.

She tries to convince herself that this thing with Kate will pass, whatever it is. She cleans the kitchen, meticulously organizes her dresser drawers. She thinks she wants to do it with Kate, but what does she want to do exactly? Would Kate be willing?

She reminds herself that she is crazy, which helps. Fucked-up childhoods have long teeth. She should tell her therapist about it. Confess. She *should* confess, but at the bottom of that thought is the idea that she might not really want to be done with it.

After days and days of contemplating and considering and intentionally staying away from drill class (*I will not go. I will not go. I will be married. I will behave.*), the obsession leaves her as quickly as it has come. She is happy. She fucks her husband. She comes. When they finish, he rolls over, tells her he loves her, loves their life.

"I can't believe we still have this kind of sex," he says, staring at the ceiling.

"Me either," she says.

"I have to go out of town again," he says.

"Why?" she asks.

"You know why, silly girl."

He is smiling at her, leaning on his elbow now. "Work," he says. "I have to pay for this." His fingertip makes a circle on her stomach. "You think a woman like you would be with a man like me if I didn't make a ton of money?"

She laughs lightly, because she is supposed to. She *would* be with him, no matter what. She wants to be with him.

Her phone buzzes. Conrad tells her to forget about it. She reaches for it anyway, reads:

KATE: I'm teaching on Monday and Tuesday. Do you want anything then?

There is an instant surge—a flash, like a light being turned on. *I want everything then*, she thinks.

She fantasizes in the minutes that follow. She stares at the phone. The fantasy is the perfect situation—twenty-four hours in a hotel room, drinks after work, but what work? Jocelyn doesn't work. Jocelyn is a mother. She can't work and do that. Her eyes must be open and attentive at all times. Not that the predators are easy to see, but they are there. She needs to talk to Maud about Mr. Baird still. She cannot let Kate get in the way of that.

"Who's texting you?" Conrad asks, still caressing her stomach.

"Tennis."

She says yes to both days. A smiling emoji buzzes in return. She wonders if she is just money to Kate, but then lets the thought go. Her husband's mouth is on her skin now. She allows it. She is thinking about Kate. The whole room swells with her. It is like Alice overflowing, her presence too big for the Wonderland house. She pushes his head down. She has decided. In the roar of a second orgasm, she will pretend Conrad is someone else: blonde hair, green eyes looking up at her from between her legs, watching her come, seeing her lose control.

"When are you leaving?" she asks, as he makes his way down.

"Tomorrow. Early morning."

THE FIRST TIME THEY TOUCH IS DURING A PRIVATE LESSON. CONRAD IS out of town. She arrives for the lesson at eleven o'clock, and Kate seems happy to see her. It feels like friendship, not business. Jocelyn likes it, likes taking instruction, likes running around and getting tired. Nerves vibrate inside her from the start.

"Be gentle with me," she says, as Kate warms her up, running her back and forth to hit balls. "I hurt myself cleaning."

"Cleaning?" Kate says, not missing a feed. They both laugh a little. "Don't you have anyone to help you?"

There is a moment of terror that pings in Jocelyn, a reminder that she might not quite be right for this life at the Miramar. She might not fit into the club and all that it represents. Or, more horribly, her wrongness might show. She does not have a maid. She doesn't like strangers in her space. She has an aversion to anyone going through her underthings. She is obsessively clean. In the past when she's tried, the women were always disappointing.

"Well, yes," she says. The lie comes. "But not a live-in."

Kate's eyes sparkle. "You'll have one of those soon enough. Once you get more and more into tennis, you won't have time for cleaning."

"Who says I'm getting more and more into tennis?" she asks.

"I say." Kate's voice is assured, bossy even. She smiles.

Jocelyn smiles back, and then they play.

At a break, when Jocelyn is getting water, Kate says, "Where did you hurt yourself exactly? Did you pull something?"

They are a foot apart—a wooden bench with an attached table is beside them. Their large tennis bags are balanced there. The question is nonchalant, and yet not exactly. Jocelyn looks up into Kate's eyes and sees possibility. She feels the animal terror of adolescence, primeval fear, and then silence. Jocelyn decides, feeling her heartbeat surge. Her hands tremble. She lifts her skirt, just an inch, but she is aware of it for what it is: an invitation.

"Here," she says and takes Kate's hand and places it on the inside of her thigh. "Right here."

Kate stares at her. Jocelyn sees surprise move across Kate's face. A ripple. A grin. She seems to be assessing: What is the risk? What is the responsibility? Jocelyn watches as Kate glances around at the other courts. No one is near enough to see. Her hand stays where it is.

"Is this the right spot?" Kate says then—very quietly. Jocelyn can feel blood pool in her cheeks. Kate's eyes are as green as the peel of a lime. She keeps her stare still but moves her body to block anyone from seeing what is happening. Kate's hand is warm and soft, not at all like Conrad's.

For a minute, as they look at one another, Jocelyn considers pushing Kate down, making her kneel on the ground in front of her. She forgets where she is. She has a vision of Kate's bruised knees.

Kate moves her hand inside Jocelyn's tennis shorts in the way that her husband has done many times before. The edge of her panties lift. There is the catch of breath. The tip of a finger. Jocelyn hasn't blinked.

"How about here?" Kate says. "You tell me, because I don't want to hurt you." Her voice is a whisper. "I want it to feel good."

"I like it," Jocelyn hears herself saying. The fingers move between her legs more easily. A wet puddle in a hand. She leans into Kate's ear, smells the clean scent of shampoo in the blonde tendrils that have come loose from the bun.

We are in cahoots now, robbers in a crime, she thinks, but says, "Yes" and then, "Please."

THEY HEAR THE HEAD PRO, HARTFORD BENNINGTON, RUNNING—THE slap of his feet. Kate pulls away quickly—all business. He is tall. It seems as if his body moves the ground. Jocelyn tries to snap out of the dream she is in.

"Sorry," Kate says.

"I just . . ." Jocelyn says, but can't finish. She wants to put Kate's hand back. She smells the edge of herself in the air.

"We can't," Kate says.

Jocelyn has to force herself not to beg, and says, "Yes. Of course."

"Go back to the baseline," Kate almost shouts.

Jocelyn tries to orient herself. She is slow to move. Hartford walks by, lifts his hand. Kate waves back.

"Please go back to the baseline," Kate says again, even more firmly. "Jesus. Fuck. What are we doing?"

Jocelyn doesn't answer. She walks to the back of the court, but she is unsteady. She finds that she is in a kind of daze. Her entire body feels swollen from the brief contact, especially the space between her legs. She is afraid to run, although Kate is instructing her to. She is afraid she will come on the court. She worries that her wetness will run down the inside of her leg, which has happened once with her period, the sheer, almost clear blood of the first day. She wants to grab Kate, move her, make her.

When they break, they both get water. They look away from each other. Kate speaks first.

"We can't do that. Ever."

Jocelyn feels her face redden. She is embarrassed, so disappointed. How could she have thought? She starts to say something, but Kate reaches out, touches Jocelyn's hip, just on the outside of her tennis skirt. She lets her thumb graze the front of Jocelyn's thigh. There is pity in the touch, and Jocelyn doesn't like it.

"It's not that I don't want to, but . . ."

"I understand," Jocelyn says, not wanting to hear any more. All of it a reminder of how stupid she is. "Don't say anything else."

"I'm married."

"Yes. Me too. Of course."

They do not mention it again. They hit balls back and forth. Kate gives instruction. Jocelyn listens. A robot inhabits Jocelyn's insides. At the end of the private, Kate looks in her appointment book.

"I'll see you tomorrow," she says. "Right? I mean I've got you down."

Jocelyn doesn't know if she should come tomorrow or not, so she says nothing.

"I've got to switch to court seven now," Kate says. She shuts her book. "They're cleaning this one. You can stay here. Take your time. You can get your stuff together. Maintenance will wait for you."

Jocelyn doesn't move.

Kate gets her bag, pushes the cart of balls. "Just text me if you want to cancel," she says and walks off. She doesn't say goodbye.

Jocelyn feels dismissed. *Crumbs*, she thinks. *She has given me crumbs, and now I am angry because she has taken them away.* Raw shame overwhelms her as she tries to recount exactly what happened, whose fault it is, whose fault it will seem. The details are vague—the quality of vision like that of being underwater.

Jocelyn sits down on the bench, looking at the spot on the court where they were standing. She wonders what this thing that has happened will mean now. Disgust at herself, at her weakness, fills her. The image of her maternal grandmother comes to her. Jocelyn wants to scream it away; knows she might cry. Old and wrinkled, she was, her wig always a bit offset. The balding scalp beneath was almost cylindrical. Jocelyn hated her grandmother. Her grandfather's erection whenever she sat on his lap, the expectation that it should be tolerated.

"Dirty little beggars!" her grandmother would say when she saw them in their makeshift Halloween costumes, and Jocelyn would feel the bottom of her stomach drop out.

She feels the same way now, sitting on the bench on her own, thinking of the touch, how drawn she was and needing. She remembers being hungry as a child. Another secret to be kept. The hidden candy melting under pillows, eaten inside sheets.

She hears the steady beat of balls being hit back and forth—a woman is laughing. She hears Kate's voice loud and instructing as if nothing has happened. *Am I the only one here?* she wonders. *In this place?* And then just as suddenly, *What if I am the only one here?*

Jocelyn stands, getting herself together. She feels sweaty and unwell, like a child who has had a tantrum. She walks to the front desk, and then realizes she has forgotten her tennis bag. When she goes back to court 3, it is there. Maud is there too.

"What's wrong with you, chickadee?" she asks. "We were supposed to meet at twelve thirty. We're all waiting. Did you forget? You look a mess."

"I don't feel very well" is all Jocelyn can think to say.

"You can play, can't you?" Maud is a bit whiny. "You have to play. We've been waiting."

"Yes," Jocelyn says. "Sure. Of course, I can play."

SHE DOESN'T PLAY WELL, AND THEY LOSE THE FRIENDLY. THERE IS TOO much on her mind, and Missy being there makes it worse. Jocelyn hates her. More now than when she first met her. She doesn't know why she is there or who invited her. Missy gloats over the win. She walks to the net. They shake hands.

"I've really got to dash, girls," she says. "It's been fun, but I've got a new girl. She's probably washing my tennis clothes in hot."

She laughs a high whinnying laugh, but no one else gets the joke.

Jocelyn walks with Maud out to the parking lot.

"That was fun even though we sucked," Maud says. "You sucked anyway."

When Jocelyn doesn't respond, Maud says, "Earth to Jocelyn. Come in, Jocelyn." Maud's voice is joking, but it doesn't lift the mood. None of them likes to lose. Ever.

"Sorry," Jocelyn says. "I did suck. I'm just . . . well, I have a lot on my mind." *Like Kate*, she thinks. *Like what the hell happened.*

"Okay," Maud says, neutrally.

"I hate losing to Missy," Jocelyn says. "She's so over the top. She'll be talking about it for days."

"Who cares? She's an idiot."

"I know," Jocelyn says. "That's why I hate losing to her."

"Don't worry about it. We'll beat them next time."

Maud says it like a woman who has had everything she has ever wanted and expects more of the same. There isn't even a hint of doubt.

"Maud?" Jocelyn says. "Can I ask you something?"

"Of course, Ms. Serious." Maud puts a hand on her shoulder. "What's that face?"

"It's about school, you know. I've been thinking about Mr. Baird. He's Lucy's new teacher. You've heard that Ms. Serrania has left, right?"

"I heard. Yep." Maud glances at her watch. "Let's walk and talk. I've got a facial at two."

"I just can't help but feel weird about him being a man."

Maud sighs. "Mr. Baird is fine," she says. "They wouldn't hire anyone who wasn't."

"Yes," Jocelyn says. "I keep telling myself that."

"They vet them," Maud says, matter-of-factly. "Also, the way I like to think of it is that it's important for girls to have male teachers before they become adolescents. I fell in love with my art teacher when I was thirteen. He could have done anything he wanted to me. That's what happens when you don't have a male teacher until your hormones are raging. He was gay, by the way." She laughs, squeezes Jocelyn's arm. "I figured that out much later. God was he beautiful though. Sort of like Prince."

Jocelyn smiles. "You're so funny," she says.

"God's truth." Maud holds up a vowing hand. They are almost to their cars.

"So, I shouldn't worry?"

"Nope."

Jocelyn feels a shudder of relief pass through her. She wonders if she could talk to Maud about Kate. What would Maud think?

"Thanks," Jocelyn says. "I suppose you're right."

"You're welcome," Maud says and hugs her. "Ask me anything, anytime, except to babysit."

Jocelyn laughs.

Maud is looking through her purse for her keys. The white Range Rover gleams in a spot three over. "You headed home?"

"I'm actually going to therapy."

"Mine is on Fridays," Maud says. "Wealthy women and our problems."

"Conrad kind of insists. I had a bit of a breakdown early in our marriage. I mean not since then, but, well my mother just died. He worries."

"Oh gosh, honey. I'm sorry to hear that. That must be awful."

"Yes, well. We didn't have the best relationship. It's just weird. I don't want to talk about it. I suppose he's right. I should go."

"Unfortunately, we've got to do what the men say sometimes," Maud says, making it light.

Jocelyn turns to look for her own car. Maud speaks: "Don't worry so much, Jocelyn. Our kids aren't stupid. They know when something isn't right. You're feeling insecure because of your mom. It makes you vulnerable."

"Yes," Jocelyn says. "Kids aren't stupid." She feels like a parrot.

They hug goodbye, and Jocelyn heads slowly to her car. She wonders and remembers. *We weren't stupid either though*, she thinks. *That was not our problem.*

She reaches in her purse. She puts on her Cutler and Gross sunglasses. She wishes she had told Maud about what happened with Kate. She just wants to let it out of her body. She wants to let Mr. Baird out too.

I will watch him, she thinks. *Closely. Whenever I come to school: pickup, drop-off, volunteer shift, assembly, classroom parties, field trips, lunchroom duty. I can do this. I have to. I'm her mother. I'm a good mother. It can't happen. Not to Lucy.* There is a quiet ruthlessness to her plan.

She sifts through possibilities, more ways to keep her daughter safe. She could add volunteer days, although she's already really involved. She gets into her car, tells herself that Maud knows. Maud is part of this world. Maud would tell her to worry if she should worry.

"I THINK WE SHOULD FINISH TALKING ABOUT YOUR BROTHER," DR. BRUCE says, but Jocelyn doesn't want to enter the past. Her brother is not on her mind after what has happened this morning. Mr. Baird and Kate. Mr. Baird and Kate. Mr. Baird and Kate. These names ricochet back and forth inside her brain, one word after the other, no room between. Which should she say? Which should she deal with? *Neither*, she thinks. She has the sense that they will break her open. *I am not ready yet*.

"Last week it seemed there was a breakthrough with your brother," Dr. Bruce says.

Jocelyn stares. She does not even remember the session. "Why do you say that?"

"I don't know. I just thought we were close to something. You've had a lot of loss—your brother, your mother very recently. In my opinion, people do not talk enough about the dead."

"People always talk about the dead," Jocelyn says, "when the dead aren't their own."

It comes out aggressively, a criticism of the doctor, but Dr. Bruce doesn't seem to notice.

"What more can you tell me, Jocelyn? You have to talk or I can't help you. What about his illness? Were you his caregiver? The story you told last week about his head on the desk." Dr. Bruce looks at her notes. "About the fat lady, made it seem as if you took care of him when he was dying. That must have been very, very hard."

She looks at the therapist. She feels herself surrendering, as if to something physical. She decides she can't fight her. She can't fight Conrad either. She must be here. Life is eternally something to behave for.

"I took care of him. He was very sick at the end. There wasn't

much that we could do. He was *the one that got away.* You know?
Ycidra and I loved watching him escape. CVG airport, across the
Brent Spence Bridge. It was like a movie. Of course, he went to
Manhattan."

In the corner of the office she sees toys. She wonders about
the children that come here: Are they as she and her siblings were
as children, damaged and unlovable? She remembers eating Chi-
nese food with her brother in bed in his apartment in Midtown.
They shared the same chopsticks, passed the same box of orange
chicken back and forth. It is a memory from the early days of
the disease, before he seemed sick, when eating was something
he still did.

"Were you comfortable with him being gay?" Dr. Bruce asks.

"Yes," Jocelyn says. "Sure. I didn't think about it. Gladys and
Uncle Al said it was a sin, but there's not much to be done about
being gay, right?"

Jocelyn tries to anchor herself on the poster again, but it isn't
working. It's too far out of her view for her to read the difficult
words. Her brother always liked men, never women. She always
liked men too, never women. The girl in college was curiosity
more than desire. She likes Kate, but that feels singular, as if Kate
is the only woman in the world whom she wants or will ever want.

"You seem more distant than usual today, Jocelyn. I felt that
way last time too," the therapist says. "Are you okay? Remember,
the fight will be easier if I prescribe something. You can always
come off of it again. We can taper off."

"No. I'm fine. No meds," she says. "I don't want to depend on
a drug."

"But why?" Dr. Bruce asks. "It will help you. Prescriptions
aren't the same as street drugs."

Internally Jocelyn rolls her eyes. Ycidra and her Vicodin.
Ycidra and her doctors, the Oxy, the Percocet, just the beginning
of things. The session ends and she has not talked about Kate or
Mr. Baird. Nor has she told the whole story about her brother.
She finds herself keeping things from Dr. Bruce more and more.

Her brother is still with her when she leaves the office, and she is angry about this. It is as if Dr. Bruce has performed a séance and has drawn down the dead. She'd like for her brother to go away. She'd like for Kate to go away too. She'd like for Mr. Baird to teach some other little girl, not her own, for Ycidra to leave her mind. The death of Gladys has opened some Pandora's box and she can't get it to close again.

She walks to her car—the car that Conrad has bought for her this year. It costs as much as a house in a good Cincinnati neighborhood. It has four doors because of Lucy, but it is sleek and fast. It is dark blue, the color of the sea that night when she and Lucy painted with Simon. It isn't the kind of car that sneaks up on you. She longs for Conrad suddenly. He is so steady. Never a blip in him. She dials.

"Hi, my love," she says. "How's it going?"

"It's okay. I miss you. And Lucy," he says. "Actors are annoying. All the extra social shit I have to do, you know."

"We miss you a lot," she says, fiddling with the air-conditioning vents in the gleaming dash. "I hope you're being good," she says, half joking, half thinking about her own sins.

"I'm being *pretty* good," he says. "Lots of temptation. Entertainment has been provided." He says this as if they are sharing an inside joke. "I'm holding out though. You'd be proud."

"What do you mean?" she says. There is a snap of jealousy. "You mean like women, like dancers?"

"Sometimes," he says. "Not all of them dance. Some just sit around and look pretty. Others bring us whatever we want. Drinks. Food. They change the music. They walk around in skimpy clothes. It's a thirteen-year-old's wet dream. You know, female slaves. The actor pays for it, I think. Although he doesn't admit it. It's totally stupid, totally predictable. It doesn't really warm me up."

"Hmmmm," she says, doubting him.

"No sex," Conrad says, firmly. "Don't worry about it, silly. You know I don't want that from anyone but you."

"I guess," she says, and then relaxes a little. She laughs. "You are so full of shit. You're enjoying it, but I like that you lie to me sometimes."

"I'm into *you*," he says. "That's not a lie."

"What else?" she asks.

He tells the rest of it. The bathing suits, the few married men who have gotten blow jobs in a back bathroom. Gossip and the landscape of Louisiana—endless rain and water everywhere, the bugs. He tells her he has stepped in a mound of fire ants. One of the women poured Pappy Van Winkle on his foot.

"Oh my God," she says. "What a waste of good bourbon!"

"Exactly, but the fucker worked. She was my nurse."

"Uh-huh. I bet," she says. All coy.

She can tell he is smiling on the other end of the phone, and thinks, *We have always been like this, have always told the truth about everything—until right now. I should tell him about Kate. I have crossed a line.* She feels tender toward him.

"There are alligators here," Conrad says, as if he is looking at one just outside his window. "It's really beautiful," he says. "I don't mean the girls."

"I know," she says. "I know."

They sit saying nothing, just holding the phone. It is intimate. The girls come to mind again, and beyond Jocelyn's jealousy, she knows they are just commerce, like Walmart, like Costco, like the shops that run up and down Sunset, like Kate and her hourly fees, they are a part of the transaction. There are so many worse things.

"The pills will make your brother better," the doctor said to her. He had stopped her in the hall at Saint Vincent's Hospital, as they made their way out of the fat lady's office. Her brother had to lean into her to stay upright. She held his thin elbow.

"Make an appointment. Come to me directly," the doctor said. "Your brother can stay home."

And then when she got to his office, a few days later; sleet as she ran up the subway stairs, almost slipping, a day impossible to forget: "On your knees," the doctor said. Just like that.

The pill bottle when he handed it to her was warm as his cock had been in her mouth. Business, she thinks. Negotiation and favors. Transactions. But still, my brother is dead.

"Jocelyn?" She hears Conrad's voice coming through the Bluetooth. "Hello? Did I lose you?"

"We used to play Monopoly on the steps outside of our building," she says. "My brother was always the banker."

She can feel herself getting shaky. His memory here, a needle in and out of the skin, making a stitch.

There is a pause because her husband knows her—twenty years is a lifetime to be with someone, and so, very gently he says, "Yes, babe. It's okay, sweetheart. Are you all right?"

"I'm not doing that great," she says, feeling as if she might cry. Her voice breaks. The day has been long and full and confusing. "Something's not right with me since Gladys. I'm just not myself."

She hears other voices coming through the phone now.

"I'm going to be home soon, okay? Are you going to therapy? You're keeping up, right?"

"Yes," she says. "I'm being good. I'm just leaving her office."

"Your mother was an ass, honey. She never did a good thing in her life, except make you."

Jocelyn feels defeated by the words. She thinks about Ycidra and William. Her brother's final zealousness. Her looking away. Groveling at the end. *God will save me*, he said. Shallowness in the voice, tapping the black Bible cover with his thin fingers. Religion—the worst last resort. They all knew God had never saved them from anything.

She sighs, feels the fact that therapy is making her worse. What was she thinking, why go back? A chain on the waist, restrictive, a boulder attached, something to carry, up, up, up. She shouldn't talk to Dr. Bruce anymore. She shouldn't return to the past. She should tell Conrad right now about everything. She should tell him about Kate and Mr. Baird, and it will be better, because she will repent. She will stop therapy and stop tennis and just mother. She will take Lucy to the park and the zoo and the pool. They will hold hands on the diving board. She will be the best mother. She will not cry anymore without meaning to.

"Jocelyn?" he says again, and she thinks, *I cannot let him hang up. If I don't tell him now, I will be punished. Lucy will be kidnapped or touched or ruined. Conrad will die in a car crash. Have I not learned to speak up?*

"Conrad?"

He is talking to someone who has walked into the room. It sounds as if there are children there. Young girls? Are the girls in the back bathroom children? She feels nauseated.

"What do you mean it's the wrong location?" she hears her husband say. "We have to scout today. Not tomorrow." And then back to her: "Honey, can I call you right back? Twenty minutes at the most, my love. I've got a screwup here, and you know, everyone just walked in." He whispers: "It's not a good time to talk."

She waits, because the answer to whether he can call her back is somewhere inside a vast black hole that she cannot find her way out of. *Speak up!* she tells herself again. The yellow pajamas, his voice, cold floors. *Please don't*, Ycidra said.

He is angry suddenly. "Jocelyn? Can I call you back?!"

"Conrad?" she asks again. She feels weak. She needs to tell him. "Please, Jocelyn. I'll call you right back."

She hears the disconnection of the phone. She sits many minutes thinking. She needs to drive the car, to get back home.

4

HE DOESN'T CALL RIGHT BACK OR AT ALL THAT EVENING. AT THE CONDO-minium, with Lucy in the white Waterworks bath, she wonders briefly if he is with one of the women. The Louisiana cottage would be large, with many bedrooms—down comforters and king-size beds. The women would be problem-free. Why has he forgotten about her? An unrelenting sorrow presses against the edges of her mind, discouragement. She had been doing well un-til just—when? A day ago, a week ago, a minute ago, when? The memory of her brother settles across her brain again, the doctor and the meds, Kate, Mr. Baird and Gladys, Ycidra. A curtain made of people, sweeping shut. All of it dark.

She recognizes the instant descent. It fills and presses, swells. Her heart aches, literally. There is the sodden heaviness of inade-quacy like wet newspaper. She tries to focus on the breathing that Dr. Bruce has taught her, the tapping for survivors of trauma. That's what she is, the doctor has defined her—a survivor of trauma. She has been named.

The Before, she thinks. *All of what has come before is demolishing me.*

Jocelyn moves through the good things. They should buoy her up. She thinks about Lucy in the inner tube, Lucy building the park with Simon, she and Lucy on the high diving board at the Miramar club, but the sorrow seems to *be* her, not some other thing, and so it will not go. The good will not right her.

She studies her daughter as she plays in the bath. The girl will be prey if she doesn't keep hold of it. There is the slim shape, the soft skin. Her fingernails are little crescent moons. Her brown eyes are clear and happy. The child is utterly uninhibited. Totally trusting. Jocelyn admonishes herself. She has to be ever mindful. She has to be focused on this one thing and let the other things go. She cannot weaken. If she can be a good mother, it will be a true thing. It will bury Gladys completely. No ghosts will hover into Lucy's future.

"Remember *Eloise Takes a Bawth*, Mama?" Lucy asks. "Remember how fun she was? She almost sunk the Plaza, Mama. What's the Plaza again?"

"It's a hotel, my love. Well, not any longer. At least I don't think so. Now it's residential."

"What's residential, Mama."

"Apartments, sweetheart. Apartments."

"What's an apartment, Mama?"

"Well, it's like this, sweetheart. Like our house." She presses her fingertips gently to her eyelids.

"Papa says we live in a condo, not a house," Lucy says. "A *luxury* condo. Papa says it's important to have a concierge, which we have at *our* condo. Papa says it's good to have a doorman too. George is our doorman and Rodrigo. Papa says it's unique to have a doorman in Los Angeles, but that we are unique. I say, 'Hello Rodrigo!' Every day."

"Yes, well. An apartment is like this, only you pay rent."

"What's rent?"

Jocelyn sighs.

Lucy splashes around in the tub. The question is forgotten as soon as it is asked. The water jumps in sharp little waves, some of it landing on the marble floor, some on Jocelyn's dark jeans. The bubbles are excessive. Dish detergent is what they had in Winton Terrace. No such thing as bubble bath in their house. Ycidra had figured out that if they rationed it, she could make Jocelyn a "day at the spa," bubbles all around her, indulgent and special. But then Gladys had noticed, and had beaten them both, calling them thieving, stinking dirty birds anyway.

A beating for soap? It seems unreal to her now, but she knows that it happened.

"Don't cry," Ycidra would say whenever they were punished.

She'd put her hand out, and when Jocelyn wouldn't take it, she'd put her palm on the top of Jocelyn's forehead, and say, "The Great Ycidranova will tell your future. You will grow up to be a famous sailor."

There was warmth in those fingers, and then she would pull Jocelyn into her own body, being careful of where the belt had cut her, and the blood was drying, and the shirt was sticking, and Jocelyn can still feel the pull of this sometimes. She can still hear the beating of Ycidra's heart, fast and afraid, although she always pretended otherwise: "I'm here with you, Jo-Jo. Don't be scared. We're going to sail away one day." But where did they sail?

"It's a bawthroom, Mummy," Lucy says in an English accent, and cracks up laughing.

Jocelyn smiles at her child, but the fight to not cry hurts and suppresses her breathing like knuckles pressed into rib bones, or a heavy body on a small one. *My child*, she thinks. But how had that girl come from her? How had something so breezy come from the solid damp of her?

The brown swirl of the Ohio River falls across her memory. The walk across the bridge to school, a crossing over, into another land. The cars whizzing by, the rocking of the bridge, its singing. She, holding her sister's warm hand. *I'm on the car side*, Ycidra would say. A following after. An imprint. She was Ycidra's duckling.

She hands Lucy the raspberry soap. *Ycidra*, she thinks. *My child doesn't know my sister's name. She does not know my brother's name.* Ycidra and William, she wants to say, but keeps both names in—protective, fearful that whatever infected them all as children might implant itself in Lucy now. Do not speak the names of the dead. Where had she heard that? Gladys, she knows. And the beg again, fight the forced dilation.

She tries to use Kate to steady her, but the image of her and what she wants from her does not lift her or come clear. She loves Conrad. She knows this, but there seems to be some trick there too. She is vaguely aware that she needs to pull herself together, that she needs to find something light, but it isn't there. The dark has been made for her by Gladys. She reaches for a towel from the towel warmer. She thinks she had better get her child out. *Get the child out of the water!* She hears an inner voice shrieking, but she can't move. She can't stop thinking about the dark. The known and familiar dark.

CHAPTER EIGHT

SIMON

1

HE RUNS INTO JOCELYN IN THE HALL. IT HAS BEEN TWO DAYS SINCE HE last saw her and her daughter, since Lucy read the book to him. They both wait together for the elevator. He has a meeting at the museum and is running a bit late. She looks gloomy. He does not like to see her sad. The child is not with her, and he worries before he can stop himself that something has happened to Lucy. Panic moves through him like wildfire. He reminds himself that he has just seen her, that she was fine when they shared the book. He knows he is experiencing his own paranoia, his own residual fears from Claudette. *She is fine*, he tells himself.

"How are you?" he asks.

"Good," she says. "Conrad is out of town still, but I'm okay."

He notices how slow her speech is. She isn't really engaged. He wonders momentarily if she is on some kind of medication.

"You must miss him," he says.

"Yes," she says. "I do."

"Maybe you could come for dinner. Lucy could work on the park some more. It might make the days until he returns go faster."

She gives him a brief smile. "We would like that. Thank you. Lucy would especially."

They stand silently, formally, waiting for the elevator. He looks at her more closely. He wants to say something more. He wants to feel close to her again.

"I was wondering," he says, trying. "I was wondering if you could possibly do me a favor?"

She does not hesitate at all when she answers. "If I can, I will," she says. "Of course."

He watches her watching the floor numbers of the elevator illuminate. She is not looking at him. From this angle, he can see the fine lines around her eyes. Dark circles.

"Are you sure you're okay?" he asks again.

"Yes," she says. "Not enough sleep. I never sleep well when Conrad's gone. Everything sort of falls on me. It's a mother thing."

She smiles, but the smile is gone as quickly as it comes.

The elevator doors open. They step inside.

"What is it?" she says. "What favor?"

"I was hoping we could play tennis sometime," he says. "I haven't played since I was a boy, and I know you love it, and I used to love it. Could we? Maybe you could reintroduce me to the game?"

"Sure," she says. A full smile suddenly. "That's not what I thought you'd ask."

"What did you think?"

"I don't know. I just thought it would be more serious. Tennis is, well . . . it's not exactly a favor."

"Wonderful," he says. He is glad that there is a slight opening.

"Do you belong to the Miramar Club?" she asks.

"I don't," he says. "But we can go to the rec center at the park."

"Or," she says, "you could be my guest."

"No," he says. "No. I might be embarrassing. It's been a while since I've played."

"You're silly," she says. "You are welcome to come with me."

He has the sense that they both know what they aren't saying. He says it bluntly. "No, I don't think I'd feel comfortable there."

She looks down. "Okay," she says. "I guess I don't really want to go to the club anyway. It's been making me kind of miserable."

"Is it something you would like to talk about?"

"No," she says. "But tennis with you at the park would be good."

She is back, he thinks. At least a little. He will not push it. He will be careful with her. She seems a vulnerable creature.

"Tomorrow?" he asks.

"Yes," she says. "After I drop Lucy at school. I will look forward to it."

THE NEIGHBORHOOD WHERE THE MUSEUM IS LOCATED IS GENTRIFIED, BUT the drive there goes through areas that are not safe. Along the edge of the highway, Simon notices houses that must have, at one time, been grand. Since he is an architect, he knows that white people have tried already to turn this neighborhood, to restore the wood floors and the gaslights and the old ballrooms of these hundred-year-old houses, but West Adams is still, essentially, a ghetto.

Because it is rush hour, traffic on 10 East is like a parking lot. He checks his phone whenever he stops. He counts the lanes—five across at a standstill, including the carpool lane. He has grown used to traffic. It is a way of life in Los Angeles. His car is set up as if it were an extension of his condo. He has a very expensive sound system. There are recorded books, favorite podcasts, old music. The hope is to enjoy the ride, even when he isn't moving. His car is comfortable, spotlessly clean. The leather seats and wooden dash gleam. In his experience, only white people have dirty cars.

In the lane next to him, in a bright red convertible Mustang, he notices a young man, Hispanic maybe. He is smoking. Even though Simon hasn't smoked in fifteen years, he considers asking the man for a cigarette. The urge is there. He'd just like a drag, the tiniest bit. He could get up, open his car door, walk over, have a little chat if he wanted. That is how still the traffic is. He taps his fingers on his steering wheel, still looking at the man, enjoying the beat of the song. The tennis with Jocelyn is on his mind. Something to look forward to.

He moves to raise the volume on his radio, a song from childhood, American rap. Joy at first, and then the pressing of violence, inextricable. Impossible to separate it from the music.

He reaches to turn the music off, turn the memory off, and as he does this, he notices out of the corner of his eye, a dog, on the shoulder of the freeway, sitting, perfectly still. He thinks at first that it might be a statue, like the tiny white crosses that mark the early deaths of young drivers. He keeps his focus on it. Is it real? And then it moves.

The dog is lean. His once barreled chest looks like a birdcage. He is what people call a fighting dog. The sort that eats babies and turns on owners. He knows from the news that they fill the pounds and shelters—a pit bull. Simon does not dislike dogs, but he does not like them either. In Rwanda, Claudette wanted a dog. A fact he has forgotten until just now.

He tells himself not to look at the dog, but he can't help looking. It is regal, even in its diminished state. It is a dog for a king. The king must miss it. Simon's brain does this sometimes. It starts on an adventure and keeps on going. The traffic doesn't move. The man in the next car throws his cigarette out the window.

Simon decides that he should do something about the dog. He asks his phone to call animal control, and his Bluetooth does its magic.

A man with a bland voice picks up, assures him they will get the dog. "What exit?" the man asks.

"I don't know the exact number. I'm on the ten . . . at Arlington . . . by the entrance ramp."

"Got it," the officer says, but his tone is dismissive. Simon does not sense that he is writing the information down.

"You understand it is a traffic hazard," Simon says to the man on the phone. "I mean what if the dog rushes out onto the freeway?"

He looks at the dog again. Rushes? No way could it rush. The dog is lying down now. He can't stop staring, wondering. How are these things abandoned? How does that happen to a dog, to a beloved house with a ballroom, to a child, to a man? In flowing traffic, he would not have noticed it. Traffic does not flow here. Life makes us see.

"We'll take care of it," the man on the phone says.

"Thanks," Simon says.

THE NEXT DAY, HE AND JOCELYN GO TO THE PUBLIC COURTS BY THE library, which are clean but worn. They cost eight dollars an hour, which he insists on paying. She has some sort of membership, even for the park system, so she reserves the court. She still looks a bit undone, but he has the sense that the game and the sport, the very sweat of it, will be good for her.

They warm up and he can tell immediately that Jocelyn is good, but not good enough to beat him. Women cannot generally beat men. She is fast and smart, but he has power and experience. He likes to watch her run around. He likes that she thinks she can win against him and never gives up. He hasn't played tennis in many years, and it is exhilarating.

As a boy, he and Abrahm played in an empty swimming pool. The pool had belonged to a government man in his sector, but the man had lost favor and was later killed. There was an abandoned house there too. The two of them pretended it was their own. They danced in an empty dining room, listened to the Sugarhill Gang. They had sex with girls there too, and earlier in their lives, they had even touched each other, exploring which touches felt best. They played soccer in the large garden—balls made of banana leaves. He remembers the slow, meditative act of wrapping them. He and Abrahm were like live wires: they never shut down. His very best friend—a Hutu. He, a Tutsi. The difference didn't matter for the longest time.

Before they finish two sets, he calls it. He is not a young boy anymore.

"That's it," he says to her. "I'm too tired. We have to do this again."

"Okay," she says. She walks to the net, shakes his hand. "Nice playing," she says.

"Thank you," he says and kisses her gently on the cheek.

She smiles. The kiss is platonic. The ball and the racquet have touched a part of who he once was. They walk off the court together. He drops his water bottle. It rolls away from him. He goes to retrieve it. He looks up. She is waiting for him.

I have a friend, he thinks. Happy. Something warm settling in him. *One that waits for me.*

THERE IS A PRO SHOP IN THE RECREATION CENTER WHERE THEY PLAY, AND she looks at skirts and tops, and he looks on. He feels as if she is his sister, and he must manage the choices she makes. She tries on a lacey skirt that is see-through, although all that can be seen are shorts. He tells her that the skirt doesn't suit her, that she is too much of a lady for it. She blushes. He can tell she is pleased at the compliment.

"You have no idea who I've been in my life," she says with a wry smile, and they are oddly intimate again.

In the recreation center, there is a freezer with ice cream sandwiches, chocolate chip cookie bars, and popsicles that are the color of the American flag.

"Shall I buy one for each of us? We can sit and eat them at the park."

"Yes, please," she says. The lines around her eyes have lessened. The exercise has reddened her cheeks.

She picks the American flag popsicle, and he picks one called a Firecracker. It is cinnamon flavored and strange. Once outside, they realize they have forgotten napkins, but she has wipes in her purse.

"Consequence of having a little one," she says. "That and hand sanitizer. I used to see my friends who were mothers with all this stuff and I'd say, 'Not me! That's never going to be me. I'm going to be stylish. I'm going to be myself'—and now, look at me."

There is a kind of longing in her words, as if the words themselves were reaching out to some lost future. Still, he thinks, the day has been a success. She seems happier than she was yesterday in the hall. He picks a bench that faces away from the children playing on the play structure. He cannot take the risk of seeing any little girls that might look like his own after his visit to Cambridge.

"How is Lucy?" he asks. "How is that wonderful child?"

Jocelyn smiles. Pride is palpable in the glint of her eyes. "Good," she says. "Good. Except she has a new teacher."

"Is the teacher not nice?"

"Oh no," she says. "He's nice, but he's a man."

He watches the color drain out of her cheeks.

"I don't like that," she says. "I can't help it."

In the *can't help it* he senses a confession, or maybe self-consciousness. There is more there than she means to say to him. He sighs.

"Yes," he says. "I understand that." *There is the wolf, the sheep*, he wants to say, but thinks better of it. "You will want to keep an eye."

She looks as if he has taken something heavy out of her arms. Relief and breath come back to her.

"Thank you," she says. "Thank you so much. Everyone thinks I'm paranoid. Well not everyone. I can't really talk to Conrad, you know. He's always working. He's always very busy, and well, my husband is from a whole different world than I am. Everything went well for him in his life. He had a magical childhood. It's one of the things I love about him, but he doesn't always understand. I talked to my friend too. She gets it, but she seems to think I shouldn't worry. I can't explain it all. I'm just, well . . ."

"It's okay," he says. "It's our job to protect our children. It is nothing to feel ashamed of. It is tiring though."

"Exhausting," she says.

There is a beat of silence.

"I'm probably being silly," she says.

"Probably," he says, wanting to sound very confident. "But better safe than sorry.

She licks the popsicle. "These are kind of fun," she says, assessing it. "There was always an ice cream truck on our street, but we were never allowed."

"Too much sugar?" he asks, winking at her.

"Too poor," she says, matter-of-factly. "My mother was mean too."

They sit enjoying their popsicles for a while, not talking, and then she says, "So tell me about your trip. Was it for fun, or for work, or what?

"I had to meet with an investigator. I received a letter. Have I told you that? Maybe I've found my daughter. She *claims* to be my daughter anyway."

"Oh my," Jocelyn says, a bit of blue popsicle drops on her chin. He dabs at it with his wipe, and she pushes his hand away. He does not think that she is averse to him, just sister to brother. "Tell me about it."

"I didn't get to meet her. Just him. I will go back though. He gave me pictures. They are surveillance pictures. Nothing up close. It is hard to tell."

"Does it seem promising?"

"It seems scary," he says. His voice wobbles. The emotion surprises even him. "This has happened before," he says. "Last time I was not careful. Last time I wanted it so much. Well . . . that one . . . she wanted my money." He looks beyond her, at the children kicking a ball in the soccer field. As if the shame of the con could be found out there, in a blade of grass. "This time I will do better, but the hope is hard."

"Yes, of course," Jocelyn says. "It would be terrible if it wasn't her. You don't want to get invested."

"Yes," he says, and then a wavering, "I am afraid it is not her, but then again, I am also afraid it *is* her."

The detective's voice repeats like a record in his head, as if he is a part of their present conversation. *She is pregnant*, the detective said, as they looked out at the quiet water of the Charles River. *If she is your daughter, she is pregnant.*

He wants to tell Jocelyn this, but he chokes on it. She reaches out and takes his hand, as if she knows his secret. He remembers his mother walking with him when he was a boy. She was already forty when she gave birth to him. In Rwanda there was so much walking. His hand in his mother's. The touching of elbows, the shifting of skirts, language everywhere. Her hands were aged. The veins were like tangled laces.

When the Interahamwe came for his mother, they sliced her forearms off first. They hobbled her ankles. She lay alive in the mangrove trees. A mission to get to the next, and the next, and the next. Speed the most important thing to the killers. Alive for a bit. For a long, long time actually. Three days, and three dark nights for the blood to seep out of her completely. The smell of her like something dead on the road. He shudders suddenly. He weeps. The work songs linger. Water in the mouth. Youth. A vision of dwarves in the woods. Disney infiltrating Africa. Off to work we go, hi-ho. We are all children until our mothers die.

He sighs. What is the use? Why fill the chasm? He wishes he could speak to his mother.

"I wish I weren't so frightened," he says.

"Yes," she says. She does not tell him to stop crying. She does not seem to care that he is making a scene in public. "I can see how that would be."

CHAPTER NINE

JOCELYN

1

SHE DOES ONE PRIVATE AFTER THEY'VE TOUCHED, BUT IT IS TOO WEIRD. They can't look at one another. They don't speak. It all feels off, as if they are stepping on each other, even when they are on opposite sides of the court. She knows they should talk, but how to start the conversation?

"Bye," she says at the end of the hour, feeling as if she hasn't even been there, as if the whole experience has happened to some other person.

"Bye," Kate says.

She picks up her stuff, heads out. She passes all the other women playing tennis and wishes she could get to that place. Those women are content. Those women are happy. They don't cry without meaning to.

Group drills, she decides on the drive home. *I have to see her*, she thinks, *but I cannot see her alone. That's it. That's the solution.* Maybe they can be friends.

A negotiation. Torture. *I have to see her. Just not alone.*

Nothing else in between.

CONRAD COMES BACK FROM LOUISIANA WITH ALL KINDS OF SWEETS. SHE has decided to be the wife of his dreams. She wants to be happy. There is still the thought of Kate, right there, like a pebble in the shoe, but Conrad's return will be the beginning of something new. A fresh start. Keep it simple. She's decided.

When he walks in the door from LAX, he drops his suitcases, smiles. Jocelyn has forgotten how handsome he is. He is beautiful, really. Other women always want him, always comment. He calls out to Lucy, and the light that shines from her daughter's face when she sees her father makes Jocelyn's heart lift. Kate is momentarily forgotten. Darkness cannot drive out darkness. Only light. She has read this before but can't think where.

In his left hand, Conrad holds a large paper shopping bag. He reaches inside the bag and reveals a box of candy. The box is almost the size of Lucy. Inside are milk chocolate turtles and pralines, dark chocolate alligators, and white chocolate frogs. There are enough sweets for four children.

"*Tortue*," Conrad says to Lucy. He is kneeling in front of her as if he is proposing to her. "It's French for 'turtle.' People speak French in New Orleans. Well, not much anymore, but it's fun to think about."

Lucy repeats it with a deeply affected accent. "Are they all for me, Papa?"

"Every one of them."

"Do I have to give any to Mama?"

"Nope," he says. "I got Mama her own thing."

"What did you get her?" Lucy asks. Her look is suspicious. The gift had better not be better than her own.

"Go get it from Papa's bag."

Lucy runs to the corner. There is always a gift for both of them. Lucy searches the leather messenger bag.

"It's a tiny blue box," Conrad says. "Robin's egg blue. Your mother will think she knows where it comes from, but I am tricking her."

Jocelyn smiles. Lucy runs back with it.

"Open it, Mama! Open it!"

Jocelyn does as she is told and inside she finds an intricate ring, shaped like a snake. The eyes are green emeralds, the tongue is a series of small, clear diamonds and rubies.

"It's beautiful, Conrad. Thank you. You always think of us."

"I got myself something too," he says, winking at her. "From La Perla."

"What's La Perla?" Lucy says. "I want to see."

"Oh, God," Jocelyn says to him. "She'll go to school and say it."

"It's French for 'a pearl,'" Conrad says.

"Not French, smart boy," Jocelyn says. "It's Italian for pearl."

"Is there an oyster?" Lucy asks.

"Absolutely," Conrad says. "An oyster shell and a pearl. I'll show it to you after school."

"Did you hear that, Mama? A pearl *and* an oyster shell. Not for you."

"Can't wait to see it," Jocelyn says, laughing, and wonders how Conrad will produce an oyster shell before the end of the school day. Lucy isn't likely to forget.

"It's just for us, right, Papa? The oyster shell is just for us. Mama can have the pearl."

"Just us," Conrad says, confirming their exclusive tribe.

"Yes!" Lucy shrieks and runs. When she gets to the opposite side of the room from her father, she turns and sways from side to side. "You owe me forty-nine spitty kisses, Papa. Me and Mama figured it out last night."

"You're kidding?" Conrad says, and starts to stalk her. He is sneaky and intense as a panther.

Lucy screams. "Help, Mama! He's going to get me."

"That's right," Conrad says. "I'm getting as many kisses as I can before you go to school."

THE LA PERLA BAG HAS THREE SETS OF LINGERIE. ONE SET IS PINK. ANother all black except a bit of purple piping. The third is forest green.

"Which one?" she asks.

"All of them," he says, lying back on their bed.

Lucy has been dropped off at school. She and her father argue as they go out the door about how many kisses are still owed.

"All of them?" Jocelyn says, feeling instantly shy, but enjoying it all the same.

"You show me all of them with heels. No, maybe boots. What shoes have you got? When I've seen them all, then I'll pick. I'll decide what you wear."

She likes how excited he is. She likes it when he tells her what to do. If it is outside her, she can let so much go.

"It's the middle of the day," she says, wanting to make him wait a little.

"I've got all the time in the world," he says, his blue eyes dancing.

She reaches for the pink panties, the sheer pink camisole.

"Not that one," he says. "I've changed my mind. I want it to be a little raunchier. A show. That's a bit sweet."

She smiles, picks the green one, holds it up for him to see. There are garters and stockings too.

"You're so beautiful, Jocelyn." He is unbuttoning his jeans, adjusting the pillows behind him. "You're so good to me."

WHEN THEY ARE FINISHED, SHE THINKS OF TELLING HIM. JUST BEING OUT
with it. He is in a good mood. Her orgasm has made her feel like
a college student—languorous and lean in bed. All things seem
possible. She wonders now if the depression she has been feeling
is hormonal, or even physical—a lack of sex and closeness. She
doesn't want to give the death of her mother too much credit. She
reminds herself that Conrad has forgiven her over the years for
everything. He forgave her the day they met for who she was, for
the fact that she didn't save Ycidra or William or herself when
she could have. It is one of the things that she loves about him.
Can he forgive her for this?

I want to fuck my tennis coach, she says internally to picture how it
will sound. *I've touched her. She put her fingers between my legs. I do not under-*
stand it, except to say that it is chemical. It is beyond me, like hunger or breathing.

If Kate were a man, she wouldn't even consider telling him.
Conrad would get a man fired, but the fact that she is a woman
makes it an eccentricity, a potential turn-on. She starts to say it,
but it feels heavier than that. It feels as if it could ruin them. *Forget*
it, she thinks. *It is nothing. He is back. I have decided to be different.* Is a
touch worth ruining a lifetime, a family? He is smiling at her.

"Wanna do it again?" he asks.

"No way," she says. The Marant boots are on her feet. They are
the only article of clothing that she still has on. She climbs on top
of him. She presses the soft suede of the boots against his thighs.
This is his favorite position for her, besides on her belly. "I'm going to be late for therapy as it is," she says, and kisses him chastely
on both cheeks. "Then I have drill. Don't you work anymore?"

"It's supposed to rain," he says. "Go to therapy and then come
back to me. Immediately!" A pretend command. "You should just
stay with me all the time, my love. No tennis today."

She likes that he says this, but the thought of not seeing Kate at all makes her feel as anxious as an addict. *I will see her. I will behave. It will be different.*

"Are you working today?" she asks, again.

"I'm always working, babe."

He closes his eyes, leans his head back. He will be asleep in one minute.

"I'm going," she says. "I really need the exercise."

Without opening his eyes, he says, "Stay here. Exercise with me."

"I'D LIKE YOU TO PUT IT IN A BOX," DR. BRUCE SAYS. "CAN YOU SEE THE box?"

The therapist is teaching Jocelyn a new strategy. It is a way to deal with inexplicable grief or sudden memories. Jocelyn doesn't want to be there. She wishes she didn't have to learn strategies. She wishes she could just play tennis, be normal. She wonders what it will feel like to see Kate today. Will it have dissipated? Will it be the same? She is frightened—roller-coaster scared—but she reminds herself it was nothing . . . *is* nothing. A touch. A fantasy. *I've decided.*

Of all the days for this to be, it seems as if Dr. Bruce has an agenda. She is pushy, piercing, more focused. She suggests that Jocelyn is not present in the moment.

"Be here now, Jocelyn. I'm trying to help you."

"I know. I know," she says.

"Close your eyes, please. We can practice here. We keep skirting issues."

Jocelyn closes her eyes. She laughs a little without meaning to. She feels like a slaphappy teenager.

"Try to be open, please."

"Okay," she says. "I'm sorry. I'm distracted. My husband just got home."

"Picture a box," the therapist says, ignoring the excuses. "Give yourself some time to see it."

Jocelyn doesn't picture a box. Jocelyn counts. She wonders. Can she and Kate be friends?

"Can you see the box?" the therapist says.

"Not really," Jocelyn says, and opens her eyes.

"Close your eyes," the therapist says, patiently. "Maybe a mailbox. It should have a lid."

"A lid?" Jocelyn asks, thinking how stupid she feels.

"Yes. Or a lock. Just try. Please. It's just off to the left of you. The box is to your left. Picture it."

She closes her eyes. She tries. Feels tense. Pretends she can see it. "Okay," she says. "I see it."

"Now take the thing you don't want to look at, or the thing that is whirling around in your mind right now, and put it in there. It can be Gladys, or Uncle Al, or your brother's death or your sister's, your husband coming home. You can get it out again, so don't worry. Don't worry, okay?"

"Okay," Jocelyn says. She tries to put Kate in the box, almost laughs. She breathes deeply to stop herself. She waits several minutes, staying still, figures this is the only way out of the office. She waits a few more seconds for good measure and then opens her eyes. Tries to seem changed.

"How was that?" Dr. Bruce says, intensely hopeful.

"Good," she says, knowing what's expected of her. "Thank you. I do feel calmer."

"Great," the therapist says. "You can do this at home, on your own."

Jocelyn reminds herself that the therapist can't possibly know she's lying. *It's only me*, she tells herself. *I'm the only one in here.*

SHE DRIVES TO THE CLUB AND FINDS A PARKING SPOT THAT FEELS AS IF it's a mile away from the entrance. She is still slightly silly from the session, but in the parking lot, she tries the strategy again. She really does want to get better. She wants to have control over the things that come into her head. She waits, eyes closed, but nothing. All of it is still right there, stalking. No box. No lock. No lid.

Her phone buzzes, startling her. She opens her eyes, looks at the screen: Kate.

> **KATE**: Are you coming? Looks like rain. Might not be a long drill.

She leans forward, looking up at the sky and out the car's front window. It's gray, but who knows? It's California.

> **KATE**: I want to talk . . . maybe?

Jocelyn smiles. Giddiness returns.

> **JOCELYN**: Yes.

Her heart beats fast. *Talk*, she thinks. Her hands tremble. She texts again with shaky fingers.

> **JOCELYN**: I'm here, in the parking lot. Absolutely. Yes to the drill. Yes to the talk.

Her breath comes fast. Her heart pounds. Just minutes before she had decided. Conrad. Motherhood. *How does she do this to me?*

CHAPTER TEN

SIMON

1

HE IS BLOCKED, WHICH HAPPENS OFTEN. HIS WORK IS ARTISTIC. IDEAS don't just fall from the sky. He feels distracted. He thinks about the future. He thinks about the dog on the road. He sits and stares and stares at the table, at the blueprints, and still nothing happens. He thinks Lucy could help him, if she were here. She has a beginner's mind, but she isn't here. He and the pygmy are the only people in the room, and the pygmy never helps.

The whole condominium is silent except for the ticking of his kitchen clock, the soft ebb and flow of waves outside his window, and none of that helps him focus. He looks at the front door. He'd like to see beyond its wood veneer, into the carpeted hallway and into the family-filled home of Lucy. Earlier, he heard the father— his return, from wherever he was. It was a jubilant one, happiness, the thud of his suitcase hitting the floor and then *Papa, Papa,* Lucy saying, and her father: *My lovey, I've missed you*, and then envy throbbing in his own body like a beating heart.

He touches the letter in his front shirt pocket, but it makes him feel heavier. He goes to get the newspaper. He'll read. Sometimes if he can relax, the answers will come.

The pygmy laughs in the other chair when he sees Simon. He requests the comics as Simon walks by. "You are not real," he says aloud, but still, he is compelled to place the comics on the chair.

He sits in his own chair, stares at the blurring page. He will read and connect again to the world outside. The front page is the same as yesterday, and he knows that if he looks at the front page every day of his life it will always be the same. The gospel, he thinks. Bring the good news, but it is never that. It is always something hideous, a parade of horribles: terrorists beheading the innocent on television, children accidentally gunned down in the street, police brutality. This time, it is a gunfight in a disco in Orlando. The man pent up, unable to face his sexual desires. They call the shooter a terrorist, but really? He's just a man, insecure and intentional like other men. Like the men in Kigali, like Abrahm, like himself.

War is everywhere now. Men and women and children are killed every day, but what was the beginning? What was the first link in the chain? A dictator's demise? The conflation of news and entertainment? An uneducated electorate? A staff and a hat and a cow? White people call themselves victims now. It is hard to hear the nonsense.

There is the claim that there will be a woman president. He knows that it will not happen, but the innocent Americans believe. He remembers her. He remembers her husband too. How could he forget? Genocide? she said, and he said, although not with their own lips. *Let's talk about the definition of genocide.* People float like logs in the river. They bubble up like pasta in a hot pot. A vision, he realizes (not really here), although he sees it in front of him on the newspaper page. He knows to stay calm. *We will send them by the river,* Mugesera said. The words and images are a truth, but not an article on the front page of the *Los Angeles Times.* It isn't happening here, now, in the penthouse on Pacific Coast Highway, he adamantly reminds himself.

He does not want to have an attack, so he must ground himself. But sometimes things come without warning. *The speed of it all*, the American president said, as if confused. My entire family gone: my mother, my father, my grandmother, my six brothers, my two sisters. My wife, which is separate. My daughter? Everyone dead so quickly.

The pygmy is laughing, a high-pitched barking. It reminds Simon of a seal. He reads a joke aloud. Simon doesn't find it funny. The pygmy readjusts himself, sits as a bird, perched—his webbed feet hanging over the edge of the chair. Simon tries again to make him disappear, and this time it works, and it is only he in the condominium, and the newspaper, and the real words come clear on the page, like a photo in a darkroom.

He forces his eyes to read, to continue, to fight back. If he looks up, the pygmy might reappear. He reads two other bits of news, and then there is this: a Nazi SS man has been tracked down in Argentina. They are returning him to Vienna for extradition. He will be prosecuted for crimes committed in an almost ancient history, in another land.

How is it possible? Simon thinks, seeing the black ink on the page, and then the paint on his hands from his work. The brown skin of his forearms is ashy and veiny. He has grown lean. *How is it possible?*

Three months after the genocide (not war—he will never call it civil war), the Hutus were free, living among them, and almost seventy years after the fact, the United States and the Jews are *still* pursuing the Nazis with the vigor of rabid dogs. Relentlessly they work to return lost works of art. Art? he thinks. Art?

Lost limbs. Lost lips, lost ears, he remembers. Babies cut out of mothers. He remembers Claudette's little coat hanging on a peg when he came home from work. A straw shared with his brother—banana beer.

Suddenly he has a strange wish to shoot someone—envy and anger and instant forlornness overwhelm him. He remembers rain in the long months, slanting sideways through the window.

Vestine, her beautiful arms, smiling across a pillow at him. He thinks about the dogs, violating the corpses that had already been violated by men. He thinks about the dog on the 10 freeway, waiting for whom? The dogs were hungry. That's all they were. How was that more offensive?

The white men in blue berets looked on while the Hutus cut them, while they dropped them with tied hands into the river, while they raped their women: *A woman on her back has no ethnic group*, he remembers. Then laughing. A slap on the back, next in line. Vestine. We are all essentially animals.

The children sat on the corpses of their mothers. The men in blue berets shot the dogs when they ate the dying. A completely quiet country after that. *Let's talk about the definition of genocide.* As if it were a question of semantics.

He knows the American difference, of course, between Jews and Rwandans and dogs, but he doesn't like to think on it.

CHAPTER ELEVEN

JOCELYN

1

SHE FEELS ANXIOUS AFTER KATE'S TEXT. THE SKY IS OMINOUS—AS GRAY as an elephant. She knows the earth needs rain, but Jocelyn wants to exercise before she talks to Kate. She wants to hit balls. She wants to run laps and then she supposes she will be calm enough to talk.

She gathers her tennis gear and heads to the court. She can already hear Kate's voice. Her body shivers. She considers turning around. They can't do this. They have to do it. *I have to do it. Talk. That's it. What will she say? We'll talk. No big deal.*

She arrives on court and everyone is already there. Maud looks at her watch as if chastising Jocelyn.

"What?" she says.

"Nothing," Maud says. "Don't be so guilty."

She says hello to all the women, even Missy. She forces herself to look directly at Kate and say hi. They get thirty minutes into the drill and it starts to drizzle. All six of them deflate.

"Let's do a sun dance," Maud says.

"I'm going to flip out," Jocelyn says.

The drops keep falling, but there aren't many yet. They keep hitting balls. The air is heavy. The balls move slowly through the court. Erica runs her tennis shoe along the baseline, moon-walking, testing the slickness. Kate watches and then stops feeding balls. She sets her racquet in the cart. They all turn to her. She holds her hands out, testing, palms up, palms down, to feel the rain, and then: Fountain Square, Cincinnati—"The Lady," a bronze, standing in the square's center. She is there in the brain for Jocelyn as clear as Kate is. Downtown is deep in Kate's pose. The statue and Kate merging now. As a girl, Jocelyn thought the statue was beautiful, an image to escape into. Kate now. Jocelyn has to look away.

Kate picks up her racquet again. She picks up a ball, as if to start, but then calls the drill five seconds later.

"It's too wet," she says. "It's dangerous."

"Fuck," Jocelyn says.

"God, you're grumpy this morning," Maud says, teasingly. "There's always tomorrow for dreams to come true."

"She needs to get laid," Theresa says, kind of smirky. "Her husband's out of town."

"Ooh la-la," Missy says.

"Believe me," Jocelyn says, "that is not my problem. Conrad is back."

They all laugh.

She feels aware of Kate. She is slightly embarrassed. Does Kate wonder about her sex life?

"I hate when my routine gets screwed, that's all," Jocelyn says.

"Wanna have lunch?" Maud asks. "Wanna screw it up some more?"

"I will," Theresa says, happily.

"Let's go to Maestros," Missy says.

"I can't," Jocelyn says. "I have to go to the grocery store, make something for dinner tonight." She knows to keep the pending talk with Kate a secret.

"Food, sex, and quiet," Maud says. "That's all a man needs."

"Secret to a long and happy marriage," Erica says, tittering.

"Yep," Theresa says.

Jocelyn says goodbye to all the women, watches them walk out together. She purposefully takes a while getting her stuff together. She fills her water bottle. She folds her towel. Kate hasn't said a nontennis word to her. The rain is a steady drizzle, warm and light, like the start of a summer rain when she was a kid. The wind picks up.

"Wanna help me put the balls away?" Kate says. She covers the balls in her cart with her jacket. "We could talk in the shed? We *should* really talk. It's weird now, right?"

Jocelyn feels incredibly nervous. She is like an adolescent again. "Yes. For a minute. Not in the shed though." The fantasy fills her head again. "I have to head home soon."

"In a big race to get that dinner going?" Kate asks, lightly, teasing her.

"Don't tease. I'm so pissed it's raining."

"We need rain. We're having a drought. This is like the driest year in LA history."

"Yes. Yes. Blah. Blah. Blah."

"Wow," Kate says. "Maud is right. I don't think I've ever seen you this grumpy before."

"Yeah . . . well . . . it's not as if we're friends," Jocelyn says. There is the edge of anger there. She doesn't know why. Why is she angry with Kate? Her nerves are at the surface.

Kate lifts her tennis bag, sets it in the cart. There is just a pause, a stutter before they go.

"I'm glad we're going to talk," Kate says. "It's driving me crazy." *Step, step, step*, the cart is moving. "I've been thinking about you."

Jocelyn's stomach flips. She worries about talking, worries about not talking, but says: "I'll wait for you in my car."

"Okay," Kate says.

They head toward the gate, side by side, in the rain. They seem to fill the huge space of court 3. Their elbows touch, their hips graze, as if they cannot get around one another. There is plenty of room for two as they go through the gate, but they bump into each other anyway. Kate nudges her.

"Excuse you," she says, and they are children with crushes again. Jocelyn feels herself redden. She nudges her back. Conrad is elsewhere. *Maybe I can just have this thing*, she thinks. *As something small and private.*

"My car's blue. It's a—"

"I know what you drive," Kate says. "Wait for me two seconds while I put this away. We'll go together. If someone sees us, we're allowed to be friends."

Jocelyn waits and then watches Kate exit the ball shed. As she steps out, she looks up at the sky as if to feel the water on her cheeks. Kate is tall—maybe five nine or five ten. Jocelyn notices this for the first time. She has the flat stomach of an athlete. The drizzle is thickening into a heavy rain and Kate's skin looks lush, the texture of a soft, smooth mushroom. She changes her tennis glasses for sunglasses that are much more stylish. She is lovely.

"We better run," Kate says. "It's really starting now."

THEY RUN LIKE SPRINTERS TO THE CAR.

"I'm going to beat you," Kate says, and Jocelyn is ten again, running as hard as she can. They laugh. She tries her best, pushing Kate back when she gains on her. She has a memory of running in the apartment when she was a kid. Gladys passed out on the floor of the bathroom. A game among the siblings. Their kingdom until their mother woke up. She catches herself smiling, but then there is a bruised cheek, impact against the rail of a table leg. Gladys screaming at them, because they've woken her up. The extension cord snapping, folded over for pain. Every scar on her body pings. She wonders if the memory is right. Whose cheek was bruised? Who hit whom? And then it leaves.

The rain is a deluge by the time they get to the car. Jocelyn hops in, unlocks the passenger side for Kate a few seconds later. Kate's body lands like an avalanche in the front seat. She is soaked from head to toe. There are droplets on her forearms, the curve of her collarbone is like the rounded edge of a rolling pin. She is glistening. Her blonde hair is stringy, and the darker roots show. The large braided bun has come loose and hangs, a rope down to her breasts. Jocelyn wants to undo it, wants to watch the hair cling and vine. They are both breathing hard.

"I won," Jocelyn says.

"You didn't unlock my door," Kate says. "That's not exactly fair."

"Who knew the rules?"

"You're a cheater," Kate says, but she's smiling. It's all in fun.

Jocelyn can see the swell of Kate's breasts beneath the white tank. The rain has made it see-through. She tries not to notice. She forces her concentration on the rainstorm, which feels biblical—the end of days, as if the whole world has been turned upside down. Would she want to be here with this woman in her last hours, talking in the front seat of the car, or fucking, moving her back and forth like a wave on her lap?

She considers turning on the cab light. It feels dark, not like night, but more like the gloaming. She can't see out, because of the pelting rain. No one can see in. It's like the automat when she was young. She has a brief vision of Kate above her. She wants to hold her arms and hands back. Keep her mouth inches away. Look at her.

"It's crazy isn't it?" Kate says.

"It will stop in a minute." Jocelyn says,

"What? You're like a meteorologist now?"

Jocelyn rolls her eyes, but she likes the teasing. "No," she says. "It just rained a lot when I was a kid."

As soon as she says it, she wants to retrieve it. Anonymity. Two separate spaces. Twenty-four hours in a hotel room. That's what she wants.

"Where'd you grow up?" Kate asks.

"Let's not do that, okay?" Jocelyn says. She tries to make her voice light, a joke even. She watches the streaming water.

"Do what? Ask questions?"

Jocelyn tries again but doesn't know how to say what she wants to say. She feels trapped with Kate in the front seat of the car suddenly, but knows if Kate leaves, she will want her back. The fierceness of the storm is claustrophobic. She has to hang on. The storm will wear itself out. It feels relentless now though.

"Nothing," Jocelyn says. "Never mind."

"God we're nervous," Kate says. "It's pathetic."

"It's not like I have a lot of experience with this," Jocelyn says.

"Yeah, well. I don't either."

Courage, Jocelyn thinks. *Be brave.*

"What did you want to talk about?" Jocelyn asks. Innocence in her voice. Can they ignore it?

"I don't know," Kate says, pretending ignorance. "The other day would be a good place to start." A smirk. Her head lowers. "I can't stop thinking about it."

"Me either," Jocelyn says.

They are both looking straight ahead. No interaction. Jocelyn thinks it makes it easier to go on. She can feel a rivulet of sweat slide down her arm, another between her breasts.

"I want to see you," Kate says. "I think, anyway."

"Yeah. Me too . . . I think," Jocelyn says. Her voice is wavy. "Look," she says. "I have a daughter." It feels like a violation to say it. She doesn't want Lucy in this space, but she has to say it. Nothing but the present from here on, she thinks. "I wouldn't want anyone to know. I mean if we did."

"I have a son," Kate says.

"You do?" Shock inside her. "Really?"

"Don't look so amazed, Jocelyn. Lesbians have children. God, you're annoying right now."

Jocelyn smiles a little. She supposes she is. It takes her a minute, but then she says it: "I think I would like it, but I would want it to be . . ."

"What?" Kate asks.

"I just think when we start, we start. When we stop, we stop. Nothing serious. Just between us. No matter what."

"Have we started?"

"Maybe," Jocelyn says, not sure if she's committed.

"Okay."

Jocelyn feels herself panic with the decisive word, as if she is crossing a physical line. She senses that on the other side there will be a difference—a staining will be left. She and Conrad are the only pure thing she has had in her life. Conrad and Lucy, anyway. There is the tap of sorrow—a finger pressed slowly and firmly into a bruise. Confusion.

"God, you look so down all of a sudden," Kate says. "Don't be so serious. Don't worry about it. We don't have to."

"I know."

"It's not like I'm going to stalk you or get crazy or fall in love with you or anything," Kate says.

Jocelyn allows herself a laugh. It relaxes her. "You might fall in love. You never know."

"You're not my type."

"Oh, I think I'm your favorite."

A degree of lightness. Kate takes her hand. "All right, you little egotist. I think we both want this. Whatever it is. But you seem sort of unhappy right now. I don't want an unhappy girl. You can have more time, and if you don't want to, we'll go back to where we were before. No biggie. There are other girls, you know."

Jocelyn waits for a minute and then just goes for it. "I don't need more time," she says. "I'm just afraid."

The sentiment is so simple, and yet she feels as if she might cry. She is embarrassed by her fear.

"It's not going to be serious, Jocelyn. We're otherwise engaged. Both of us. Don't worry. You'll—"

Jocelyn interrupts, feels the importance of defining what she wants. "Let's not do that thing where it's deeper. I don't want that. No history, no nothing. Just physical. Let's pretend we barely know each other."

"We do barely know each other."

Jocelyn grabs Kate's hand. They look at each other. She thinks they will kiss, but then they don't. Jocelyn reaches out, gives in to the urge to touch Kate. She cups her breast, feels the soft skin of her thigh just below the tennis skirt. She turns her body toward her. She can hear her breath, can feel herself relax into her decision. The car is small. There isn't going to be much room.

"You are so weird," Kate says. "You are the strangest person I've ever met. No falling in love. No talking even." She is pretend-serious now. "I promise——" she lifts her hand as if swearing in court "——I don't really even want to talk. What I want to do with you has nothing to do with talking." Kate grasps either side of Jocelyn's tennis shirt, lifts it gently, puts her hands on her waist. "You're not that great anyway." Smugness is there. Kate is as coy as a schoolgirl.

Jocelyn leans in. She kisses her. They touch through clothes. Pawing and petting like high schoolers. The rain keeps falling. Jocelyn thinks, *When the rain stops I will stop.* She kisses Kate's neck, her collarbone, her breasts through her tank and then through the lacy bra, which is pink and surprising. The rain keeps going. Jocelyn keeps kissing. The car is cramped, but manageable.

Kate slides the passenger seat back, and they both laugh. Still nervous, but intent. Jocelyn pulls Kate's skirt down, kisses her belly, her thighs, her knees. She works her way back up and kisses through panties. The light is dim in the car, but bright enough to show the building lust on Kate's face. Kate adjusts her whole body, opens her legs, holds Jocelyn's head gently at first and then more fiercely. Jocelyn teases her, licks her, breathes. Kate moves the panties aside. Jocelyn watches her. Sees her eyes close, her hands trying to push her back down again.

I want to make you beg, she thinks. *I want you to think of me while you are with your wife.*

Jocelyn kisses again. She hears Kate's desperate breath. *Say please,* she thinks. Jocelyn begins, feels fingers in her hair, pulling, the sigh and sound. Kate grows hectic, desperate. And then there are the swiveling twitches of giving in.

LATER, WHEN SHE IS AT HOME AND LUCY IS PLAYING WITH HER FIGURINES, Jocelyn can't stop thinking about what has happened with Kate. *When we stop, we stop*, is what she'd said, what they'd agreed to, but she is not sure if that is true. So many things in her life have refused to end, refused to go away.

She feels herself redden as she thinks about the kiss and the car and the rain. She is thinking about rope, its texture—nylon or cotton, which will feel like what? How can she bring it? *Tether. I will tie her to a chair. I will tether her to the bed. What bed? Hotels don't have those kinds of beds. Will we be at a hotel?* She thinks of Kate's neck and wrists, kisses on raw skin. Making it better. A long-sleeved shirt, zipped up to here, so the tennis ladies don't see. The abraded skin. She is giddy, going too far.

Conrad is cooking dinner, whistling as he cooks. She wonders what the next time will be like when she sees Kate. Will Kate want her or ignore her? How do you act when it is just sex, just physical, no past, no future? It's been a lifetime since that was all she wanted. She and Conrad deal with all the extras, the miscellaneous nonsense: bills, tuition, deep fryers, death, and dinner.

Lucy brings her a little plastic Jasmine figurine as if to remind her of what is real.

"She's so pretty, Mama. She's my favorite. Would you like her?"

Jocelyn looks at the little doll. Even here in their lovely condominium, with her husband cooking for them, and her daughter vying for her attention, she can't stop thinking about the car, the woman. *I would like her. She is pretty. I would like to have her.* There is the vision again that has to do with possession and control, freedom for herself, but Kate on a shelf, and even, she realizes, a luxurious lack of memory.

"Would you, Mama?" Lucy insists. Jocelyn comes out of her daze. "Would you like her?"

"I want *you* to have her," Jocelyn says. "Mommies want their girls to have the best things in life."

Lucy kisses the tiny figurine. Jocelyn watches the sea outside her window and watches her daughter too. There is so much light in the child. This is what she needs to keep intact. Can she do this and the other thing with Kate?

"Do you love me the most in the whole world?" Lucy asks.

"Yes," Jocelyn says. It is a conversation they have all the time.

"More than Papa?"

They both look toward the kitchen—spies engaged in some espionage against the whistling chef.

"I'd sell Papa down the river to keep you safe any day," Jocelyn says.

"What river?" Lucy asks.

"It's just an expression, my sunshine," Jocelyn says, and draws the girl up to see her more closely.

As she looks at her daughter it becomes clear that there is nothing in Lucy that is like her. The girl has might. She's less sensitive. She is confident and sure. Mr. Baird crosses Jocelyn's mind, but the girl is even safe from him tonight. It is a good thing that she lacks her mother's qualities.

Her daughter giggles with the squeezing. "What river, Mama? I want to know."

"The Ohio, then," Jocelyn says, and is brought back like a sinking elevator into darkness.

PART II

Sometimes love does not have the most honorable beginnings, and the endings, the endings will break you in half. It's everything in between that we live for.

—ANN PATCHETT

CHAPTER TWELVE

CLAUDETTE

1

NOW THAT SHE IS HAVING A BABY, THE BOX IS SOMETHING SHE THINKS about all the time. Her stomach grows. The heartbeat in the doctor's office is loud and fast. She is sick for most of it. Unable to eat anything but citrus. She drinks water, grape juice. She tries, but then throws up the prenatal vitamins the doctor gives to her. They are as large as almonds, impossible to get down. She has lost twenty pounds so far.

She cannot understand how the baby grows while she thins. A tapeworm, a leech, some other parasite seems more durable than a baby. She cannot sleep, because of worry. If her mother were alive, she would ask her, *Will this baby live?* If her father were alive, he would bring her ginger, a cool washcloth. He would place his hand on the small balloon of her belly and try to feel the spastic kicks and punches, but they are both dead now, an accident, a young girl, sorrowing for a boy. A young girl crossing the center line on the Tobin Bridge in her car after sending a suicide text message. Her parents' car lifts, is suspended in air, zero gravity, and then hits the water. What are the chances? Such a busy bridge. More than a million cars drive across it yearly. She has looked the number up.

The girl driver is uninjured and later indicted. She is given fifteen short years (a child, they say), but has left Claudette without a family, unless, of course, she counts the man in the magazine. *I am a child too*, Claudette wants to scream at the sentencing. *Before this girl, I belonged to someone.* The war, the sorrowing girl—both strangers with long arms. They have pruned her family members away as gardeners prune fruit.

She is in her third trimester, but still hasn't heard from the man in the magazine. She has been waiting seven weeks and three days for him to respond. She has the sense that someone is following her, maybe him, but she isn't sure. He must think she's a crank. Has he hired someone?

On the day she sends the letter, she doubts herself. Her hand trembles above a blue metal mailbox. The handle burns when she touches it, the white heat of the sun is trapped inside. The mailbox seems to exhale hot breath when she opens it. And as if the letter were glued to her fingertips, she has trouble releasing it from her grasp. As soon as she drops the letter, she wants it back. But it is irretrievable, as so many other things are. She walks away from the mailbox in a daze. Concrete disappears out from under her, and she is toppling down the stairs. She falls, one step after another like a toy she remembers from childhood—a Slinky on the carpeted stairs, Christmas morning, the family farm in Newton. She thinks the baby is lost. She sits at the bottom of the stairs and cries.

A woman, gray haired and stout, leans down to her, tells her not to worry.

"Hormones, child. Just hormones. That wasn't much of a tumble."

She remembers being stood up, dusted off, as if she were a winter coat left too long in the closet. The woman aimed her in the right direction. The baby was alive. The baby *is* alive.

She thinks about the box all the time now, the identity card inside, the birthmark. She is like the box: she has one small life, mysterious and separate, hidden inside.

2

SHE IS HER FATHER'S FAVORITE. HER MOTHER DOES NOT LOVE HER. SHE knows this from the time she is old enough to contemplate these things. She is a smart child, a curious girl, used to being able to work things out to a satisfactory conclusion. Because of this, her mother's indifference to her seems surmountable. In the beginning, she tries to be the best, because she thinks it will please her. She makes straight As. She behaves. She keeps her room and bed clean and made, but none of it matters. It is as if she and her mother exist on separate planets—no butterfly effect between them. Through their bedroom door, she hears her father trying to talk her mother into loving her. She is a product; he, the market research specialist. Even as a child, Claudette knows that her mother does not love her father either.

Neither of them can move her mother to love. Her neutrality is as sure as death. She sleeps a lot. She does not have friends as other mothers do. When she wakes, she drinks until she sleeps again and stays asleep for many hours. Even as a small child, Claudette makes her own breakfast. Her father washes their clothes. A maid comes in on Wednesdays to try to make the house livable. The maid glares at her mother in her beautiful canopy bed. Claudette does not know why she does it, but she makes up excuses to protect her mother against the maid's harsh tongue.

Claudette has many memories of her small self standing in her mother's bedroom. The bed is antique. It is fancy, as the house is. It is meant to show how American they are, as if these things have been passed down for generations, instead of bought on weekends from flea markets and dealers. Her father has hired someone to do this, to make their home beautiful, to make it more American.

Claudette watches as her mother sleeps. Her mother's breathing is not smooth and restful. She sputters and snores. Spit pools on her pillow and leaves the lingering smell of cherry NyQuil and Listerine. If she dares, Claudette reaches forward and gently touches the soft skin of her mother's forearm. She doesn't want to wake her. She just wants to touch her. She stares at her mother sleeping, a beautiful woman with dark skin. Both of her parents are dark. Claudette has the light complexion of her grandmother. At least that is what her father tells her when she asks.

If she wakes her, her mother sits up in a panic and looks around. When she sees that it is just Claudette, she sighs resolutely and rolls away from her onto her side. She tries for many minutes to fall back asleep, and if she can't, she wakes, never looking at Claudette, and makes her way to her bedroom vanity. She sits at the vanity and stares at herself as if she thinks it is possible that a different woman might emerge from her bed after a bit of sleep. Her back is to Claudette. Claudette looks in the mirror waiting for her mother to look away from her own reflection and look back at her. She heaves the brush up from the table as if it were a very heavy thing. She brushes her thick black hair, leans her elbows on the vanity table, rests. She never looks at Claudette. It is as if Claudette were a ghost, something to look through in order to see something else. Claudette wishes for a hug. She wishes to hold her mother's hand. She watches for these opportunities, for recognition and then joy.

Now, as an adult woman, she practices the look that she longed for in the mirror for her own baby. She is afraid she will not do it right. She knows how important it is, because she waited so long for it from her own mother. But it never came. Not even once. Claudette knows that a child cannot see itself until it has been seen by its mother.

3

IN HER TEENS, CLAUDETTE CHANGES TACK IN THE SAME WAY THAT SHE and her father change tack sailing the Charles River. She fails calculus and stays too late at parties. She has boyfriends who aren't appropriate. Her mother does not notice any of it. Her life is in the ice she retrieves, the slide and slick of Ketel One vodka. Her father tells her she will lose her chance at Harvard if she doesn't get it together. He says this at the kitchen table one night when he finishes in his fields. The kitchen chairs are a fine birch, spindle style. They are early American, as the canopy bed is.

Her father is a large man. When he moves in the chair, it creaks. He talks to her and as he speaks, he looks at his thick, callused hands. Dirt and earth reside in the wrinkled knuckles and life lines of the palms. She wonders if he was born that way.

He laces his hands together. A weaving, she thinks. *This is the church. This is the steeple.* His hands, her hands. A soft grip, the fingers wrapped about her own, the wiggling people. For her whole life, he has been the one to teach her. Still, she wants her mother. She wants a woman.

There are random memories, which crash and clang like dropped plates, of *another* woman, a nanny maybe, someone else whose world she was, but these memories fade and dim as the years go by. By the time her parents die, the only thing she can recall is the woman's scent—oranges. Oiled fingers, and a bright smear of citrus along Claudette's cheeks.

When asked about the woman, the nanny (What happened to her? Who was she?), her mother stops the conversation. She claims there was never such a woman. Claudette remembers her though, wonders if it was in that other time, the time in Africa, but the memories are uncertain. The nanny *could* be a dream.

Even when pressed, her mother will not talk about that other time. She cannot dip into the past of Rwanda without falling to pieces. If Claudette asks, she lifts a hand to her, blocks her from speaking, explains that she just can't. *Ask your father*, she says, and then goes into her room to sleep.

Claudette supposes the final attempt for recognition from her mother is this pregnancy. Only another woman can understand. Men will never and have never been able to do this. The child in her belly is not the child of her husband, Larry. It is the product of a brief affair. No one knows this except Claudette, not the man she loves or the man who has impregnated her.

"It's your life," her mother says when Claudette hands her the image of the sonogram. No blankets knitted. No heirlooms passed along. "Having a child is the hardest thing you'll ever do. I don't know why you'd want it."

She looks through Claudette again as she hands the digital picture back. Claudette takes it, follows her mother's gaze out the long windows of their second floor. The night is dark and cold as it can be in the Northeast. Her students will be coming back soon. She will have to tell the dean. Her father is bent, harvesting the last bits and pieces of his crop. His is the last working farm in Newton. Soon he will turn, and condition and supplement the soil. Wealthy white people come and help with this. They pay to put their hands in the manure, to work the land. Her father laughs at them, revels in it: "Only white people do this crazy thing."

Her father's assessment of white people in general is that they are strange, weird birds. He and they are not the same species. When there is a serial killer, a cannibal like Jeffrey Dahmer, for example, her father looks up from the paper and says to her: A white man. Of course.

As different from them as cows are from horses. As different as Tutsi, from Twa, from Hutu, he explains to her. His accent is still strong, even though he has tried for years to lose it. Africa will not let him go.

Her father does not need to work as hard as he used to. He can watch the white people, red faced and sweating. He can collect their fees and dole out their share of organic food. But Claudette believes he cannot exist without it. He has to stay with the land. It is the womb that he came out of it—the dirt and calluses, a part of his soul. She watches her mother watching her father as he inspects something he has pulled from the ground. What does she see there in his hunched back? It is as if she is looking to a place that she has left long, long ago. A place to which she wishes to go back. But there was nothing in Kigali. America is the land of opportunity.

CHAPTER THIRTEEN

JOCELYN

1

THEY MEET AS TENNIS LADIES DO FOR EXPENSIVE LUNCHES AND DINNERS. This time at Jacob's Place. Inside, the restaurant is lit like a bar, but it is a restaurant, recommended by the *LA Times* as the new, hip place to go. Jocelyn feels beautiful, has barely been able to get out of her own condo because of her husband. Conrad almost tackles her when she leaves the bedroom. Plucks her up as she passes him, kisses her, and carries her back to where she came from. He tries to hold her down on the bed.

"This is the fee for babysitting," he says. "I want this. Not money. How much is your daughter's safety worth?"

"I have to go," Jocelyn says, giggling. "She's your daughter too." He makes her feel happy. "You're messing up my hair."

"I like you all disheveled."

She thinks briefly about staying with him, but can't. She has committed. She hopes to see Kate. She hopes to slide into the world of her, sit by her, talk with her, touch her hand beneath the table.

She struts to the elevator, takes it down to the lobby, where the valet has brought her car. Simon is handing off his keys, just as she is receiving hers. He hugs her. They chat.

"Should we play tennis again next week?" he asks her.

"Sure," she says. "Yes. That would be great."

They check to make sure they have each other's numbers.

"I'm running a bit late," she says. A hug goodbye and she's off.

At the restaurant, the women arrive one by one, each outdoing the other. The clothes are designer, the jewelry outrageous, the makeup perfect. She looks up when the waiter brings her drink and there is Kate. Jocelyn feels as if she is choking on the sight of her. The blonde hair is, as usual, restrained in a braided bun, but tonight she has subtle makeup on, diamond earrings. Jocelyn cannot speak to her, not even to say hello. She cannot move. She is set, immobile, like some heavy piece of furniture.

They avoid each other's eyes, although the other women don't notice. Kate is at the center of all of them—each of the ladies is vying to sit next to her. All are spellbound as she tells her tennis stories and drinks her drink. She recalls her days at UVA, the bitchy girls on tour.

The women ask questions, get silly. It's the first time Jocelyn has noticed how enthralled they all are—not just her. She feels compelled to call Kate out, but keeps quiet. The conversation circles and returns, always back to Kate. Kate, like a queen, holds court.

As the dinner conversation dies down, and the end of the night is pending, Jocelyn feels her heart beating. Will they speak at all? Has she been thinking about her? They haven't seen one another intimately since the car. Cash is being passed around, math problems are being worked through. And then they are up, most of them gone, just three of them remaining, finishing up cocktails.

"Bye then," Jocelyn says to the table, draining her drink.

"I'll walk out with you," Kate says.

There is a flicker, a light in her eyes. Jocelyn is aware of her shortened breath.

"I'm going to the restroom," Theresa says. "Don't wait. I valeted. I'll see you guys tomorrow at drill. Practice makes perfect."

She and Kate walk out together. Jocelyn shivers. It is surprisingly chilly with the wind, which is not uncommon for the Palisades because of the beach, but they are inland, the Valley, where it is almost always warm.

Jocelyn has parked around the corner from the restaurant. She is glad that she is farther away.

"I'll walk you to your car," Kate says.

"Okay," Jocelyn says, feeling shy. She turns to look back at the restaurant. Theresa is nowhere to be seen.

By the time they get to her car, Jocelyn's hands are ice cold. She puts her hands under her cashmere poncho and leans back against the driver's side door.

"I'll see you then," Kate says. "I'm parked the other way." She points as if Jocelyn can follow it like a map.

"Okay," Jocelyn says, but neither of them moves.

"My hands are freezing," she says, looking at Kate. "Gloves seem silly though, right?"

"Yeah?" Kate says. "Let me feel."

She holds her hands out, and Kate takes them.

"You're a wuss," she says.

"I am not."

The hands remain where they are. Kate is a step closer. Their bodies are almost touching. Jocelyn looks back again toward the restaurant. She lets the held hands slip down beside her, but Kate doesn't let go, she just moves a millimeter nearer.

"I'm afraid someone's going to drive by," Jocelyn says.

"Not likely," Kate says. "Even if they do, it's pretty dark here."

Jocelyn wants to kiss her but is suddenly nervous. "What are we doing?" she asks, and they both start laughing.

"I don't know," Kate says. She seems a bit defeated. She lets go of Jocelyn's hands.

Jocelyn reaches out, touches the bottom edge of Kate's blouse. It is silky and light. Too light for the cold weather. It peeks out of the bottom of her leather jacket. Jocelyn pulls the fabric and then reaches under it and places the flat of her cold hands against Kate's back. Kate draws in breath.

"You're right," she says, squirming, but Jocelyn holds her tight. "Your hands are freezing."

Jocelyn kisses her. It is a kiss like the ones she had in middle school, before she knew what she was doing. Not at all like the one in her car. Their teeth click as they both smile. And then they kiss again, feeling bolder. This time it's better, more lingering.

When they pull away, Jocelyn says, "I think I better go," but there's not a lot of conviction. She gives Kate a few more chaste kisses on her cheeks and neck.

"I don't want you to go," Kate says.

"I don't want to go either."

She is happy and terrified at the same time.

Jocelyn holds her, until she feels Kate's cold fingertips, climbing her stomach, her ribs, and then pushing up her bra, circling the tips of her nipples. She presses her mouth more intently against Kate's, and her body too. And there is the smell of cold air on her skin and Jocelyn pulls her into her body. Kate lifts her hips. Jocelyn thinks of sliding down onto the ground. Letting Kate climb on top of her.

"We should go somewhere," Kate says. "I was thinking about it."

"I want to, but . . ." Jocelyn looks at her watch.

Kate reaches in her back pocket, and hands something to her.

"I was thinking about you all day," Kate says. "Thinking about coming here and seeing you. I wouldn't have come, but I wanted to see you."

"Yeah, right," Jocelyn says. "It wasn't for all your little groupies swooning all over you? Listening with bated breath?"

Kate smiles, not denying it. "I like that too."

Jocelyn looks down at the thing Kate has handed her. At first, she thinks it is a note. A Dear John note, maybe. It is difficult to see in the dark night. She retrieves her phone from her purse.

Kate stands staring at her, eyes glistening, while Jocelyn does her little investigation. She shines the light of her phone on the rectangular white object. She can see now what it is—a paper sleeve, a hotel key card, a room number, the Channel Road Inn.

The breath in her body leaves her.

"I better not," she says. "I told Conrad I'd be home soon."

"It will only take a little bit of time," Kate says, and the heat in Jocelyn's body expands.

Their fingers find each other again.

"How long?" Jocelyn says, teasing.

"As long or as short as you like," Kate says. "I'm not expected back until later."

Her hands are inside Jocelyn's shirt again. "We'll be alone. No one will be able to hear us. No one can interrupt us."

A pulsing begins between Jocelyn's legs.

"Okay," Jocelyn says. She hears herself exhale. She has not been aware of holding her breath. "Okay. Hurry, before I change my mind."

IN THE HOTEL ROOM, IT IS LIKE HIGH SCHOOL AGAIN. JOCELYN COMES before she means too, and then she works on Kate, who has an orgasm on Jocelyn's leg.

"We're ridiculous," Jocelyn says. She is happy and lusty still.

"We need to practice," Kate says. "Practice. Practice. Practice."

"I'm in for next time," Jocelyn says. "I wouldn't want to be the slacker."

She puts her bra on, the simple black dress. She hasn't taken off her heels and she slides her panties over them.

They walk out together, but they've parked away from each other.

"See ya," Kate says, as if they are leaving the tennis court. No kiss. No hug. Definitely not a high five.

"Yes," Jocelyn says, a silly smile on her face.

She watches Kate walk away, the blonde hair like a light in the dark. She had taken it down in bed. The hair is long and thick, with the slightest wave to it. The tendrils run almost to her waist. A pleasure to undo, one braid after another, falling on naked breasts.

She doesn't look away from Kate until she has gotten into her car, and then she finds her own car and settles into the front seat. She turns the ignition on and sees the taillights of Kate's Tesla leaving the parking lot. She thinks: *Kate is off to her mystery family, and I am off to mine. I am so close to home, just fifteen minutes along the beach, the blue, the bluff.* Invisible at this hour.

Jocelyn drives away from the hotel. Ten minutes later, she parks her car down Via de la Paz, rolls her windows down, hears the water crashing against the shore. She takes a few moments to think about what she is doing. What is an affair? She wishes she had been able to spend the night. She chides herself for having the thought. She wants her family too, early-morning eggs, a hug after a bad dream in the dark night from Conrad. She sits a few minutes more, realizing she wants both. She rolls up her windows, puts her car in gear. She has to get home. She does not want to worry her husband, and she wants to kiss her sleeping daughter goodnight.

CHAPTER FOURTEEN

CLAUDETTE

1

AT FIRST, WHEN SHE FINDS THE VARIOUS ARTICLES, SHE ASSUMES HE IS her mother's lover. As unlikely as it is that her mother would get up for anything, she thinks she might get up for a man like this, a man from another life, one before now. She presumes they were lovers first in Kigali.

In the pictures from the magazine, he sits at a glass desk. An office with a view of the city. He is handsome, tall, and lean as a dancer. He is relaxed, smiling, with a small-scale community of buildings in front of him on a large worktable. He is the color of wet sand, short curls peppered with gray. She reads about him— Rwandan refugee, no children, no wife. Her father has explained to her that a wife and a child were a burden in the war. Before he died, he told her, time and again, how lucky he was to have saved them both, because, at war, it is not good to have someone else to worry about. She knows all about refugees. Her mother, her father, and now this man.

The man in the magazine is a renowned landscape architect: Simon Bonaventure. There is a list of his accomplishments, and she has heard of some of his more famous projects: Griffith Park's equestrian center, the outdoor pavilion at the new Getty, and of course the Greenway in Boston. She is sure that he is the kind of man whom her mother would like. He is absolutely other to her father, who has the scent and stain of manure on his hands. A smirk alights on her face, a vision of her mother, that version of her that she has never known, sneaking around for sex (she must have been alive once). Why else would she keep all these articles? Why has she tracked him for all this time?

She reaches into the box for something else to look at, something as unimportant as a souvenir, maybe love letters. Anything that will teach her more about her parents. There is so much to riffle through, a maze of memories. Later, she will find an undoing of self.

BUT BEFORE THAT, THERE IN THE CRATES AND BOXES AND ALBUMS, IS HER history. Exhausting, unfamiliar. Her parents have never shared these treasures with her. She wonders what else she will discover now that they have died. As she looks, it takes some time for her to see what she is seeing. She lifts the evidence of her family carefully, as if it were delicate glass.

Tiny black-and-white photos of places she doesn't recognize, people she does not know. She inspects each thing carefully. Like a philatelist with tweezers, she could be sorting stamps. Each photo laid there on the attic floor: two boys with kites drawn behind them, six young men with glassy eyes, drinking something in a bowl from a straw. All holding machetes. She cheers when she finds one of her mother smoking, smiling, holding a baby in her arms. She is proud that she has recognized her mother, so unlike her is the picture. On the back, her mother's name is there, just for confirmation. *Legato*, she thinks, settling down to stare at the picture. *Tied. Feel where you come from.*

She knows she must look at these things, fill her mind in order to defer her grief. The heft of her parents' death has not yet hit her, and so she organizes and works and delays and sees what is here that she can hold on to, what is here for her to take with her into the future life that will be just hers, her husband's, and the baby's.

She doesn't leave the attic, not even to eat. She cries often and falls asleep from exhaustion. Dreams find purchase. Sudden liquid, filling gaps. The dreams are of blazing fires, of breathing underwater. Babies sliding headfirst out of their mothers' wombs. Always wet, slick floors. She wakes, her body sore against unfinished walls. She wonders what her parents might have been thinking as their car skidded off the Tobin Bridge, the water sucking them in like an intake pipe, the doors of the car as heavy as cinder block walls. Her father was a strong man. He would have tried. Opening the windows just an inch. Waiting, waiting, for the balance—there must be almost as much water inside as out. Knowing there would be just the one chance, the one breath to take and then go. The car sinking still. Maybe giving in, maybe embracing. What must he have seen other than the rising water and her mother's panicked face? A white light, perhaps. Her own birth. The hills of Rwanda—his childhood home. She hopes he's seen the fetus inside her as a formed child. He had longed for a grandson.

She returns to her task when she wakes. Cardboard smooth as sheets. A monogrammed shirt. Expensive and out of place. The identity card is something she feels first and then sees. It is rough, the size of a passport, dirty and wrinkled, a thing of war. She wonders why her father has kept it, but the things we keep—hair from our dead loved ones, rooms like shrines, pictures of people we do not know—are impossible to understand. She opens it. Sudden night and must in the attic, but even in the poor light, she sees that it is not her father at all. It isn't even her young father. She opens the little pamphlet wider, stands at the attic window to get the last of the setting sun. A series of Xs. Tutsi marked. Her father was a Hutu—a historical underdog. He has explained everything to her, and she understands in a way that is deeper, more complex. A life lived inside history is different from a life lived outside it.

A name is there on the card, the name that she has seen in the magazines: Simon Bonaventure.

What? she thinks. Her brain unable to catch up. *Her mother's boyfriend?*

Her high school French is good enough to get by. Sector: Kigali. Birthplace: Kigali. Wife: Vestine Bonaventure.

Wife? she thinks. In the magazine, he said he didn't have a wife.

On the opposite page, she reads her own first name, her own

middle name. Category: Children. Beside it in the same swirling handwriting, her own birthdate. She flips the card, flips it back. Rereads the names. She feels her legs weak as noodles. A cat is mewling somewhere in the night outside the attic window. She presses her forehead against the card. Feels woozy. *Why haven't I eaten all day?*

One daughter, it reads: Claudette Simona Bonaventure. Quarter-size birthmark on collarbone. She reaches up, touches the spot. Fingers hot against her skin. She is afraid they will leave marks. *Claudette*, she thinks. *But that name is mine.*

3

SHE TRIES NOT TO BETRAY THEM: *IMMACULEE. ABRAHM. MOTHER. Father.* She tries to forget about the man in the magazine, the words on the identity card.

Her parents, the debris of them, are found bloated and pale and trapped inside their Chevrolet Corvair. *They* are her family. *They* are the ones who have raised her. She does not need anyone else.

When the full weight of grief comes to her, the awareness that her parents are never coming back, she doesn't know what to do with it. There are so many questions, and yet no one to answer them. Certainty is a sinkhole that makes her lose her footing. One person can never know another. She touches her belly. *Will I know this child?*

She goes to the box over and over again, looting its treasures. She stares at the identity card as if the words can miraculously change. "My father was a good father," she says in the attic, but there is no one to hear. "My father loved me." A pen in an empty room. A bare desk. A white page: *I believe I am your daughter.* But no, that isn't quite right. *Biological daughter* is considered, but again, it is wrong, like something made in a petri dish. So many limits to language.

I am the child of Abrahm, she says to herself. *This I know, and yet I know it is not so.*

She has perfect cursive handwriting, taught to her by her father when she was just seven years old. His hand wrapped around her own, quiet, a prayer—the soil stains in the folds of his thumb. Dark skin against light. *I do not know. Will you know?*

CHAPTER FIFTEEN

JOCELYN

1

AFTER THE CAR AND THE HOTEL ROOM, AND WHAT JOCELYN LIKES TO think of as their "agreement," they meet every few days, mostly to have sex, but also for the pleasure of each other's company. She continues therapy, but by half, using it as an excuse when Conrad asks where she is going.

One morning, she and Kate decide to hike along the trails of Santa Maria in a small hippie community just north of the club. They hold hands for half the time, knowing no one they know would be caught dead in this town of Buddhas and peace signs. When they've almost made it back to their cars, they sit down on a large boulder, just looking out at the view. Jocelyn holds Kate's hand in her lap and rubs the slick polished fingernails with her thumb. She remembers that first day in the car. She remembers after, thinking of ropes and knots, a lack of reciprocation. Only her doing, making.

She looks at Kate, the fine skin, the flushed cheeks, and realizes she doesn't even know her age. She resists asking. She likes that they are strangers. Within the anonymity lies control.

She wants to ask her if she would like it, if she would be willing, but she is afraid. It is not easy. She does not fully understand what she wants or why she wants it, but she has to. She leans closer to whisper.

"I want to tie you up," she says.

She doesn't look at Kate. She is shy with her desire. It is different from what she feels with Conrad; with Conrad there has been time, growth, years and years of getting to know one another, like a tree growing outward, steady and slow and secure. With Conrad there is expectation, history, a dead mother, dead siblings, obligation, all her sins between them known, except this one. He sees who she really is. It is tiring to live with a witness.

"Seriously?" Kate says. She laughs, almost snorts. She is too old for the laughter. It is the laugh of a fourteen-year-old on the back of a bus giggling with girlfriends about blow jobs. About fucking.

A blush of red comes into Kate's face, and Jocelyn notices the freckles that speckle the globes of her cheeks. The tow-blonde hair blows. She has asked her to take it down.

"Is that a no?" Jocelyn asks. A singular twitch. There. Waiting. Silence then for a long time. Jocelyn worries, but then:

"Okay," Kate says. The word is a breath between them. Vulnerability. Excitement. "Yes," Kate says. "Please." She is pretending submission. She is very, very intense. Waiting. Wanting too. "When?"

"Later," Jocelyn says. "A different time. When I haven't asked you. When I've told you. When I make you."

Kate covers her face with her hands. She runs her fingers through the long hair that Jocelyn likes to feel and smell, especially in bed. Release, open, fall.

Jocelyn pushes Kate back gently against the flat edge of the rock. Below them there is a long drop into the Santa Monica Mountains, but they've got plenty of room. Their legs graze. Jocelyn rolls on top of her. Kate kisses her, pulls her down fiercely. The talking has made them want one another.

"I hear a dog coming," Jocelyn says, looking behind them out onto the trail.

"Fucking hikers," Kate says.

"Who cares?" Jocelyn says, and starts with Kate's shirt.

BECAUSE IT GOES ON DAY AFTER DAY, AND BECAUSE NO ONE SUSPECTS them, and also because it feels so good, the affair gains a certain morality. No one knows, so who could be hurt by it? It feels destined and outside themselves, as if it has been ordained by the universe, as if they cannot help it.

There is a kind of urgency to it too. Deep down they know it must come to an end, and so they want to get their fill.

Sometimes they are gentle with one another. Sometimes they are violent. There are rules, which they make almost immediately. Jocelyn will not be spanked. She will not be tied down. Kate likes a rope but not metal handcuffs. Kate likes to be hurt, to take the sting of what they do together back to the court.

At drill, after particularly rough sessions, Jocelyn warms when she sees Kate in long-sleeved shirts and long pants. She knows the wrists are red where the rope has held her. The skin is pink on the bottom of her buttocks, the tops of her thighs. She wonders briefly what Kate tells her wife but finds that she really doesn't care.

After the quiet domination of these sessions, they make love and talk and then make love again. There is never enough time for them. They are dizzy with want. Their only worry is that they will be found out. But when they are together, all of it is without shame or struggle, or history. Each time, they are absolutely uninhibited. It is absolutely new. They are strangers who meet and fuck, sordid and open with their desire—uncaring, because they know they will never have to face each other again.

JOCELYN WAKES IN THE DIM LIGHT OF THE HOTEL ROOM. SHE IS STARTLED at first. She sits up quickly, naked.

"You said Lucy had a playdate," Kate says. "I canceled my afternoon lessons. I didn't want to wake you, lazy girl."

"Jesus Christ. I had no idea where I was. How long have I been asleep?"

Kate shushes Jocelyn, calms her. "We have time," she says. "I've been watching the clock." She smiles a bit. "And you."

Jocelyn is lying on her belly, groggy and weak from the sleep and the sex. Kate's eyes are on her, a dark green in this light—so different now than they are on the tennis court. Jocelyn feels fingers tracing the ridges and scars on her back. She flinches. She pulls inside herself. She pushes Kate's hand away, tries to turn, but Kate holds on to her—a hand on her hip to stop her.

"What are those?" Kate asks.

Jocelyn does not move. She feels a wall, hard as concrete, erect between them.

"I didn't want to ask, you know. I mean before," Kate continues. "Did Conrad do that to you? He doesn't hurt you, does he? That doesn't look like fun."

Jocelyn tries not to move, not to hear. She thinks if she holds still, she can keep it out. She can be in this space with her lover. She wishes for perfection. Complete separation between here and before. Between now and later. Just this—a daydream of pure. She closes her eyes. *Take it back, take it back, take it back.* The air is chill in the room, and she feels the scars as if they are something nailed to her body.

"It's nothing," she says, feeling Kate's fingers moving along the back of her thigh now, finding and feeling her way along the branches of another atrocity, trying to understand.

"You shouldn't let him hurt you."

Jocelyn turns her head on her pillow, facing away. In this space too, with a precise blade, a sharp knife, Gladys has managed to cut a hole. Even in death she is powerful. *The residue of her pierces through.*

"Conrad would never hurt me," she says, simply. "Conrad saved my life."

The skin is tender again, as if slit open by Kate's painted fingernails. Fresh, even. The body has a memory for pain.

4

JOCELYN KNOWS TO PROTECT HERSELF AGAINST TENDERNESS AT ALL COSTS. *Do not love*, she reminds herself; this a lesson taught to her as a child by her sister. *Do not grow interested. Do not share.*

But sometimes it is hard. Sometime she forgets to find distance. Sometimes, to the tip of her tongue the words come, and she thinks she might say, *I love you*. She thinks she might ask, *Can we be something more?* When that happens, and as it happens, she fights to gain purchase again. She sits on top of Kate, and she pretends that Kate is something to be had. Just for her. She draws out a scarf, an item she brings with her for just this purpose. They are grown-ups. They do not have to pretend that they do not want these things. The scarf is a long one—Hermès. She blindfolds her lover and then pulls the two sides of its length, crisp and taut through Kate's lips. She ties the ends behind the slope of Kate's neck. Kate always protests, just a bit, never very convincingly, and then she allows her hands to be tied by rope, she allows her shirt to be unbuttoned. Jocelyn watches for minutes, seeing the rise and fall of breath, saying nothing, not touching her for many moments, after the rope.

In Kate, there is always the squirming need, the dirty girl whom Jocelyn likes, whom she had hoped for so many months ago. Jocelyn is pleased by this. She senses balance again. Confirmation that what they have is not love.

She kisses Kate lightly and then withdraws. She touches just the tips of her nipples and sits back. Jocelyn moves her hands and fingers between Kate's inner thighs, like a feather there—light and then less light. She listens to the signals of Kate's breathing and then pinches her nipples gently, and then harder, over and over again. Kate writhes, moves in ripples. Jocelyn waits for her to ignite, for the small flame of need to expand and make her desperate. Then she pulls away. She studies her. She is like something she would make. She undoes the scarf that keeps her quiet when she is almost beside herself.

Jocelyn, she hears, but it is breath, not a word.

Jocelyn licks one nipple, then the other. There is a cry of pleasure from Kate, which Jocelyn takes into her own mouth, and then she takes Kate's tongue too, and then she tastes the hollow of her neck, of Kate's belly, the space between Kate's legs. She hears the rope, the whisper and rub of it, as Kate tries to move her body more intensely into Jocelyn's face. Jocelyn pulls back, just a bit. She is certain Kate can feel only the warmth of her breath. Kate cannot reach her anymore. She is safe. She presses her body forward, almost there.

What do you want? Jocelyn asks. They are not shy. *You can have whatever you want. But you have to ask for it.*

"IT WASN'T A HOLIDAY, SO WE KNEW," SHE SAYS IN THE SMALL OFFICE. "WE never got gifts anyway. Holiday or not."

She is loose and free from the sex with Kate. She wishes she could go straight home, enjoy the day. She doesn't want to be here bringing in the past, but she is here again for Conrad. For help he thinks she needs, and Dr. Bruce is invading, asking, pressing. She is always trying to put her back.

"So, you never really celebrated Christmas or birthdays?"

"Sometimes Gladys would put something on layaway and get it out after a long time. Then she'd sell it to a neighbor or a dealer for drugs or just take it away. Nothing belonged to us. We learned not to get excited."

"Did that bother you? I mean not to ever get anything from your own mother, on your birthday, let's say."

"Yes," she says, lying.

It didn't bother her. It was worse when there was a gift. A trick. Power. Things they never wanted. A theme even. Once, in June, there were blow-up toys, bats, balls, a clearance sale of beach things, a naked blow-up doll to embarrass William with. Where it came from, they couldn't tell, but Uncle Al found it funny.

He and Gladys had been at a thrift store all day. A thrift store in Norwood. *Just white people there*, Gladys saying. Uncle Al saying, *Hey! I'm white.* They were high. Gladys and Uncle Al had a look of conspiracy in their eyes.

She and Ycidra and William were still as stones, all staring at the table, at the stale things they'd brought back. Not wanting any of it. Just wanting to go back into the room that they shared. *Can't trust your fucked-up ass with your sisters*, Gladys would say, but all of them knew that William hadn't thought of a girl in that way his whole life, much less his sisters.

"We thought you could hit the dogs with them," Uncle Al said seriously, his eyes glassy, his mouth wet. "They need a bit of training."

Jocelyn remembers the looking away, the floor falling out beneath her.

There were no dogs at the apartment in Winton Terrace, but Uncle Al rented a house in North College Hill. Jocelyn hated to go there.

There is this cold place for us, she used to think.

Jocelyn feels it now, as she felt it as a child, sitting at that table. It is weighty, the taste of copper, a tightness always in the shoulders and the neck, a cowering. The dogs behind gates in the yard—a concrete slab under bald bellies. The space, three by five at most. They were large dogs. A ground full of piss and feces. Stink in the air. Always there were smells when she was young, smells that she couldn't get away from.

She has seen them many times in her mind, but she cannot bring herself to talk to Dr. Bruce about them. They are pack animals that are afraid to socialize. As a child, Jocelyn loves them for a second before she realizes she cannot love them. They exist behind secret memories of their own that do not allow them to lift their heads. They do not make eye contact when Uncle Al is in the yard. He parades their fear to the children. When they please him, they are beaten. When they rebel against him, they are beaten. On occasion, there is the soft touch for absolutely nothing. Their confusion makes them docile and isolated. They push their bodies into corners, crawl along the floor. Jocelyn tells Ycidra that she loves the dogs the first time they go and see them. The blow-up toys come later, months and months after.

Do not love them, her sister says. *You can love me. You can love William.*

"Which one of these do you like the best?" Uncle Al says, fondling the blow-up bat. He throws the beach ball at William's face. There is glee beneath his question as he shows off each item. He walks behind Jocelyn's stool, and she feels his erection, as hard as a broom handle, against the back of her head.

Gladys lights a Newport.

"Jocelyn?" Dr. Bruce says, gently.

"Can I get a glass of water please?"

CHAPTER SIXTEEN

CLAUDETTE

1

SHE HAS ALWAYS HAD A CONTENTIOUS RELATIONSHIP WITH FOOD, AND pregnancy makes it worse. At fifteen, she intentionally starves herself in the hopes of getting her mother's attention. Her breasts, her butt, the pad of skin that feminizes her waistline shrinks away, leaving rib bone, tailbone, and a feathery coat of hair. Her father takes her to the doctor, but there is nothing they can do. She likes the glassy look of her eyes, the sharp peak of her cheekbones. She likes how wispy she is, and loves the meticulousness required to enact her eating plans. It takes wit and intellect to starve herself and yet stay alive. It is power. If she can do this, then there is nothing she can't do.

She counts calories, she pins her pants. She peels her grapes. In the morning for breakfast she has twenty flakes of cereal. She drinks loads and loads of water. For lunch, she has two saltine crackers, carefully picking the kernels of salt off them. Water retention is the nemesis of the scale.

Her mother does not set down her coffee cup though. She

drinks the vodka and Diet Coke she always drinks. Her mother remains as emotive as a houseplant.

Her father though, is her father. A man of deep love and notice. They are close, even during these years of adolescence, these days of starvation. Even at fifteen, at night, most nights, she and her father still read together. They have had this habit since she was a small child, beginning with *Stellaluna* and *Green Eggs and Ham*. He stutters and cries when they finish *The Secret Garden*. *This is the magic*, she remembers him reading. *This is the magic.* She is nine.

He sits at the edge of her bed in the years of her anorexia. They are reading Achebe. He holds her slim self against his own muscular body when it is time to say goodnight. He is gentle with her, as if she really were a bag of bones.

"Eat," he says, the glimmer of tears in his eyes. "Will you eat for me, my dearest one? Will you eat for your father?"

NOW SHE TRIES TO EAT FOR THE BABY, BUT IT DOESN'T WORK. SHE LAYS the food out on the counter, all of it clean. Raw cucumber, heirloom tomatoes. There is kale to tenderize, to massage between her fingers with sea salt and olive oil. Her sense of smell is magnified, so meat is out of the question.

At the university, while teaching, she is certain she can smell the dried sperm that crusts the inside of Landon Hill's underwear. She leans down to help Allison Wray with her rhetorical strategies and smells the sour scent of yogurt—rhubarb and raspberry, mixed with her morning toothpaste. She is like those bees that can sense cancer in the body, dogs that catch sweating criminals in bushes, or pigs that dig for truffles that have been held in the earth for hundreds of years. The smells send her gagging to her desk. She steps outside the hallowed, heavy, wooden doors of her freshman comp room to throw up into a bag that she's brought for just this kind of emergency. In her office, the clear scent of bile and phlegm is present no matter how much she cleans. She'll have to tell the dean she is pregnant soon.

When she goes to the doctor's office, she explains that she cannot eat, because she smells everything. The doctor says she is dehydrated, that she will be hospitalized if she doesn't find a way. She explains that she is trying, but he knows her history. I would never put my child at risk, she says, but he looks at her with disgust—a baby killer, a woman with deep-seated issues. A crazy lady who still thinks she's fat.

She explains that food alights on her tongue and then, like a projectile, shoots out when she swallows it. She can look at vegetables, handle them, but all she can eat, in very small doses, is citrus, grapes, and grape juice. That's better than nothing, the doctor says. He hooks her to an IV, rehydrates her, and tells her to come back in one week.

She leaves the office. At home when her husband is at work, she undresses, looks at herself in the mirror. She cannot help but gasp with habitual pleasure: She is starved and yet alive. She is slim and yet full. She stands on the scale countless times, but nothing changes except her belly. The baby lives on air. A sparrow, a snipe, dipping and pecking, eating the fat from her brain. It grows into a tiny ball.

At the appointment one week later, the doctor warns her of anemia.

"I cannot eat meat," she says. "No way."

He sighs, insists, but the slick surface of a raw chicken breast makes her stomach turn. The texture is muscular, uterine even. It recalls a memory—camp, a girl, the two of them touching each other inside a tent. Claudette's fingers inside the other girl, pressing, feeling. The texture, the walls of the girl's insides, until this moment, absolutely forgotten.

CHAPTER SEVENTEEN

JOCELYN

1

On Wednesdays, Jocelyn volunteers in Lucy's class. Her shift starts after lunch and ends at dismissal. She has time on these volunteer days for tennis and sometimes time for Kate at the Palisades Inn. Their habit is expensive, more than three hundred dollars a week. Nothing in the Palisades is cheap, and Jocelyn doesn't like that they have to stay local. She is afraid that someone will see them. Kate reminds her that she has to be close enough to work. She snickers at Jocelyn when Jocelyn suggests the Culver Hotel or the Ritz-Carlton in Marina Del Rey. She calls her a kept woman, and reminds her that *she* has to work for a living. They pay cash, but must show IDs. They leave in separate cars, in good moods, not guilty anymore. Kate heads back to the club, and Jocelyn races to school to pick up Lucy or to volunteer. The scent of Kate is on her fingers, her clothes. The secret of Kate swells inside her. She feels light and young when she sees Lucy and the other children. It takes a minute to become the woman who is a mother again, a wife, a protector.

Lucy's teacher, Mr. Baird, is always happy to see her. He is very obliging. He is a good-looking man with straight brown hair and clean-shaven skin. He is very tall, as Lucy said. He keeps a friendly classroom, filled with art and tiny desks and the alphabet. Little Wanted signs for fairy-tale creatures hang on laundry lines that run down the center of the ceiling. He seems like a decent man, but Jocelyn knows better than to trust him.

Today, he has given her the task of making papier-mâché globes with the children. She sits in the back of the classroom and calls each child up to help her with the newspaper and liquid starch. Some of the children are squeamish, especially the boys, who do not like the slimy texture of the starch. As she greets each one, there is the feeling that she is seeing the same child over and over again—blonde and blue eyed, white and skinny. They all have a whisper of wealth behind them. Lucy is the only girl in the classroom who isn't white. *And yet she is white in a way,* Jocelyn thinks. *Just not in this country.*

As early as kindergarten, Jocelyn has heard other little girls starting sentences with, "No offense, Lucy, but my hair is blonder than yours," or, "No offense, Lucy, but my skin is more like Claire's. Your skin is darker, so *we'll* be sisters and you'll be a friend."

Lucy doesn't seem to notice or mind, but Jocelyn's heart breaks when she hears it. She is thirteen again and wants to tell the pale white girls that they'll pay for skin like Lucy's one day, that they'll wrinkle and shrivel and scar years before her daughter will. That the stringy blonde hair they have now will dull and grow brown as they move into puberty. *You're an ugly white girl,* she whispers to Brooke Borman one day after she overhears her tell Lucy she can't be in their family. And when the child's face drops, Jocelyn tells her she's looking a bit big. She doesn't worry when the girl starts crying. If Brooke's mother or Mr. Baird asks what she's done, Jocelyn will just lie. Adults lie about children all the time.

She keeps an eye on Mr. Baird while she volunteers. She is compelled to assess him. Does he really need to read with one of the girls right next to him? Does he touch Lisbeth Salen's leg unnecessarily when he bends down to tie her shoes?

At the end of the day, the children line up to hug him goodbye. One after another, he lifts them up in the air above his head. They giggle, and sometimes the girls' skirts float up, revealing the smallest line of panty before he places them back on the ground. Does this mean something? she wonders. She isn't really sure. If it were obvious, she could stop worrying. She could act. She will not miss the opportunity to protect Lucy as she missed the opportunity to protect Ycidra, William, herself.

When it is Lucy's turn in line for a hug, Jocelyn tenses up. Her daughter is dancing while she waits, shaking her hips with the excitement of the end of the day. Lucy and her best friend, Ali, squeeze each other's hands in anticipation—of what? Of anything, Jocelyn realizes, and she earnestly wishes she could keep Lucy right where she is: happy about almost anything.

She studies her daughter to see if there is any sign of the flaw that she and her own siblings have inherited, but it is still not there. Jocelyn looks quickly at her own reflection in the classroom mirror. She cannot see it in herself today either, but it's in the blood. Her mother has taught her this. She worries that maybe it is invisible in Lucy too. Is it a seed, waiting to bloom? Has she been gone too long from Winton Terrace and all that survives there to still see it clearly? All she sees in the mirror is a wealthy woman with good hair, good makeup, good boots. She is carrying the python bag from Conrad.

Mr. Baird picks Lucy up, and her daughter squeals with laughter. A flash of Gladys comes to her then, but why?

"She's trash," Gladys said to Conrad when he asked for Jocelyn's hand in marriage. Uncle Al was long gone by then, but Conrad had insisted on being ridiculously romantic, as if his urge, his own sense of the importance of taking Jocelyn as his wife, would make Gladys rise to the occasion. One more time Jocelyn had been shamed.

"Why her?" Gladys had asked through an exhalation of Newport smoke, "when there's so many girls in the world?"

The hurt is still there. Its persistence, miraculous. *Gladys is dead*, she says to herself. *My mother is dead.*

Lucy runs to her, hugs her tightly, brings her back to joy. They go to collect her things—the tiny backpack, the water bottle that's the color of the Caribbean sea. Outside the classroom door, she sees Maud. They air-kiss and smile at one another. Jocelyn is grateful that she and Maud are friends. Maud helps her navigate this world.

"Are you coming to dinner tonight? Third Friday of the month."

"Oh crap, I forgot," Jocelyn says. "If Conrad will come home, I'll be there. Otherwise I'm out."

"You can drop Lucy at my house. The kids can play. Aurora is there. You know she's great."

"I'll let you know," Jocelyn says, knowing she'd never leave Lucy with a stranger. Not even a stranger whom Maud recommends. *When you least expect it, expect it*, she thinks. *They're out there, everywhere.*

2

"Go," Conrad says, pushing her out the door.

"Go, Mama!" Lucy says, and then there is the carpeted hallway, green waxy plants. The shiny stainless-steel elevator doors that reflect her image back to her—a good outfit, a sparkle from the diamond ring on her finger.

"Papa?" she hears her daughter say, as the doors of the elevator slide open to swallow her. "Let's play, Papa."

The restaurant is expensive. It is positioned right on the water, before Coastline Drive and along Pacific Coast Highway. Parking is horrendous. Jocelyn leaves her car a quarter mile away and walks back to the restaurant, avoiding the speeding cars that come very close to her. By the time she arrives, her hair is a swirling mess.

"Where's the valet, for God's sake?" Maud says in a huff, catching up with her.

"That was so tiring," Theresa says.

"We're so spoiled," Jocelyn says, and they all laugh.

There are five of them out for an MNO, or "Mothers' Night Out." They do it monthly. They talk about parenting strategies, about ways to do things better than their own parents did, which is laughable in the case of Jocelyn. Jocelyn has fictional parents for dinners like these—there is no Gladys. No Uncle Al.

She and the other mothers are seated immediately at a table by the window. The water from the sea is close enough to leave the residue of spray along the windows, which are foggy, dirty even. Jocelyn thinks the restaurant seems a bit shabby. She goes to wash her hands.

When she returns, the waiter is there, and Jocelyn orders

a vodka with soda and lots of fresh limes. It is the drink of the hour—low calorie and potent. The others order variations on it. When the drinks come, Erica gets the meeting started. It is her turn to lead. Her turn to pick a significant topic.

She clears her throat. "Let's talk about how we can protect our children," she says. "How can we keep them safe?"

Jocelyn doesn't speak. She hates subjects like this. She instantly thinks of Mr. Baird but knows not to bring it up. She wishes the mothers could just talk about the weather, gossip, get drunk.

"Safe from what?" Maud says. "We live in the Palisades. We don't even have a police force. Get real, Erica."

Jocelyn grins at Maud, loving her.

"Well," Erica says in a pissy tone. "You never know what's out there."

Jocelyn takes a sip of her drink. It is strong. Her phone buzzes. She looks at it. It's Simon. She's surprised.

> **SIMON**: Wanna come over and watch the men's finals?
> **JOCELYN**: Would love to. Am in boring mother's meeting. Can't escape.
> **SIMON**: I will save you. Tell them your neighbor is locked out of his apartment.
> **JOCELYN**: I can't. I'll stop by after. Very briefly. Can't make Conrad jealous.

She sends a winking emoji with it. Conrad is never jealous.

"What do *you* think, Jocelyn?" Erica asks. "About safety. I mean, if you're done texting."

Jocelyn feels put on the spot. She doesn't know what to say. She doesn't want to talk about safety. Safety is a tricky thing. All she knows how to do is to be with Lucy, to interrogate anyone whom she feels suspicious of, to not allow sleepovers. Ever. Even then, the perpetrators might outsmart her. Even then, they might ruin her child. She has the sense that this isn't something she should say. It might expose something in her. Present Gladys and her smell. Gladys and her leering. The answer feels as if it might take the form of a spotlight and announce her childhood secrets. Her differences.

"I'm not really sure," she says. "I'm a bit distracted. Sorry. My neighbor locked himself out of the house. I've really got to go. I don't mean to be rude, but well."

"I've got to head out too," Maud says. "Thank God for your neighbor," she whispers in Jocelyn's ear.

They all leave after paying the bill. She and Maud laugh about Erica as they walk to their cars together. It is gentle gossip.

"You going to tennis tomorrow?"

"Yes," Jocelyn says. "I'm officially addicted."

"We all are," Maud says. "How about the retreat? I'm thinking about it. Scott says he'll watch the kids."

"I don't know," Jocelyn says. "Palm Desert is so hot, and I hate leaving Lucy. Also, I can't share a room. I just can't."

"Nobody's asking you to share a room," Maud says. "I mean, except Missy. I heard Missy is dying to stay with you. You're her favorite person."

"She's going?"

"Oh, come on, Jocelyn. Stop being a child. Missy is still the official Kate stalker. Of course she's going. No excuses though. She isn't going to bother you, and you don't have to share a room. We're adult women. We're beyond room sharing. Besides, I might have to take home one of those tennis cabana boys."

Maud is joking, but Kate crosses Jocelyn's mind. Could they have a night together? Is there room for privacy? In a flash, she imagines waking up next to her, a whole night spent.

"If Conrad will come up Saturday, maybe. Lucy still has bad dreams sometimes. Three nights is too long."

Maud sighs. "Oh, leave your poor daughter and husband alone. Let them have a weekend together. You never give yourself a break. That's why you get so crazy and worried. Let them be a bit by themselves."

"I don't think it will work. I mean, Lucy, she'll want me."

Maud sounds disgusted. "You should have had more kids, Jocelyn. You'd flee from them as I do if you had five of them. They're animals. Don't you see that?"

Jocelyn smiles and shrugs her shoulders at Maud.

Maud continues, "Think about it, okay. We'd have fun. We'll ask Kate to keep us together. I don't mean in the room. I mean for the drills."

"Maybe," she says.

"I'll tell Scott to come up with Conrad. How's that? I know some of the girls are bringing their nannies."

"That might work," Jocelyn says.

"Oh my God," Maud says. "I just went insane for a minute. Those heathens are not following me up to Palm Desert to ruin my girls' weekend."

The two women laugh. Jocelyn knows how much Maud loves her children. She knows that they are always first in everything she does. She sometimes watches Maud manage it all, wonders how, and wants to be like her. If Ycidra were alive, Jocelyn thinks, she would want her to be like Maud—a good life, a good husband, lots of money and children. The loss of her sister pricks at her like a tiny pinpoint.

"I'll let you know," Jocelyn says and hugs her friend. "Either way, I'll see you tomorrow."

ON THE CURVY DRIVE HOME FROM THE RESTAURANT, JOCELYN TRIES NOT to remember. She tries not to let the voices in. But something in the dinner, in the conversation, in the sisterly feel of her friendship with Maud, has made her lose control, has let the past eat the present.

Find the box, she thinks, feeling the panic rising as she drives the car toward home. She has had a good night. She does not want it ruined. Palm trees sway and move as if alive in the windy night. Find the box, she says again. Put the past inside.

She knows from her history that she needs to get a handle on it right away. There is urgency in the touch of the gas pedal. The car goes faster. She blinks against the pictures that come to her. PCH winds and winds. She is a little bit tipsy after drinking her vodka so fast. Lights streak by. Close the box after. Close the box. And then a lock. With a chain? She tries to remember what Dr. Bruce told her. She tries to see each link, the combination numbers. She tries, but it doesn't work. She focuses on the road, the hills beside her. A fun tennis match watched with a friend. She rolls the windows down. A rock then, something to beat it down with. Level it. If she can just get home. If she can just make it up to her floor.

She imagines an animal, ravenous, a wolf. Yes. An animal to eat it. Some weighty, growling thing. Then there is Ycidra. Uncle Al. William. Lucy. Mr. Baird. *But what did I do wrong?* Then, Gladys, *You know what you did wrong.* Her confusion. No. No. And no.

As a child, it was a television set inside her head, many stations, the noise of it, running on top of all that other noise. The noise in the bed above. The noise of her siblings being whipped. She would blink to change the channel. The sheets that were never washed had the smell of her own fear in them. She tries now, but time has left her unpracticed. A cave, she thinks, a rock rolled in front of it. She rolls the windows down even farther, but nothing helps. The sea crashing against rock makes her afraid.

4

In the elevator up to her penthouse, this is what she hears:

I will feed you when your mother will not.

I will pay the gas bill, so you won't be cold.

I will be your mother's boyfriend.

I am your friend's father.

I will keep your mother high.

I will forget your sleeping bag. You will shiver in the cold, before you finally get inside mine with me.

I will check your naked body for mosquito bites. Not just you, but Ycidra, and William, and all the other children, one after another, in a line. This is what you will remember about Camp Christian. This is what God will give you. But I will linger on you, because there is no one for you, no one to protect you. Just the cold plastic of a Hefty bag.

I will put a pillow over your head so you can't breathe or scream, even when you are beyond the noise. Even when you no longer believe in protesting.

I will touch you like I touch your mother.

I will rape your sister. You will know better than to tell. I will spend most of your childhood teaching you that lesson. Shame will make you behave.

5

SIMON'S DOOR OPENS AS THE ELEVATOR DOORS OPEN. HE MUST HEAR IT. Tears warm on her cheeks. A dizzy feeling. He is expecting her, of course—the men's finals, the tennis. All of it suffocated under. She is too disoriented to care what he thinks, to figure out what brings it on. Why can she never control the hurt?

He walks toward her. His face strains. *What is it?* his eyes ask. "What has happened?" his voice says. He grasps both of her arms gently, walks her back to his door, leads her in through the entry, past the marble island, and then sits her down on his couch. A blanket around her legs. Her high heels in his hands and then on the ground. Within minutes, he places a glass of warm brandy into her hands. She cries and cries. He sits beside her. Quiet. Facing forward. No words. The tennis is on but muted in the background. Large brown hands hold her own. Hands like William's, strong, slender. *My brother was a pianist. I used to turn the pages for him when he played. A short nod of his head, a signal between us.*

"I miss my brother," she says to him. "I miss my sister. They are both dead."

"I didn't know," he says. "My brothers are dead. My sisters are dead too. My whole family. So many families."

Snot runs down from her nose. He gets her a tissue. She wipes her eyes, her nose. They sit, in no hurry, for what feels like a long time.

CHAPTER EIGHTEEN

SIMON

1

Before she goes, when she's finally calm, when she has washed her face, and fixed her hair, he hands her the letter. It is a commitment that he is making to her. The sharing of blood in order to make them blood siblings, a cut to the palm, a shake. It is important, he knows—the only way to avoid certain regret in the morning. He must equalize the relationship. He must make it so that they are both absolutely vulnerable, absolutely naked in front of one another.

She unfolds it. She is careful. It is as fragile and important as a rare museum piece. She handles it as if it might disintegrate in her hands. He lays the pictures out too—the grainy, blurred bits of them. She looks at them. She reads the letter. When she is finished, she speaks.

"She is your daughter," she says to him. "I can feel it. I just know."

"Do you really think so?" he says.

"Yes," she says. "I really do."

He puts her shoes back on for her when she is ready. He steadies her. He opens the door for her. He watches her as she makes it safely to her own door.

PART III

I will arise and go now, and go to Innisfree,
And a small cabin build there, of clay and wattles made;
Nine bean-rows will I have there, a hive for the honey-bee,
And live alone in the bee-loud glade.

—WILLIAM BUTLER YEATS

CHAPTER NINETEEN

JOCELYN

1

THE IDEA OF A CABIN IN THE WOODS CLAIMS HER IN THE SAME WAY THAT Kate does. The Palisades Inn is expensive, staid. They worry about maids and other patrons hearing. It's too close to the club. Intrusion is just outside the door. She can't stop thinking about an imaginary place to be. *Our own space*, she whispers to herself. *It must be completely separate. No one will know.*

On Wednesday, after she drops Lucy at school, she heads north on Pacific Coast Highway, past her condominium, and then right onto Topanga Canyon Boulevard. The town is less than fifteen minutes from the club. The road is dangerous, something to slip off of in a light rain. There are no guardrails. There is just nature, mountains, and sky for quite a long time, and then suddenly, a sign that says SLOW DOWN THROUGH TOWN.

Town is a lumber store, a grocery store, a liquor store, and a specialty store with oversize Buddhas and hippie-wear. There is a post office, a feed store selling baby chicks, and a real estate office, tiny, not even the size of a small shed. She passes it, heading into the Valley, and then changes her mind, makes a difficult U-turn, and heads back, parks in its parking lot.

She steps out of her car. It is actually cold here, much colder even than by the beach. She knocks on the real estate office door. A man invites her in, tells her his name is Walt, offers tea, yerba maté. He hands her a blanket.

"Fourteen microclimates here in Topanga," he says to her, as if she's asked. "You're in the coldest one."

The office, he explains, is an old forest ranger's cabin that was built in 1907. Jocelyn takes a seat, puts the blanket on her lap. She likes the smell of the wool. She watches as the Realtor starts a fire in an old-fashioned stove. A dog is asleep on a dog bed in the corner of the room. It is a standard poodle—a show dog with ribbons on each ear and a pom-pom shaved into its tail. Not at all what Jocelyn would have expected in a cabin like this. When he lights the flame of the stove, the dog makes its way closer to the fire.

"She thinks I'm making it for her," the Realtor says. He rubs her black muzzle. "I am, in a way."

Jocelyn likes the dog. She's heard the breed is smart.

"What can I do for you?" he asks. "On this fine, fine, cold morning."

She smiles, sips the tea. It tastes awful. "I'm not sure," she says. "I just had this idea. I've always loved it here. I need a retreat."

She doesn't want to say, *I need a place to tie my girlfriend up. I need a place where no one knows me, where we can do things to each other and not worry about the noise.*

"Big?" he says.

"Just for me, really."

"I've got a few larger ones, but only one studio," he says, "It's very *original*. It takes a certain kind of person."

She likes the sound of that. She pretends she likes the awful tea.

"It's got eighty steps, which are okay on the way down the mountain. But on the way up—" he smiles "—that's the bastard." He digs around in the desk. Pulls out a flyer.

She takes it from him, sees the photograph, feels as if it's something precious in her hands.

"It's small," he says. "Not even five hundred square feet. All one room, but the rent's good. No heat, just a wood-burning stove like this one, but you can imagine."

She is already feeling the heat in this room. The cottage would be three-quarters this size.

"It's inexpensive and on one acre. Forgive me," he says, looking at her bag and her boots and her coat. "I've got better things. Larger. Less rustic. I mean, you don't seem the type for this one. I hope that's not offensive. You don't seem like you've done much camping, and this isn't much better than camping."

She smiles. Looks at the dog again. "I want something rustic," she says. "Something different than what I'm used to." She resists the urge to tell him where she lives.

"Well then," he says. He writes something on a Post-it note. "Here's the owner's information. It's five hundred a month. It's month to month."

"I'd want to pay cash," Jocelyn says, knowing this is just a portion of her shopping money. Conrad will never notice.

"Last time I looked, that would be up about everyone's alley," the Realtor says. "Still, you'll have to get in touch with the owner, Lois."

"Great," she says, looking at the flyer again, feeling drawn already to the place, as if it were already hers.

He presses the Post-it with the owner's information into her hand. "It's what we call Topanga funky, and Lois is a bit, well, different, but so's everyone around here. I sure hope you'll fit in." He says it kindly with a bit of laughter at the end.

"Thanks very much."

"Are you going to call her right now?" he asks. "She's always home. She'll show it to you right away. It's just that . . ."

He looks at her boots, the soft suede of them, the fine Italian leather. They are flat, but fragile.

"I'd change your shoes," he says. "Before I'd go out there.

We've had rain here recently. Sometimes it just rains here, and nowhere else in LA. Like I said, fourteen microclimates. Because we're in a canyon. The mud stays for days."

"I will," she says, standing up. "Is there a place nearby where I could buy something?"

"I don't think for shoes," he says. "I could give you a couple of plastic bags."

She laughs, imagining herself plodding through thick mud with her Chloé boots wrapped in grocery bags.

"Sounds good," she says, and he reaches in a drawer and hands her two plastic bags and two zip ties.

"Well." He offers his hand. "Welcome," he says. "It's kind of a live-and-let-live community."

Jocelyn gets her keys out of her purse, shakes the man's hand. She smiles. "That's exactly what I'm looking for."

She leaves the real estate office and goes to the little market. She is excited, shrieky, like a girl who's gotten her first kiss. There is a butcher in the back. She buys sausages and steak fillets to grill at home. The butcher sells her an insulated bag. She orders a cup of coffee and sits outside in what is almost a parking lot and looks at the ads posted on the wall—healing is offered, chakra readings, animals that need shelter. She likes that she doesn't know anyone in the canyon. She is fearless and anonymous. She is making it happen—a whole other existence. She watches a couple kissing. A horse is being ridden down the main street. There is a man coming out of a handmade tile store with a blue macaw on his shoulder. It's like being transported to another time. It wouldn't be weird, she thinks, if someone walked down the street naked. She sits, picturing herself in the cabin. She imagines clean, bare space, hardly any furniture. No past. *It's just for me*, she thinks. *For me and Kate*, her brain reminds her.

2

SHE CALLS FROM HER CELL PHONE, NOT WANTING TO LEAVE THE CANYON without leasing the cottage. The landlady confirms that there is just one big room and a minikitchen and full bath. She reiterates that there really are eighty stairs. She explains that the cottage's share of the property is one acre.

"I live on the other side of the creek. It's a long walk for me. I want a single person. I hope Walt told you that," she says.

"It's me. Just me."

"Okay then," the landlady says.

"I wouldn't use it full time," Jocelyn says. "I'm looking for a retreat."

"Even better," Lois says. "Are you an artist?"

"Yes," Jocelyn says. The lie comes easily. It makes her happy.

Lois says, "I'm going to warn you now. No point moving in if you aren't up for it. The stairs are a bit of an issue. I mean you have to be in good shape. No drugs either. I mean a little pot never hurt anybody, but I don't want drugs on my property."

Jocelyn cracks up. "I'm in good shape. I don't mind stairs. No drugs."

"It's very remote, and not for everyone. You can't be calling me because you see a snake. Remote is actually a bit of an understatement. This is *in* nature. On septic."

"When can I see it?" Jocelyn asks, cutting to the chase. She looks at her watch. It is Kate's late day. Will she be able to see the place, shower, change, tell Kate? Two hours before drill. She wants to surprise her. Have her come and see.

"I'll make a point of meeting you. I already sort of like you."

"Thank you," Jocelyn says. "Thank you so much."

"How's eleven thirty?"

Fifteen minutes from now, Jocelyn thinks. Maybe she can lease it quickly, get the keys. She has cash in her purse. The universe is on her side. "That's great."

"It's up Grandview Road," Lois says. "And then down a private drive. I will text you the directions. Your GPS won't pick it up, so make sure you write it all down right now before you get out of town."

Town? Jocelyn thinks again, wryly. She sits, staring at the phone. She waits.

SHE IS HAPPY SHE HAS DRIVEN THE PORSCHE. IT DOES BETTER ON THE windy roads, and she thinks it might be more impressive. The road is narrow and dangerous. There are blind curves around every corner. She is glad to have the control.

She parks her car between white lines on what seems to be the crest of a huge hill. She waits, worries that she is in the wrong place, but the text says to park by the flying pig mailbox, and there is a mailbox in the shape of a flying pig. She waits and waits, feeling tense, worrying that the landlady has changed her mind. What if someone else has rented it? What if—

"Nice car," she hears a voice say from behind her.

She exhales, unaware that she has been holding her breath until that moment. "Thanks," she says.

"You must be quite an artist," the woman says, looking down at Jocelyn's hands, lifting a brow. "You aren't married, are you? I only want one person here."

"No," Jocelyn says, grateful she's thought to take her wedding ring off for drill class. "No. No. I'm not married."

3

THE MINUTE SHE HAS THE KEYS IN HER HAND, SHE CALLS KATE.

"You can't be serious," Kate says. "Are you crazy?"

"Oh, please, come and see it," Jocelyn says. "It's so great."

"I don't know," Kate says, and Jocelyn finds herself feeling slightly annoyed.

"Please," she begins. "Why are you such a grumpy old lady?"

She gives Kate directions, and she and her Tesla are there in under thirty minutes. Jocelyn leads her down the eighty stairs. At the bottom, they are both out of breath.

"Thanks for coming," Jocelyn says, overly polite. A bit embarrassed, suddenly. Now that Kate is here, and they are looking at the cabin together, it seems less of a good idea. It seems very, *very* rustic. The stairs are insane.

Kate looks around the property. The woods are like those in a fairy tale, close to the house. The ground is wet. They have to leap over leftover puddles.

"I shouldn't be at your beck and call," Kate says, teasing Jocelyn. "I mean, look at me. You call. I come. I come. I come."

They laugh. They go inside. It isn't exactly clean. They make plans: an iron bed, antique, very feminine. They don't need anything except the bed, they joke. Well, the rope, the ruler, the other paraphernalia.

"And two wooden chairs," Jocelyn says, pinning Kate to the wall and kissing her. She has already pictured her, perched and naked, blonde hair cascading down to her waist. Her ankles and wrists tied to slick wooden chair rails and spindles. Waiting. A tall table to bend her over.

They both stand looking into the middle of the room in their separate fantasies. Jocelyn finds that she is trembling as if it is their first time together. She takes Kate's hand as little girls take each other's hands to play. They walk the small space together, step by step, walking out the measurements. Kate will go to work. She will coach, but she will be distracted by the possibility of total privacy. Jocelyn will spend the hours shopping for furniture, for home goods. She will spend her leisure time in the study of knots.

CHAPTER TWENTY

SIMON

1

THE DOG IS ALWAYS THERE WHEN HE DRIVES TO WORK. ANIMAL CONTROL has not come for it. It cannot belong to anyone. It grows thinner and thinner, more sedate. He calls animal control again and again, and then on his day off, he drives east along the 10 freeway to see if the dog is still there. It is. He can't believe it. He feels a surge of anger. He calls again, sits and waits on hold. This time he shouts. An officer assures him they will go and pick up the dog. They ask for more specific instructions. He gives them the exact exit number.

On his way back to the museum from lunch, he sees that the dog is still there, and he calls again. He has the sense that the animal control officers are laughing at him. They know his voice when he calls. He curses his accent. He does not know what to do. He imagines he will drive by one day and the dog will be there unmoving, dead, on the shoulder of the road.

He finds that he can't focus at work at all. He decides to leave the museum early, retrieves his drawings from his desk, and goes to the Pet Express on La Cienega. He enters the store, buys a dog bowl, a bottle of water, and a small bag of food. He does not have a plan exactly. He loads it all into his BMW and drives back to where the dog is.

He parks the car on the shoulder when he sees the dog. His heart beats fast. The dog looks at the car. Its head seems bigger than his own. It does not move until he steps out of his car, and then it frantically runs away from him to the other side of the grassy berm and behind a row of brush. Simon makes his way toward the area where the dog has gone, slowly and carefully. He is afraid of this kind of dog.

When he gets close, he places the bowl down, fills it with water. He lays the bag of food on the ground. He looks again for the dog, but it has disappeared. He sees a run-down business on the other side of the entrance lane. A dilapidated greenhouse is there—all the windows are broken. He wonders if the dog has gone inside. He wonders if his daughter was ever able to have a dog. If so, was it like this one? He doubts it. He opens the bag of food with his car key, constantly keeping his eyes in front of him, in case the dog returns to bite him. The kernels of dry dog food spill out. *I am free*, he thinks. *I can go now. I've done all I can.*

He walks back out to the freeway's shoulder. He gets inside his car. He puts on his seat belt.

"It is meaningless," he says to himself, turning off his hazards. "Foolish. Maybe even cruel. The dog has come so far already on a journey toward death."

He starts the car. He can't help wondering, how old is the dog? Where did it come from? Will he find the food? For the whole drive home, it is there in his mind. The way the dog sits, proud and regal, even while starving.

CHAPTER TWENTY-ONE

CLAUDETTE

1

SHE HAS TAKEN TO TALKING TO HER DEAD MOTHER. *IMMACULEE?* SHE says in an empty room. *How much did you hate me?*

Immaculee? she says, while drawing up her lesson plans. *Did you want your own girl? A real daughter? Am I all you got?*

Residue. I am residue, Claudette thinks. The word is exactly right. She can see her mother's stare—always away—even now. She thinks she will see it until she dies. Intellectually, she knows this isn't true. The dead are forgotten more quickly than the living like to admit.

Claudette wishes for a boy. *Please let there be a boy in my belly.* Boys are better. Boys are simple. To be born black, and a girl—she would not wish that on anyone.

SHE IS TEN WHEN HER FATHER WALKS WITH HER ALONG THE BRIDGE THAT runs between the Boston side and the Cambridge side of Harvard's campus. He is a serious man. He treats her seriously. Even when she is a small girl, he asks her opinion. He listens to her voice, acknowledges the things she says. There has never been baby talk between them. They sit at night and read the paper together. The news of the world. She on his strong lap. He asks her who she prefers for president.

"Princeton is a fine school too," he says, looking out at the river. Even at ten years old, she still holds his hand. "It isn't far. Just New Jersey. Still the East Coast."

She is quiet, thoughtful. The roof across the way is blue. Another is red. Another is green.

"Why are they like that, Papa? Why are they different colors?"

"I don't know," he says. "You'll find out when you get to Harvard, if this is where you go. Shall we walk across and ask them? College is where life is about questions."

She stops in the middle of the bridge and looks over. He has not attended college. He has always been a farmer. First in Africa, and then in Newton, Massachusetts. He has dreamed of college though. She imagines it herself. Sitting up late at night, discussing Shakespeare and Chaucer. She has recently discovered American southern writers—Agee and Wright. Her father wants her to read Emecheta and Bâ, but they are too didactic, she tells him, too boring. She wants to say *too African*, but does not.

"When they graduate, the students jump into the water from here," he tells her, pointing down.

She stares at the river. It doesn't seem so very deep.

"Brown or Penn," he says. "You could attend Columbia too.

There are only eight colleges in the Ivy League. You are meant for one of them. I am sure of it."

"I want to go here," she says, looking at him and at Harvard.

He places a hand on top of her head.

"It is a good thing to see the world," he says to her. "It is good to leave home. It is a kind of learning too. You don't have to go here. This is just the first place for us to visit."

"I won't go anywhere else," she says.

Panic. She remembers the feeling even now. There is nowhere she wants to be that isn't near her father. Her heart beats like a bird in her chest. "I am meant to be here. By you. It is the place that I belong."

3

THE DETECTIVE IS AT HER DOOR.

"He would like to see you," he says. "The DNA. It's a match."

She feels a bit smug. "I see," she says.

"Can we set a time? A date?" The detective says this bluntly. He stares at her small belly. From the living room, her husband, Larry, asks who it is.

"It's sales," she says, although there is no such thing anymore. No traveling salespeople like the ones she finds in old southern stories.

"Can you travel?" he asks.

"No. I can't. I'm too far along. The baby could come early."

He looks at her slim hips, her belly the size of a child's Nerf basketball. There is judgment there. She pulls her sweater shut.

"Do you know if it's a boy or a girl?" he says.

"No," she says. "We want to be surprised."

They stand staring at each other. The detective is white. His skin is pockmarked. His eyes are a sharp blue, as light as the sky.

"What day is best for you?"

"My next school holiday. I wouldn't want to take off work. I can email you."

"Okay," he says. "Thank you. I will tell Mr. Bonaventure. Would you want to meet here?" he asks. "At your house?"

"God, no," she says. She still needs to explain it all to Larry. "I'll figure out a place. A place that I can walk to. I'll text you."

He stands there. "Okay. That would be good."

She goes to shut the door, but then the detective's voice stops her.

"Um," he says. "He's asked me to ask if I can take a picture of you. Do you mind if I take a picture for him?"

She touches her hair, straightens out her dress. "I look a sight," she says, all old lady.

"You look great," he says.

"I guess it's okay," she says.

"I will text it to him right now. If you have a selfie you'd like to send, I could send that. Or I can take it right now."

"A selfie? Not likely."

She poses quietly. Not wanting to draw the attention of Larry. She does not want him in the picture.

The detective snaps the photo of her before she has a chance to really smile or protest again. Her father is there with her sud-denly: It is picture day at Newton Elementary. She is maybe eight years old. He is making sure her braids are just right. *When I was a boy*, he says, *we did not take pictures. I was taught that a camera would take my soul.*

She feels this now, contemplates grabbing the detective's phone. She feels stripped, as if the man in the magazine, Mr. Bonaventure, has taken something deep and vital from her. The very essence of who she thought she was.

CHAPTER TWENTY-TWO

SIMON

1

HE RETURNS AFTER MANY DAYS. THE DOG IS NOWHERE IN SIGHT, BUT THE food is gone, so Simon is inspired. He goes again to the Pet Express and buys a bigger bag. He has scheduled a visit with his daughter, now that they know it is true, and he wants the dog to have food while he's away. He returns with the bag just as before. He has brought additional water too. He opens the bag as he did the last time. He places the food closer to the broken-down greenhouse. He stands from his kneeling position and looks at what he's left for the dog. It is a feast. He can't help smiling.

He walks behind the row of bushes and waits, hiding, hoping to spy the dog. He is quiet. Within minutes, the dog comes out. He glances all around and then runs toward the bag. The animal throws its face into the food. As he eats and after every bite, he looks up and around him, as if afraid that some other animal will come and take his bounty. The dog settles his eyes on the spot where Simon hides. He pauses for a second. Simon believes that he has been seen. The dog stops eating. He is frozen. He stares and stares. He lifts his pink, moist nose into the air and sniffs. Simon is sure he knows he is there. In minutes, as if he has made a decision, he goes back to the kibble. He growls incessantly as he eats the food, claiming it, daring Simon to take it away.

After he leaves the dog, Simon calls Jocelyn from the car. He asks for advice. Tells her the good news.

"What should I wear to meet my daughter?" he asks. *After so many years?* he thinks. *After a lifetime?*

She realizes immediately what he is saying, and she congratulates him.

"So, we were right," she says. "I told you."

"I know," he says. "But now I am nervous. What should I wear? I'm asking you, because you are always so stylish."

She laughs, but he can tell from the tone of her voice that he has flattered her. She tells him business casual.

"Don't scare her by being too fancy. Maybe even nice, dark jeans."

He feels content suddenly: The dog has food. He has a daughter. He has a friend to call for advice. His daughter will like his clothes.

CHAPTER TWENTY-THREE

JOCELYN

1

THERE ARE THE CONTRAPTIONS. THE THINGS THAT THEY BUY. THE CABIN in the woods makes so much more possible. There are the beads. The clips. The leather. The soft cuffs. The belts. The cantilevers. The eye hooks. The rope. There is the equipment that allows them to fuck in the way that she and Conrad fuck.

But when Jocelyn is alone and remembering it all, when she is able to judge it, to relive it, to lose herself in the daydreams of it all, the thing she likes best is when Kate is on top of her, kissing her, when she begins to lower her whole self and then reaches up and pinches Jocelyn's nipples, and then lowers her head some more, and lowers her head some more, until her face is right between her legs, and there is the soft tongue and the gentle sucking and then a little harder, and sometimes the flat of her teeth until all that is left is the feeling, and the coming, and the moan of her voice and her lover's voice, muted and trying to push through. Like being underwater in the roll of a wave.

2

THE TENNIS SKIRTS ARE A HASSLE TO GET OFF, THE TIGHT UNDERSHORTS that come with them, the synthetic material. It all catches smell. Jocelyn feels dirty sometimes after, but neither of them seems to mind. There is something base about their attraction that Jocelyn likes. Sweat and come, sticky fingers and mouths, all parts of each other merged into one. There is nothing off limits.

Jocelyn combs her hair before they leave. She puts on light makeup. As she dresses, they talk about Palm Desert.

"If you come a day early," Kate says, "maybe we can have a night together."

"I was thinking the same thing," Jocelyn says. "Maud wants to go, but I can't go if Conrad can't be home."

"Get a babysitter," Kate says.

"I don't really use babysitters."

"Ever?"

"Not really."

"Why?"

Jocelyn ignores the question. She wouldn't want to say. "Maybe you can keep me and Maud together if she comes up. I don't want to just be up there with no one I know."

"I'll be there," Kate says.

"We're not exactly hanging out."

"Yeah, well, that's true."

Kate starts to dress. Jocelyn watches her. The athletic body. The thick thighs. She decides to just ask.

"What about *your* family? I mean, are they coming up?"

"They'll come up on Friday. Some of the families come up after the first day."

"I see," Jocelyn says.

"Don't mope," Kate says.

"I'm not moping."

"Don't pout then."

"God you're a narcissist," Jocelyn says. "It's unbearable."

Kate laughs, but the mood has changed. Jocelyn knows what she feels is jealousy, and she doesn't like it. She doesn't want to let that in. It is as if a cloud has passed over and shadowed a favorite tree. She washes her hands regretfully. She would like to keep the smell of Kate with her for the rest of the day.

3

SOMETIMES AFTER THEY MAKE LOVE AND KATE IS ALREADY OUT THE door of the small cabin in the woods, Jocelyn thinks about getting dressed, packing a bag, putting up a fair share of water, and walking. In the daydream of it, the journey is unceasing. She does not need to rest, and she walks on and on, like a stick figure on the edge of a globe. She goes around and around like a Ferris wheel until she ends up right back where she started from, and then she begins again. She is always alone. There is no Conrad, no Kate, no Lucy, no Gladys, no Mr. Baird. She is always going nowhere, just circling.

In the journey's ceaselessness, she knows that she will find the girl she used to be before the damage—the girl who is completely clean, undefiled and able to be. She will sleep on the ground, cook meat over a spit. It will be a long walk. As a child, it was a ride on a bus that never ended, hours at the library finding doors and paths inside books. In sleeping dreams, it is a train ride, rendering eternal life. Now, as a mother, it is this walking around the world in her imagination, or sometimes an exhilarating jump into a bottomless sea.

MOST NIGHTS, LUCY HAS BAD DREAMS, AND THIS IS WHY JOCELYN WORries about Palm Desert.

Jocelyn wishes she could stop them. During the day, she spends her time keeping her daughter's life protected and sweet, but night is its own master. Even with Jocelyn in the room, on the small couch, Lucy is afraid of all sorts of things, and especially afraid of the monsters that live inside her closet. Jocelyn explains to her that bad dreams are a sign of brain development and that none of it is real.

"You're getting smarter," she says. "Your brain is getting bigger."

When Lucy seems unconvinced, Jocelyn tries a different strategy. "Nothing is bothering you at school, right? You can always tell Mama anything."

This line of questioning seems to confuse Lucy, and she doesn't answer. Instead she tells Jocelyn the contents of her dream—hiding in the green leaves of a dark bush, a riot of children surrounding her. There's a boy and his friend, both with long, dirty fingernails. She has a ball in her hand, and as if the boys have planned it together, they set upon her and take it away.

Jocelyn tries to assure her. She reads to her, wanting to change her daughter's focus. She dozes without meaning to and is wakened by Lucy's intense, "Mama! You're not sleeping are you?"

"No," she says. "You're all right, sweetheart. I'm here."

When her daughter finally finds sleep again, Jocelyn goes to her own bed, but she's slept just enough on the couch in Lucy's room to make it hard to sleep in her own room. She tosses and turns and tries to think of good things. She tries to press away the pictures that come to her in her own dark night. Not even Conrad, lying next to her, can protect her from the memories that come. She tells herself, *I am good. I am good. I am good*, at least fifty times before her eyes fly open, and she's in a kind of state, remembering what it is to be helpless, to need Ycidra, to want to escape from the things in the bunk above her.

It was like this: A head covered with a pillow. A prayer not to hear. Counting. What channel now? What instead of right now? Please. No. And then another kind of please, not from that moment. One she can understand only now, because she is an adult.

The ceiling in her room is gray. She will turn on the light, try to sleep with it on. Conrad doesn't wake for anything. She should have the men come, paint the ceiling white. White is soothing. If she sleeps at all, she will wake in the morning and wonder why the light is on for a half a second. She will have forgotten her fear, but then the light will remind her, and then the pictures will be back and she will wonder if it will ever end, or if it will always be a life of deferring, a life lived outside now, energy exerted in the pushing away. Lucy is bleary-eyed in the morning and Jocelyn thinks, *We are twins.* Afraid of the dark. Still children. *It is okay*, she says to herself as much as to her child when she comes into her room and they hug a good morning. *My little lamb and I.*

CHAPTER TWENTY-FOUR

CLAUDETTE

1

SHE PICKS ART BAR, A MODERN RESTAURANT WITH AN OUTDOOR PATIO and a view of the Charles River. It is appropriate for their first meeting. They shake hands as if they are colleagues at a convention. She knows that she does not look overly large even at this late stage of pregnancy. He looks at her belly immediately, but does not say anything. They sit. They are together for minutes, but neither of them speaks. Even though she is not looking at him, she can feel him staring at her, holding himself still, studying her. It is unlike anything she has experienced before. His eyes dig into her, excavating, trying to unearth something.

"I would like to call you Simon," she says, quietly.

"Of course," he says.

The waiter comes. They order.

"You look just like your mother," he says. "It is strange for me. I always thought you would look like me, but you don't. It is as if you are her ghost come to dinner. When I last saw her, she was about your age."

"Really?" she says, but it means nothing to her. She cannot

remember her mother, would not know her if she walked up to her in the street.

The lobster rolls come, the heavy white bread buns. She must focus on getting the food down, keeping it down, so she eats very slowly. In the end, she gives up on the bread and rinses each piece of buttery lobster in her water glass before ingesting it. Simon notices. She thinks he will say something, but he doesn't. They are as distant as strangers. Besides, she doesn't care what he thinks.

They eat in silence. Her birthmark a touchstone between bites. She sees him look at it, finding it on her collarbone. Evidence, she supposes. She glances at him. She has questions, but is unsure of what to ask, and in what order to ask them. What can she tread on? She clears her throat.

"Did my biological mother die in the war?" she asks. *"'Biological mother' sounds space age*, she thinks. *I am an alien."*

He pauses. "She did," he says.

"And my father, Abrahm?" she asks. *He is my father*, she thinks. *I will claim him in front of this imposter.* "How did you know each other?"

She leans back in the contemporary chair, testing its support. On the Charles River, kayakers skim. She can see them over Simon's shoulder. The yacht club is just in view. The beauty of Boston is on the other side of the river.

"He was my best friend," he says. "We grew up together. Like brothers were we."

She shakes his hand when they leave each other. There aren't any more questions to be asked tonight. They will get to know each other slowly. It is an unsaid agreement. They are both wary of one another, not knowing what to expect. Why this is the case for him, she doesn't understand. There can be no doubt now that she is his own blood. The Q-tip does not lie. Science *is*. There is no ambiguity.

She walks along the river by herself. The weather beacon is a steady red. Storms ahead, she thinks, and her father is there with her even though it isn't possible, and they are looking at the old John Hancock building, which will always be the old John Hancock building to her and to him, no matter what the citizens of Boston call it now.

Every summer, they vacationed in Boston or Cambridge. They rented a room in a better hotel. Her father called it cultural. Every night of vacation, for as long as she can remember, the two of them would look out the window, in search of the light pattern. Her mother was always asleep already, always gone from their world.

"What is it, Claudette?" her father would ask, and she'd tell him the colors. Together as if they were the same person, in stereo, they'd say the rhyme: "Steady blue, clear view. Flashing blue, clouds due. Steady red, storms ahead. Flashing red, snow instead."

He teaches her so many things in her lifetime. When to plant, when to sow. Mathematics. Literature. He is self-taught, learning most of what he knows at the local libraries. Her acceptance at Harvard hadn't moved her mother at all, but her father came each weekend to walk the square with her. They went for coffee, the Museum of Science. She has a picture of herself, at twenty-two, in front of a moose diorama. He posed her so the two antlers came out of her own head. He is there with her at the river now. The cormorants duck and dive and disappear. How could he not be her father? So much of her *is* him.

"A farmer's daughter at Harvard," he says in the weeks after she gets her acceptance letter. He is more perplexed than proud. As if the moon on a morning, instead of the sun, has decided to shine.

CHAPTER TWENTY-FIVE

JOCELYN

1

THE GIRLS ON THE TEAM ARE PLANNING FOR PALM DESERT. SHE HAS visions of Merv Griffin and Frank Sinatra, acres of green in the middle of the desert. Hotels are booked. Babysitters reserved. Nannies shared and discussed for the tennis hours. Maud tells her she is buying matching outfits for them.

"Stella McCartney," Maud says. "Are you a size six?"

Jocelyn has reservations about going. She has never left her daughter before.

"All of it will be fine, babe," Conrad says, hoping to soothe her. "Lucy loves being with me. It's really just one, well, two days. Then we'll come up. Then we'll be together."

She and Conrad have sex the night before she leaves. She is distracted, unable to come. She senses that something terrible will happen while she's away. She shouldn't go. She shouldn't leave her child. It is what she promised herself when she was finally able to get pregnant, that she would be the best mother in the world. She would not leave her child when her child needed her. Only mothers can protect their children from the villains that are hard to see. She is aware that she is breaking that promise.

"It's all going to be okay," Conrad says. "You have to let go of us sometimes."

THE PLAN SHE MAKES WITH KATE HAS HER ARRIVING THE NIGHT BEFORE, rather than the day of. Conrad assumes all the women will arrive on Thursday for the Friday retreat, and it is true that some of the other women will come early. They will want to be rested for endless days of tennis. They will want some alone time if their families are coming later. They will book a facial or a massage, get a good night's rest, for the fun they've planned, but Jocelyn is coming only to spend the night with Kate.

> **KATE**: Were you able to work out 3 nights in Palm Desert?

She is in her bathroom, filling up her toiletries bag.

> **JOCELYN**: Yes.
> **KATE**: I'll be there at 4 after I teach. I can't wait. Delete, delete, delete.

As if Jocelyn would ever forget to delete her messages.

She drives up the 10 freeway in her fast car, and into the dry city of Palm Desert. She calculates a fourish arrival, not wanting to be at the resort early or alone. In the last half hour of the drive, she finally lets herself relax. *What's done is done*, she thinks. *No turning back now*, and there is a jolt of excitement and letting go. She listens to music, loud and blaring, a bit of rap, some old-school James Brown. She even dances a bit in her seat. Maybe she will go dancing. Probably not with Kate, but maybe with Maud. Maud seems as if she might be a white girl who can dance. Jocelyn hasn't gone dancing since her twenties.

When she gets there, it is as she's expected. A series of streets named after singers, an oasis of lush and green in spite of the

California drought. It is perfect for rich ladies, she thinks. An affirmation of what for them is a truth: almost anything can be made more tolerable, more beautiful, with money.

Lucy flashes in Jocelyn's mind, but she forces herself to have rational thoughts. *She is with her father,* she tells herself. *You have already gone. Her father loves her. He will not let anything happen to her.*

As she parks her car, she is aware of the line that she is crossing: spending the night, sharing a bed. *These are the things I do with my husband,* she thinks. The thought of it makes her afraid. She tries to repress the fear, but before she can stop herself, she thinks, *These are the things I do with someone I love.*

THERE IS THE BRIGHT LIGHT OF THE SUN AS SHE STEPS OUT OF HER CAR with her tennis bag, her small Longchamp travel bag. Her luggage is whisked away. The doorman opens the door of the hotel lobby for her. The lobby is dark after the blinking-bright light of the desert sun. It is like walking into a cave—cool and air conditioned. She takes a few minutes to allow her eyes to adjust. She walks forward, pushing through, not allowing herself to lose her nerve. There is a line at the check-in desk, and even as her eyes adjust, she sees her. The hair is down, unbraided, thick and bright—transparent as the sun's rays. There is the lushness of the hips, the thick thighs. Jocelyn starts to walk toward her to touch her, to surprise her with hello, but then there is a hand in her line of vision, a hand and a finger where hers should be, and they begin to wrap and twirl the hair, and Jocelyn has the feeling of being submerged in a viscous liquid, and of not being able to breathe, and of not being able to see or understand. She stops walking.

She follows the twirling fingers, the arm, the torso, the shoulder, the neck, to a face, and her eyes find a woman. The wife, she thinks. Who else could it be? And Jocelyn watches them for a minute. What do they look like unawares? There is playfulness. There is happiness, and for Jocelyn there is just shock and confusion and shame.

CHAPTER TWENTY-SIX

SIMON

1

THE DOG IS THERE WHEN HE RETURNS FROM CAMBRIDGE. SIMON sits cross-legged beside the bush, not hiding anymore. He has named the dog, Lion. He watches the dog eat. The dog allows it now. If Simon stands, Lion growls. Simon tells the dog about his daughter. He says, "I have found my daughter. I am afraid. You have lost your master. You are afraid."

Beneath the dirt and the muck and the grease of its life in the streets, Simon can see that Lion must have been a golden brown at one time. There are dingy white spots around its muzzle, and a puddle-shaped white patch on its chest. When the dog drinks water there is the pink of its lolling tongue. The dog eats and Simon watches. It does not fill out, not even a bit. A parasite, maybe. He remembers his brother's diaper when he was just a child. A night's sleep, the heavy warmth of it. He remembers opening it and finding a tapeworm as long as his forearm inside.

"That is how it was when I was a child," he says to Lion. "I had many brothers and two sisters. I had a best friend . . ." He cannot finish.

At three o'clock, he stands up, dusts the dirt off his tailored pants. He admonishes himself for staying so long. He hears the crack of his knees.

"Goodbye, Lion. I have to go, so I can beat traffic," he says, and the dog looks at him. It doesn't take a single step toward him. It just stares and growls.

"You are welcome," Simon says, as if the dog has thanked him. As if the dog were his friend.

CHAPTER TWENTY-SEVEN

JOCELYN

1

SHE CANNOT FIGURE OUT THE TRICK OF IT. WHY WOULD KATE BE THIS mean? Why hasn't she called her, warned her? Has she checked her phone? Not in some time.

Kate pushes the hand away, signs something the desk clerk is giving her. A boy stands between the two women. He is maybe three or four. Jocelyn watches, but hopes not to be seen: there is the couple, there is the child. She studies the boy, who is handsome, more like the wife than like Kate. Dark, with eyes like chocolate and tiny white teeth. He holds on to the edge of Kate's tennis skirt as she checks in. He leans into her as a tired lover would. *I am in love with her,* she wants to say in his ear, but that isn't exactly right. *I can't stay away from her.* That is more exact, but still not fully true.

The wife is maybe thirty. Thirty at most. Looking at her makes Jocelyn feel ancient. She has the complexion of youth. Everything about her body is slim, maybe too skinny. She has the body of an Italian model who smokes rather than eats. Did the boy come out of *her* body? It makes Jocelyn wonder what Kate has possibly desired in a body like hers. Not bad for forty-five, but forty-five nonetheless. The wife's hair is long and chestnut brown, almost down to her ass. She has so much of it that Jocelyn wonders if it is real, but then thinks, *Of course it's real.* She wants to put her fingers in it and pull.

In a moment of splintering shame, she sees that Kate has seen her. Her own head snaps down, but the wife sees recognition between them.

"Hi," Kate says. It's uncomfortable.

"Hi," Jocelyn says. A pause then.

"I'm Leilah," the wife says, putting her hand out. "Are you here for the weekend retreat?"

Jocelyn feels herself blinking, but knows she needs to say something. She looks over at Kate, who has turned away. She is getting the key cards to the room now. Her son is in her arms. She has picked him up and he is settled. Kate keeps her eyes trained on the desk person. It seems as if time is passing very slowly. What does she expect? They are two people who barely know one another, after all. That is the agreement. She tells herself to get it together. The boy is gripping Kate's hair in his fingers. Jocelyn has the irrational thought that it is *her* hair. That the light, bright gold of it should not be shared.

"Yes," Jocelyn says. "I'm here for the weekend. It should be fun."

Leilah smiles. She has a little chip in her front tooth, so slight that it is sexy.

"It's great to meet you," Leilah says. She leans closer to Jocelyn when she says it, a hostess now to a lovely weekend, and there, just at the edge, under an Altoid or a stick of Doublemint gum, Jocelyn smells it. It is Gladys all over again. Deep in the breath, alive there, is the smell—light and sure—of alcohol. Jocelyn wonders if she and Kate have celebrated before leaving, if they've had bloody marys together for lunch.

"See you later," Kate says. Her voice is brittle as ice. "Great to have you here for the weekend."

Jocelyn watches them leave—the lovely family. Business,

Jocelyn reminds herself. She lifts this idea out of herself from some point in her history, from that other girl whom she has always been able to count on when she has needed to go away. The solid one. She exhales. She steps aside, letting that girl in. That girl will keep her steady. That girl will make it so she does not cry. That girl is always just under the surface, on the lower bunk with her. She is a more capable self.

It's business, the girl reminds her. *You had an agreement. Things come up. You can't take it personally.*

"Bye," she says, but Kate and her family have already walked away. She turns to the lady behind the desk. *Bye? Why did I say bye?*

"May I have your name, please?" the woman asks.

"Yes. Thank you. Mrs. Morrow. I'm here for three nights."

SHE SITS IN HER ROOM, TRYING TO FIND DISTANCE. NAIL UP WALLS. SHE hangs her clothes. She makes folded piles of the others and puts them in drawers. She checks her phone, but there's nothing. *Fuck her*, she thinks. *I hate her. What was I thinking? Why? I have such a good life. I have Conrad. I have Lucy. Am I insane? I have left my child for this? Not even the decency to text.*

She tries to read a local magazine, but can't. She calls Conrad, but he doesn't pick up. She is angry. Irate. She feels dirty from the long drive. She looks at the room service menu, but there is nothing. She resents the expense of bad hotel food but doesn't know if she can get herself out of the room. She should drive home, she thinks. She should get in her car. She begins taking off her clothes, just trying to separate herself from everything. She decides to take a shower. She can try to get clean. The girl inside her exerts herself more strongly, tells her a shower is good, a new Jocelyn. Draw a line from here forward and emerge. As with all the lines before, she takes this step.

The water from the shower runs hot and prickly. The soap is mint. The girl inside her is armor to pull on. She is the girl who gets her through beatings, through baths she does not want to take, line after line of cocaine, through her sister dead, the smell of bile in the air. They haven't seen each other in a while, but she will always be there, familiar. Jocelyn is an old house, with new paint, but the same house nevertheless. The water warms her. She allows herself to have other ideas. Ideas that will banish the mortification she feels after the lobby.

I will make myself beautiful, she thinks. *I will dress myself in money.* She thinks of heels. *I will find another girl to fuck tonight.* There are plenty. A sea of them, right?

Buy one, she thinks. A beautiful one to walk around with. To demean later. Earlier, at a gas station when Jocelyn was getting gas, there was a girl with a man by the bathrooms. Shorts so short that it hurt Jocelyn to look at her—all friction and rub, an almost burlap-looking fabric and fierce pink blotches on her translucent thighs. She was thirty years younger than he was, if a day—seventeen maybe. Pure white women are ugly, she decides. Something in the woodpile, Uncle Al used to say when he looked at the three of him. Then he'd laugh.

She turns off the shower. She steps out. Steam is everywhere except the mirror. She wonders if this is some new technology. A mirror that doesn't steam. She looks at herself closely. She sees the swell in her cheeks and the red around her eyes. The fine lines. The jowls that are just starting to seep. *I will not cry over her. I will not make myself ugly for her.* Such a job to stay beautiful. Toner, moisturizer, sunscreen, aging, antiaging, Retin-A, Retinol, Botox, Restylane, Thermage, highlights, lowlights, makeup. Leilah *is* as beautiful as she is. It is not outside her, bought and paid for. In youth, it is there. It is free.

She stops thinking of Leilah. What can she do? She will get dressed, she will eat dinner. She lifts her phone, scrolls through. There are always acquaintances—a perk of marrying into a good family. She searches. She stops at one finally: a friend in Palm Desert, a relationship made close in LA years and years ago, because neither of them could have babies naturally. A simple thing. *Any dog can do it,* her mother would say, but not Jocelyn. Not Jen. Money, medicine, period blood shot across a white room, gloved hands inside them, injections, scrapings, bruises along their bellies and behinds—Conrad weak and fainting, pressing the plunger in, breaking the needle tip beneath her skin. She and Jen share these violations one day at a charity luncheon, and in fifteen minutes they are like best friends.

She dials and Jen picks up. There is surprise on the other end of the phone. Delight. *You're here? I haven't seen you in ages,* the voice says. *Well, it's a spur-of-the-moment trip*, the girl inside her says brightly, in Jocelyn's happy voice. She can hear herself saying, *Dinner? Of course*. Conversation. Pretense. *Goodbye*.

"I do not need that bitch," she says aloud this time, after hanging up the phone. Like a whisper that only she can hear: *I am always with you*, the girl inside her says. *You'll be fine*. A comb in her hand to bring back beauty. Lace panties, heels. Just put it on. Become something else. If you put it on. Breathe.

THEY MEET AT CIAO BELLA—AN ANCIENT ITALIAN RESTAURANT THAT can exist only in Palm Desert. It is tacky and boothed. She allows herself the slim, impossibly high snakeskin heels that have cost a thousand dollars, a leather skirt, a silk cream blouse. All meant for Kate, but why waste it (the other girl says). She feels sexy, which is somehow easier now that she is older. That single thing.

"You look beautiful," Jen says, and kisses her on both cheeks. Jocelyn says thank you, but what she looks is expensive.

"Let's do appetizers and drinks," Jen says.

"Let's."

It takes a few rounds of drinks before Jocelyn can really settle in, really enjoy herself, really let go of what Kate is doing right now. Is she with her wife? Are they having sex? She is glad she has decided to get away. She is happy to see Jen. They gossip, catch up. She does not tell her about Kate. She lets Kate go.

At the end of the dinner, Jocelyn feels certain that she can get through the weekend. She can enjoy it. She has redirected herself. It will be about tennis. She is not putting up with it. *I will be good*, she promises herself. *I will place myself back inside my family.*

Jocelyn pays the bill for both of them, and then they head to the valet. Jocelyn calls the hotel from her cell phone, summons a car.

"Please, let me take you," Jen says.

"No way," Jocelyn says. "I like to be picked up. It feels fancy." She smiles. "Conrad's paying for it anyway."

Jen smiles back. It is a joke that wealthy women make all the time. Something they can come together on—the ways they spend their husbands' money.

While they wait for Jocelyn's driver, the sky goes dark, the air picks up, and Jocelyn is reminded of summer tornado weather in

Ohio, basements, trees lifted like weeds out of the ground. To her delight, it starts to rain. A sudden, intense, desert rainstorm. The first drops steam up when they hit the pavement. Jen puts her arm outside the awning. Drops bead and multiply on her clear skin and hands.

They watch the rain, mesmerized by it, until the valet brings Jen's car. They hug, kiss cheeks, make promises to not let the time pass.

The hotel car service pulls up less than four minutes later. It is a huge GMC. Ten people could fit inside. The driver has an umbrella for her. The scalpel of memory opens her, the flash of Ycidra, all three of them racing around in a pelting rainstorm. No raincoats. No umbrellas. Just Hefty bags—another one of her sister's make-dos.

The driver opens the door for her. She settles into the back seat, watching the droplets hit the windshield. She wishes for lightning, and then for thunder to follow. *Sound is slower than light*, her sister taught her. *One Mississippi, two Mississippi*. Ycidra dividing. *The storm is five miles away.* But why was this important? What did it do for them to know when the storm would arrive?

She is tipsy from the drinks at dinner. The memories are all neutral, tinged with an aquatic feel. She calls Conrad. They speak for less than five minutes. She feels deeply in love with him. Deeply grateful that she hasn't been caught in her affair with Kate.

He hands the phone to their daughter. "When are you coming home, Mama?" Lucy says. "Me and Papa are having fun, but when are you coming home?"

"You're coming to see me," Jocelyn says, and finds that she is really joyful about it. She misses her child, wishes to be back home. "I can't wait until you get here."

Conrad's voice is abruptly back on the line. "That's it," he says firmly. "Go have fun. I know if I let you two talk for much longer, you'll be back here before morning."

He is teasing her, and she likes it.

"How's the tennis?" he asks.

"No tennis yet," she says. Better to not lie. They say their I-love-yous and hang up. She leans back into the large bench seat of the GMC. It is nice inside the car, the leather luxury. She thinks she might schedule a facial for the morning. She will form a new idea about what is ahead of her for this weekend. She will make a tiny circle, place her family inside, place herself inside with them, seal it. She will let go of Kate. Her phone buzzes and she knows it is Conrad. Surely he has forgotten some bedtime ritual—which sweet is allowed, which story needs reading. The alcohol makes her feel in tune with everything—telepathic even. She looks at her phone, but it isn't Conrad. It is a text.

KATE: Where are you?

She feels instantly angry. She doesn't want to respond. Doesn't want to talk. Wants to tell the driver to stop the car. She should find another hotel.

JOCELYN: I'm out. Out to dinner.
KATE: When will you be back?

The car is almost to the hotel. Maybe she can get inside, sneak in. The confidence she felt just minutes before is waning. *Don't text back*, she tells herself, but then she's already started it.

JOCELYN: I don't know.

The driver pulls into the hotel parking lot.

Jocelyn looks up. The fierce rain has died down to a drizzle. The lobby is ten paces away, and though her visibility is lessened by the rain, she can clearly see the outline of Kate's blonde hair. The hair, the hair the hair. It is stark, almost white in the gray weather. It is down, wavy in the humidity. Kate is standing under the overhang texting her. Jocelyn's body stirs.

The driver slows, then stops. She hears the car go off. Her

door is opened. The umbrella is there again. She slides out of the back seat. Her skirt lifts above her thighs, raindrops touch her skin. She rifles around for a tip, gives the driver a twenty, and before he has a chance to walk her inside, Kate is on her.

"Where have you been?" she asks.

"Dinner. I told you. Thank you," she says, excusing the driver.

"Can we talk?" Kate asks.

"I don't really want to," Jocelyn says. "Thanks though."

She begins walking away, happy with her snarky tone. Kate keeps pace beside her.

"Just a minute, okay? I want to explain. Let's go to your room?"

"Explain about what?" Jocelyn asks. *Room, room, room*, she thinks, even though she doesn't want to think it. *The things that will happen in my room.*

"A minute?" Kate asks again, almost whining. "Please. You've got to have a minute for me."

Jocelyn would like to punch her.

"Where's your wife?" Jocelyn asks. "Why are you here bothering me? Where does she think you are?"

"I thought we weren't doing that," Kate says.

"Why didn't you tell me?"

"She surprised me. I didn't think she was coming up until Friday," Kate says. "Let's talk in your room."

"Whatever," Jocelyn says. "You could have texted me."

"I couldn't have. Please."

Jocelyn feels herself giving in. "Hurry up, please. I don't want anyone to see us together. Especially not *your* someone."

"Don't be smug," Kate says.

"I would have brought my husband if I'd known," Jocelyn says.

"I said, don't be smug."

"You're an asshole. You could have texted me," she says again.

"I could not have texted you. She was waiting in the car for me when I got home from work. She took the day off to come. The whole car was packed up. My son was in his car seat. She thought she was doing something nice, something for the family."

Jocelyn can't look at her. She stares at the ugly hotel carpet, which, she thinks, is always ugly no matter how expensive the hotel.

"Nice shoes," Kate says.

"Fuck off."

"Nice shoes," Kate says again.

"God you're annoying," Jocelyn says.

They reach the room, and Jocelyn puts the key card in. The door doesn't open. She tries again, sliding it in and out. Nothing. She looks up and down the hallway, worried that someone might come. She tries again, slowly this time, but the red light just blinks. She feels herself starting to panic.

"Let me try," Kate says. She puts the card in the slot, and she is in the room in a flash.

"You're clearly experienced at hotel room doors," Jocelyn says and smirks.

"Only with you," Kate says. A light smile is on her face.

Jocelyn refuses to laugh, but it's harder now. The room is dark, quiet. It is almost peaceful. She walks in, behind Kate, pushes the door shut, and leans against it, just breathing. *What are we doing? Why is she here? Tell her to go.*

"What do you want from me?" Jocelyn asks. "I don't want to waste time with you."

Kate steps closer to her, reaches out to touch her, but Jocelyn flicks her hand away.

Kate grins. "I want to know where you were. I want to know who you were with."

"No way," Jocelyn says. "It's none of your business. We're just fucking, remember? I mean when your wife isn't here anyway."

"Where were you?" Kate asks again.

Jocelyn glowers. Her lover's face is an inch away from her own. She can feel warm breath. It is almost in her mouth. Kate wraps her fingers around her wrists. Jocelyn wonders irrationally if she will be safe in the room. If she can get out of the room before anything happens.

"I want you to go," Jocelyn says.

"I'm not going," Kate says. "I'm definitely not going. I understand that you're mad at me. It's kind of cute."

"You're an ass."

"You're mad, Jocelyn. That's all. It's okay."

"I want you to go," Jocelyn says again, but isn't quite so sure.

Kate leans in, presses her mouth against Jocelyn's, and then pulls away a bit. "We had an agreement," she says. Each syllable is slow. "We're fucking. *I* want to fuck. You agreed."

Jocelyn starts to protest, but Kate's body is a wall. She doesn't like the change of roles. She doesn't like when she isn't in charge, but she feels pulled, dragged in like a kite in a fierce wind. She feels a flicker, a switch turning on, even though she doesn't want it to happen.

"I—"

"Don't speak, okay?" Kate says, kissing her again. Her tongue is light, almost licking. "Just take your panties off for me."

Jocelyn opens her mouth. She feels her breath heave up and then down. She feels Kate's tongue, likes it. She wants to be angry, wants to deny her, but also wants to keep going.

"No," she says.

"Don't say no," Kate says. "Just do what I say. No guilt, remember. No responsibility. Just sex."

After each sentence she kisses Jocelyn, softly, lightly. She lifts the leather skirt, bunching it inch by inch up either side of Jocelyn's hips. She traces the outline of her behind, moving her thumbs in toward her inner thighs, but just barely, making Jocelyn long for her.

Once more, she thinks. *I will do this once more and not again.*

She feels the pull of her panties being moved aside. She tries to call up the image of Kate's boy, Kate's wife, but it doesn't work. She tries to think of Conrad and Lucy, but it's no use. Her own fingers come to life and she starts to undo the leather skirt. The buttons are difficult. Her fingers are not adept. She tugs. There are too many. She feels Kate's hands now inside her shirt, warm on her waist. Talking and kissing her neck.

"Not your skirt," Kate says, pushing her up against the door, lifting Jocelyn up on her tiptoes, so her hips are leaning into her. "Just the panties." A finger runs gently, almost tickling her along her back. "Do you need help?"

"No," Jocelyn says, pulling the underwear down, letting it fall free. She feels it pass over her thighs and then her rain-wetted calves. Her cheeks are warm. She can sense Kate's intensity growing. She is kissing her harder.

"Open your mouth for me," Kate says, and Jocelyn does as she is told. She feels the soft edge of Kate's lips. Her tongue tipping inside of her mouth. They are the same height now, with her heels on. Jocelyn kisses back, and Kate pulls away.

"Just open your mouth," she says. "I'll tell you what to do."

She starts to unbutton Jocelyn's shirt. She leaves the skirt where it is. Jocelyn lets go. *I'm here. I'm in.*

"Keep your shoes on," Kate says, at Jocelyn's ear now. "The whole time."

Her silk shirt falls open. The cool hotel air-conditioning chills Jocelyn's skin. Kate lets the shirt slide off Jocelyn's body. Goose bumps prick her.

"Who did you have dinner with?" Kate asks again, insistent. "These pretty panties and bra aren't for just anyone." She moves the bra, pushing the cups down, lifting the swell of her breasts out of it. Her nipples are hard, elongated. Kate is sucking on Jocelyn's nipples between questions, lightly and then more intensely. "A girl? A boy?"

"A friend," Jocelyn says. She feels impatient, awash with lust. She wants to push Kate's head down. She wants to sit on top of her. She likes and doesn't like the power Kate has over her at the moment. Kate is sucking and kissing, but keeping Jocelyn's hips and body anchored against the door. Jocelyn feels like begging, but won't. Might. Isn't sure.

"Let's get on the bed," Jocelyn says.

Kate lifts up her skirt, pulling it roughly. "Don't speak," she says. "Unless I ask you a question."

Jocelyn feels a hand between her legs. She sucks in breath. It's just there, just barely, skimming. Kate is watching her face. "Is your friend pretty?"

Jocelyn looks away. The finger is there, a constant, circling. The small flame inside her ignites, expands, breathes.

"Please," she hears herself saying.

"Look at me, Jocelyn. Is she pretty?"

Jocelyn looks. Kate pushes the finger an inch inside her, and then out, each time a little more. Jocelyn hears her own voice, moaning. It is almost like fucking, but very, very slowly, outside and then in, and then back on the tip of her clitoris.

"I want you to answer me."

The word *tonight* sticks in Jocelyn's brain. She feels disoriented.

"Yes," Jocelyn says. "Yes. She's pretty." And it is as if her friend is there too. Jocelyn feels herself unspooling, pressing herself now against Kate's finger. She is balanced on her high heels, up and down. The tempo picks up. Kate is licking the tips of her nipples, moving from one to the other. The cool air of the room is like a breeze on her body, exaggerating the tingling in her nipples. All of it connected like a string being plucked gently, activating everything at once.

"Whatever I want, right?"

"Right," Jocelyn says. "Yes."

"You understand, right? You'll do whatever I want?"

"Yes, yes," Jocelyn says. She pulls Kate's head away from her breasts and pushes her mouth into her own. They kiss deeply. Jocelyn is so close to coming—moving, and pressing. Kate pulls away. She holds Jocelyn with one hand against the door, watches her, pressing and teasing with the other finger the whole time.

"Please," Jocelyn says. "I'm going to come."

Without warning, Kate pulls her finger out.

"No," Jocelyn says. "Don't stop. Don't stop." She is kissing Kate, pulling, begging. She feels as if she'll die. "Please."

"Sit down," Kate says. "Right here. Sit down."

Jocelyn feels faint. She sits down on her haunches, waiting, running her hands up and down Kate's legs.

Kate undoes her own pants and steps out of her own panties. She stands just in front of Jocelyn.

"Up on your knees," Kate says. "You have to wait a bit. I like to make you wait."

Jocelyn sits up, leaving her legs apart, not wanting the contact.

"Put your legs together," Kate says. "No, wait, a pillow for you. Two pillows."

She leaves Jocelyn kneeling and weak. She retrieves two pillows from the hotel bed. She makes a neat pile of them. "Get on top of these. Spread your legs. Don't come. Not until I say. Not until I let you. Do you understand?"

Jocelyn can't think how that will be possible. She may come at the words. She sits gingerly, barely pressing, settling into the soft cushions as if into a cloud.

"You're such a good girl," Kate says, and rearranges the pillows slightly. Jocelyn feels both of Kate's hands on her shoulders pressing. "I want you to come later. Be a good girl."

Jocelyn is warmer and wetter than she's ever been before. "Oh God," Jocelyn hears herself saying.

She lifts herself up a bit from the pressure of the pillows, trying to put the orgasm off. She cannot be in contact with anything. She leans her face into Kate, holds on to her behind. The taste of her is sticky and salty and animal.

"What are you going to do for me?" Kate asks, but Jocelyn knows she knows.

"Anything," Jocelyn says, licking, beginning. "Anything at all."

KATE HOLDS ON TO JOCELYN'S HEAD AND JOCELYN FEELS EVERY PULSE OF her body as it creates pace. She keeps her mouth there, her face steady. Kate pulls her into her, moves faster and faster against her, holding, pulling hair, shrieking. Jocelyn gently sucks, even slows the pace. She likes that she is in charge again. She tries to make it better, longer lasting. She is slick with the wetness of Kate. Not minding at all. When she finally finishes, Kate collapses onto her knees in front of her, kisses her, laughs. She looks at Jocelyn.

"You didn't come, did you?" she says playfully.

"No. I'm being good."

Kate smiles at that, takes Jocelyn by the hand, lifts her up from her knees. Jocelyn is unsteady. She grips the hand tightly and follows. The ache between her legs is intense. She has to walk without letting her legs touch. She has to work to keep from coming.

"Let's get you washed up then," Kate says, and Jocelyn wonders at the possibilities of water and warm hands. So much to look forward to.

Kate says it casually as if Jocelyn is a dirty child, something easy to be dealt with. Jocelyn allows herself to be led. She is sticky faced and sticky fingered, in need of a washing, she supposes. She loves all of what they do. All of what they've done. The smell of Kate, the tackiness of her hands and lips. She feels wild and weak. Full, as if something warm has been poured inside her.

"Sit right here," Kate says, and Jocelyn sits on the edge of the ceramic bathtub. Her entire body reacts to the cold temperature. An incredible shiver moves through her.

"Straddle that please," Kate says, smirky and polite.

"Look, really," Jocelyn says. "I can't take it anymore. I'm definitely going to come." A shiver moves through her.

Kate smiles, pinches each nipple gently. "You'll be fine, sweet-heart. You'll come when I tell you to come. Straddle."

Jocelyn turns her body—one leg inside the tub, the other on the outside. She reaches out, grabs Kate's arm. "Please."

Kate kisses her. "Just a few minutes more," she says. She turns the faucet on. She flicks her fingers under, takes her wet hand and rubs it on Jocelyn's breasts, down her back, along the ridge of her rear.

"How does this feel?" she asks.

"Good," Jocelyn says. "Good."

Kate reaches up, pulls down a handheld nozzle. Jocelyn thinks if she looks at it, she will break apart.

"How does this feel?" Kate asks, letting the water run up and down the leg that is inside the tub.

"I want you to rub against the bathtub wall," Kate says, filling up the tub. "I want you to move back and forth until I tell you to stop. Put your hand in the water when I tell you." Kate leans in to kiss her, to hold her steady, and Jocelyn rocks. She is so close. About to.

"Shhh, shhh, shhh," Kate says, plucking at her nipples. "Stop moving. Stop." But Jocelyn can't really hear, can't really stop, and when she keeps going, Kate says, "If you don't stop when I tell you to, I'll stop everything. I'll make you beg."

"Oh, Christ," Jocelyn says. She stops rocking, stands up, legs still apart. "I can't. I'm telling you." She presses her swollen mouth against Kate's.

"Sit in now. Sit in the tub." Kate tells her.

And there is the warm pool of water and she tries not to think about it. She holds the edges of the tub as she sets her body down, not wanting to make a ripple. She holds on to Kate—her arm, her hand, and lays back.

"Spread your legs," Kate says, and Jocelyn does.

"Okay." And it all is building inside her. "You can come now," Kate says, and then there is the gentle flow of just warm water, and then a bit more spray and the temperature and the pressure of the water and the nozzle between her legs, and she can't wait anymore, and she reaches up for Kate's head for her tongue, for her mouth, and Kate brings the nozzle closer and closer and the pressure of the water is firmer and harder, and that finally makes Jocelyn scream, and come, and move wildly and reach out for the hand that has the nozzle so she can take charge of it, and Kate says, "Say thank you, now. Say thank you to me." And Jocelyn can hear her own voice outside herself saying, "Thank you, thank you," and then Kate is kissing her, and is letting go of the nozzle, and it is the flat palm of her hand between Jocelyn's legs, and she is holding her tightly now, where the spray of water used to be, and she is pressing and managing her, until finally there is the clench, the twitch, the pulse, and the thrill, and then it's over.

AFTERWARD, KATE WASHES HER GENTLY WITH SOAP AND WATER, BEING careful with the space between her legs. She tells her to wait a minute, to relax, and she brings whiskey from the minibar. One for each of them.

"Let's get drunk," she says. They clink glasses and throw back the drinks.

"Did you do that when you were a kid?" Kate asks. She sets down her empty glass and touches the washcloth to Jocelyn's body.

"Which thing?"

"Come, in the bathtub."

"I did," Jocelyn says, and they both laugh, remembering water, and faucets, and warmth.

Kate adds warm water and attends to every part of her. She washes and conditions Jocelyn's hair. When she finishes, she helps Jocelyn out of the tub. She dries her with the thick hotel towel, everywhere, even the soles of her feet. When she needs to, she turns her. She pauses, she speaks when she comes to the scars on the back of Jocelyn's body.

"Are you ever going to tell me what these are?"

Jocelyn does not want to answer. She sits heavily down on the closed toilet seat. She waits, watches. Kate's eyes stay on Jocelyn's body. She spills lotion into her hands. She rubs it into each section of skin, up and down each arm and leg. She files Jocelyn's newly brushed nails. She massages each of the fingers. There is nothing erotic here, just care, and Jocelyn finds that the tenderness is both wonderful and frightening.

Finally, she answers. "My mother had a boyfriend. He used to beat us. My mother used to tell him to do it. With everything. Extension cords, belts. He had a dog leash. We didn't have a dog then. Not until later."

She tries to make this last one a joke, but it doesn't work. She sees the dogs. She sees herself hitting. She squeezes her eyes shut.

"I'm sorry," Kate says.

It is like an egg cracking. The wet and slime of the past, wanting to scoop it up, but unable to put it back.

"I don't want to talk about it. I don't want to do that, really. Please."

They move to the hotel bed. Jocelyn is naked, but Kate has put the plush hotel robe on. The room is cold. The AC is blasting. They burrow into the covers, into each other.

"I'm sorry," Kate says again, and pulls Jocelyn closer. "I'm sorry it happened. I won't bring it up again. I just didn't know."

Jocelyn allows herself to be held and then they doze. When she wakes again, she finds herself wanting Kate again. She turns to see if she's awake. They grin at each other, knowing what to do. Kate pours each of them another whiskey. They are drinking in bed, making silly toasts to tennis. Fun and casual. People will clean up after them, change the sheets if there are spills.

"You aren't going to be able to coach tomorrow if we keep this up."

"You aren't going to be able to play," Kate says back.

"Who cares!" Jocelyn says. The alcohol is relaxing. It's a parallel universe.

"Who cares!" Kate says, affirming that she's inside it too.

On that night, they cannot get enough of each other. They cannot be satisfied. They laugh. They drink. They fuck. They sleep.

It is five fifteen when they wake. In minutes, they realize they have overslept. Not by much, but Kate wants to be back in her room by five thirty.

"Leilah'll never wake before six. She—"

"I know," Jocelyn says. "My mother was a drinker. I'm shocked that you drink."

"Not around her," Kate says, pushing back covers. "I just have to get there before Mathias wakes. She'll be grumpy."

"I get it," Jocelyn says, feeling a pang for Lucy, and surprisingly for Conrad too.

They both have headaches. Kate's hair is a mess, but Jocelyn helps her find her clothes, her underwear. She uses Jocelyn's toothbrush, even though Jocelyn protests.

"Just think of all the places my mouth has been," Kate says, brushing.

Jocelyn throws her jacket at her, her shoes. Kate spits in the sink, finishing. She retrieves the rest of her stuff, walks over to Jocelyn. They are face-to-face, and Kate gives Jocelyn a kiss on the cheek. Jocelyn feels slightly nauseated, but happy. She opens the door. Kate walks out, turns toward her, staring. It feels as if she might kiss her again, might come back inside.

"Go!" Jocelyn says. "Quick!"

Kate rushes at her, gives her a playful kiss, almost smashing into her. It's teasing and Jocelyn laughs, and just as they pull away, the exit door at the end of the hall opens, and both she and Kate blink in its direction to see who might be coming.

For the first moments, everything slows. Everything tilts. Jocelyn finds focus, but it can't be real. She looks, squints, and there, in the door, is a woman, familiar, and yet not so. She is walking quickly toward them, all Lululemon, ponytailed, and sweaty. She is all smiles when she sees them. Up early for exercise, Jocelyn thinks, aware of how delayed her brain is as she makes the connection. The woman lifts a hand to Kate, and then sees Jocelyn leaning out of her door.

"Good morning, ladies," Missy says. She looks back and forth between them. Her voice full of insinuation. The cat with the canary.

Kate waves as if nothing is going on. Jocelyn lifts a hand, processing it. Are they far enough apart? Could this be a coincidence? They are both disheveled, tired looking. Jocelyn is in pajama bottoms. They should have been more careful, she thinks. How will they explain Kate, just outside her hotel room door? No newspaper in sight. Everyone knows Kate's sexual orientation.

"Thanks for the talk," Kate says, as if she and Jocelyn have had an early morning powwow.

Jocelyn doesn't speak, but watches Missy's reaction. Missy looks at Jocelyn, waiting for her to respond, and then away. Kate walks away, disappears through the exit door that Missy's just come through, and Jocelyn feels ridiculously abandoned.

"You two are up awfully early," Missy says, looking straight through Jocelyn. "I didn't realize you two were such *good* friends."

Jocelyn doesn't say anything. She hates Missy. Of all the people. Of all the times. It is too early. They are too much of a mess. Missy isn't stupid, she thinks, feeling a strange certainty, a lid closing.

She shuts the door without speaking to Missy. She turns her back, lets herself sit on the floor, just in the spot where they fucked the night before. What will she do? she wonders. What will Missy do? What will happen if Conrad finds out?

CHAPTER TWENTY-EIGHT

CLAUDETTE

1

HE LEAVES A VOICE MAIL ON HER PHONE. AT LUNCH BETWEEN FRESHMAN Comp and Argument and Research, she listens to it in her small office. He is nervous. He speaks too quickly.

"It is me. Simon," he says. And then, "Well, it is I, Simon. I must do better with my grammar, now that I know my daughter is a professor. Well, I mean you are a professor." There is a second or two of silence, before he says without much confidence, "I was wanting to come for another visit. Maybe I could meet your husband. Maybe it could be for the birth of the child. I do not mean to be pushy."

She wants to call him back and say to him, *There is nothing to my husband.* She wants to say, *My child is not his.* She wants to say, *I have committed the same crime that has been committed against me. My baby will not know its true father.*

What would he think of her then? A woman who has had an affair, a woman with a PhD, and yet hasn't had the sense to use birth control.

She thinks texting might be better, but then changes her mind. *I will call him when I know my answer. He will not impinge on my life.*

HE SHOWS UP WITHOUT NOTICE A WEEK LATER. SOMETHING ABOUT A PRI-vate plane. A feeling about the baby. Fears that something had happened. Apologies. She does not know how he has found her here, at her parents' house in Newton. Maybe the detective is still paid to follow her. It can't be legal. She thinks briefly about calling the police.

"I am very upset," she says. "You can't just show up here. This is my life. This is a violation of privacy. This is not cool. Are you having me followed?"

He flinches back from the doorway as if she has hit him.

"You are right," he says. "I am so sorry. I don't know why. I really just had to see you. I had this thought that something might be wrong. That something happened to the baby and you. You didn't call me back. Now I will go. You are right."

He turns to walk down the steps of the porch. She sees that he is thin. He is not at all like her father. He is tall and lean and even a bit frail. Pity rises in her although she tries to resist. How often has she worried that something was wrong with the child inside her own belly? How many times has she lain awake at night? How often will she do this later on in life when she is an old woman?

"You can come in for just a moment," she says. "This is my parents' home, but I guess you know that. I am finishing up, getting it ready. It's too far from Cambridge for me and my husband. We may sell it."

"Do you want to sell it?" he asks. "Maybe you would like to wait and rent it."

"Maybe," she says, but feels as she has for some time, especially indecisive.

"I can help you," he says. "I mean, it is just me, so I can help if you ever need anything. I would love to help you."

She does not like his desperation. It scares her.

"Maybe," she says. She holds the door open for him. He walks cautiously ahead of her.

3

HE THRUSTS A LAVENDER GIFT BOX AT HER ONCE THEY ARE INSIDE. SHE locks the front door. She sees his trembling when he hands her the box.

"Thank you," she says.

"You do not have to open it now," he says, staring at the dark foyer that they enter through, the winding stairs, the millwork.

She presses the box inside her purse, wondering briefly where it has come from, what could be so small.

They make their way through the empty house, he scuttling behind her as if he were a much older man. She is happy most of her parents' things are boxed up. She does not want him rooting through their belongings, even with his eyes.

He asks her nothing, and she tells him nothing, and he waits patiently as she packs up her mother's favorite chandelier—white tissue paper, Styrofoam peanuts. Each crystal carefully wrapped. She has no idea why she has decided to take it with her. It's too ostentatious, too large for her small apartment, but she can't seem to leave the shining suns of glass behind.

Before they leave, she fumbles around in a box marked KITCHEN, draws two glasses out, and fills them with water from the tap. She places one glass in his hand and slides down the living room wall and sits on the hardwood floor. He looks at her and does the same.

There is something heavy in the house that she feels, something in need of being aired out. She glances out across the fields, takes a long sip of the water, which tastes metallic and cold. The shadow of her father's body, the great mountain of the man he was, is out there, expanding, full and busy across the vegetable garden. His head a darker shadow even than the fallow land.

Simon sips his water. She sees the fingers on the glass. They are shaped just like hers. Her long limbs, her light skin. How has she ever believed she was Abrahm's child?

"It will take me some time," she says to him.

"Yes," he says. "I have time."

INSIDE THE BOX, A TINY RING. A RING MADE FOR A LITTLE GIRL. SHE presses it onto her pinky, but it is too small. Thin as tin and lined with scratches. The number 333 is in the inside band. It is definitely real gold. She can tell by its color. A garnet, tiny and protruding like a pen nib. It is modest. Not very beautiful.

No memory of it, she thinks, *but it must have been mine.*

How strange to look at so many things that have always been mine, and yet not to recognize them.

A miniature bed of aged cotton is inside the box to keep the ring safe—yellow as pee. She lifts the box to her nose. Citrus smell, subtle and sweet. Orange.

CHAPTER TWENTY-NINE

SIMON

1

WHEN HE FLIES INTO LAX, HE DOESN'T BOTHER GOING HOME. HE GETS food and water and goes straight to see Lion. The dog is not on the shoulder of the highway. It is true that he is visiting at a different time of day, but he couldn't wait, not after such an emotional trip. He finds that he has missed the dog. He wants to sit with the dog.

He walks about the grassy berm calling, "Lion, Lion, Lion," but the animal doesn't come. Simon sits on the ground waiting. He tries to assuage his panic. He has opened up the food bag. The water is fresh. He calls again. He thinks of fast cars, of people texting. Once, he saw a village dog with its uterus out. The car that ran it down didn't even stop. Pets are a luxury. In Kigali they do not live inside. No barking after the genocide, he thinks again, as he often does. The corpses of the dogs were piled up, solid as cords of wood, like some strange taxidermy exhibit.

"Lion," he says again, but he is certain the dog is dead.

The food is there. The water is there.

"I am here," he says. "Please come," but the dog is nowhere in sight.

CHAPTER THIRTY

JOCELYN

1

CONRAD AND LUCY ARRIVE EARLY, BUT THEY ARE NOT IN THE ROOM when Jocelyn comes back for lunch. The morning has been full of tennis. Kate has managed to keep Missy in a different group. The lack of contact makes it seem as if they might get away with it. There's no evidence. Her word against theirs.

Jocelyn assumes Conrad and Lucy are swimming or eating or getting into whatever trouble the two of them get into when she is not around. *When I am not around*, she thinks. *There is no habit here. This is the first time. My daughter is fine. I will not be hard on myself.*

There are tiny shoes strewn all over the floor and toys dumped by the French doors that lead outside. Jocelyn sits on the edge of the bed looking at her daughter's things. The maid has turned down the bed, scrubbed the bathtub. There is no trace of Kate here.

She counts six tiny pairs of shoes—too many for one weekend. In the bathroom, there is a tiny pair of Hello Kitty underwear. Without being beckoned, thoughts of Conrad and Mr. Baird and men come to mind. The moments her daughter might be violated when she is out of her sight. She hates this—the full-color memories, the potential present, the half-formed future. She sits, closes her eyes, starts the tapping before the trauma takes hold.

The imprint of Jocelyn's perpetrator lives inside her. She is aware of this. The girl too. They are like conjoined triplets. If she tries to kill one of them, she will kill them all.

She opens her eyes. Her heart rate has slowed. She focuses. *This is my life*, she thinks, staring at the tiny shoes. *I can keep her safe. This is what I really want.*

But there is that other thing too. She wants it and doesn't want it. There is that other thing too.

PART IV

Always you will arrive in this city. Do not hope for any other—
There is no ship for you, there is no road.
As you have destroyed your life here
in this little corner, you have ruined it in the entire world.

—C. P. CAVAFY, "THE CITY" (TRANSLATED
FROM THE GREEK BY RAE DALVEN)

CHAPTER THIRTY-ONE

JOCELYN

1

THEY ARE BACK IN THE PALISADES FOR JUST A DAY WHEN MISSY GOES TO
the director of tennis at the Miramar Club. She speaks as if she is
concerned for some moral code within the club's rules. Coaches
and students, she says, especially when married. Jocelyn can picture it: the press of intent, the joy of the revelation, even without
proof. Missy reminds the director that Palm Desert is a charity
event with sponsors, not a brothel. How will it look for the Miramar Club? *My concern is for the children in transition*, she might say. Jocelyn has heard her say this phrase on court.

Kate is questioned. She texts Jocelyn after her meeting, giving
more brief details:

> **KATE**: If I were a man, if I were straight, can you imagine
> how many tennis ladies have been fucked by the tennis
> director?
> **JOCELYN**: I'm so sorry.
> **KATE**: I told him it wasn't true. But Missy isn't letting up.

We'll have to take a break. They threatened my job. Delete, delete, delete.

You mean stop, Jocelyn thinks. *You just don't want to say it to me.*

JOCELYN: I understand. I'll see you soon.

She waits and waits for another text. She can't imagine that
they will just go on without even texting.

When there is nothing more from Kate that day, she scrubs
the kitchen floor. She worries that Conrad might find out. The
malaise she feels is like a heavy anchor tied to her waist. She feels
herself sinking. The depression is familiar. Fear exerts itself. She
knows what it can lead to. *I am bound to the Before. I cannot undo myself.*

We'll have to take a break, she reads again, over and over,
and then lies down in her bed.

I don't know if I can stop, she thinks. *I don't know if I can be without her.*

THE SCHOOL CALLS. "BRING A CHANGE OF CLOTHES." SHE HEARS THE voice like a throbbing. *Bring clothes.* It takes her a moment to register meaning. She goes with a tiny outfit. The nurse's office. A brown paper bag. Tiny panties, wet with urine. The bag has an animal smell to it, something other than pee. She leans her head into the bag sniffing. The nurse looks at her with disturbed eyes.

"It's not unusual," the nurse says, pointing down the hall. Jocelyn rolls up the bag.

Lucy is on a little cot. Jocelyn's heart is in her throat.

"What happened, my love?" she asks, gently.

Her beautiful daughter looks away.

"What happened, my love?" she asks again. "Did you have a little accident?"

Her daughter sighs. A flash of embarrassment. Jocelyn grips her tiny hand, wanting her to feel that it's all right.

"I was playing," she says. "And, they all started laughing." Tears are shining in the beautiful brown eyes.

"Oh, sweetheart. It happens. It happens."

She does not ask about the details until later. She waits until they are at home, having a snack. The scenarios move in and out of her brain before then.

"Where'd you get the bag from, lovey?"

"What bag?"

"The bag that had your panties in it."

"Mr. Baird," Lucy says, and Jocelyn can't tell if she looks away.

"Oh really?"

"Yes."

"Did Mr. Baird help?" Jocelyn says, trying to be neutral.

"He told me to take my wet panties off. See, my uniform was long enough," Lucy says.

She watches her daughter take a slice of cheese and a cracker. She constructs a little sandwich, nibbles. Lucy hasn't lost a tooth yet. The baby teeth are firm and set in her little jaw, although the dentist says it is unusual.

"They got a little stuck, but he helped me. We have a bathroom in our classroom. Did you know that?"

Jocelyn holds still. Of course she knows that. She is there all the time, with her eyes wide open.

"Was the door open or shut?" she asks.

Lucy looks at her as if she were speaking a different language.

"Shut," she says, and then a little panic. "I don't know what you mean."

A dullness settles over her. And she sees the hand, and its inevitability. The hand she has seen her whole child life. *Why my child? Why my child? Why my child?* And the question grows and grows. And the answer blurs and comes clear. *You have done this to her. You are me and she is you.* Gladys and her consequences. All the things that Jocelyn deserves.

Kate crosses her mind. Another trick. Another setup. A reason to punish her, a sin to suffer for. *Why my daughter? Why my daughter?*

Fly right, Gladys used to say, and I won't have to hit you. Why do you make me hit you? A T-shirt, Saturday-morning cartoons. Panties. Young enough not to be thinking about how exposed her body is. She weighed forty-eight pounds when she was eight years old. Six times eight is forty-eight, Ycidra would say. You got to be smart to get out of here, Jo. A hairbrush, flat and hard on the back of her head. Ycidra begging, screaming for her mother to stop. *Hit me. Hit me.* The sparkle of stars in front of her eyes, like fireworks, a cheerleader's pom-poms on the third hit. Flintstones—Meet the Flintstones. And then Gladys, a word for every stroke. Get-Some-Clothes-On-You-God-Damn-Slut.

"Can I have some more cheese?" Lucy asks.

"Yes, my little darling. I'll get it for you right away."

SHE CANNOT SLEEP FOR MORE THAN FORTY-FIVE MINUTES AT A TIME. When she wakes, she can think only of Mr. Baird and Kate, think only of the punishment she deserves. She goes to the balcony and looks out at the sea. *Why didn't he just send her to the nurse? Why did he undress my daughter?* She feels dazed. She thinks about going to the principal, but what can she say? How can she stop this? There will be another one, another school, another man, maybe the principal. She knows they are everywhere.

Minutes go by and then hours. There are animals in the sea at night, pelicans, gulls, and even the shadow of whales unmoving, maybe sleeping, in the water. She sees Kate at the bottom of the ocean, her mother deep in a grave, a man's fingers, pinching tiny panties.

A tap on her shoulder. She jerks and flinches.

"It's just me," Conrad says. "Please don't be afraid."

She has fallen asleep in the chair.

"Come on, honey," her husband says. "Come to bed now. You've got to get some sleep."

HER HUSBAND WATCHES HER. SHE KNOWS HE IS TRYING TO CONTROL HER descent. She would like to tell him it is impossible, but he is such a hopeful man.

"Stay busy," he says. "It's physical, Jocelyn. It's just something you have, like straight teeth. You have to fight against it. Are you going to therapy?"

She listens to his lists, his invitations, his solutions. She takes Lucy to the club. She is patient with her homework. They drink Shirley Temples and order on the family tab.

I am doing what he tells me, she says to her reflection in the club's bathroom. Her cheeks are flushed like a fanatic. *I am doing what he tells me. Am I being good enough?* Around every corner, she is worried she will see Kate.

Following the directions will keep her safe. Behaving will work to protect her daughter. *I should not have sinned*, she thinks. *If I am willing, if I behave, then it will stop.*

She doesn't go near the courts, but just stays in the pool area. She and her daughter jump. One high-dive jump after another. *I am the best mother in the world*, she tells herself, devout as a zealot. She jumps again and again, as many times as Lucy wants. She will do anything for her daughter. She does it for her daughter, until Lucy is tired.

THE RELATIONSHIP IS OVER. THEY DO NOT TEXT. THEY DO NOT SPEAK. IT ended when it ended, just as they said. It is a rupture, without transition. It is the tearing away of flesh. It takes a while for her to realize though. She is like the machinist who in the minutes after losing his arm, still feels the itch on the wrist.

CHAPTER THIRTY-TWO

SIMON

1

HE LOOKS FOR THE DOG EVERY DAY. HE WANTS TO DRAW IT TO HIM. HE brings a large travel crate, a soft cushioned bed inside, his own dirty shirt. *He will smell me, even when I'm not here.* He leaves.

He comes back every day, even though he tries not to. He realizes it's a compulsion. Insanity. How long will it go on? On the seventh day, he brings a pig's ear and a cow's hoof—two very smelly items. The Pet Express employee claims dogs cannot resist them. He sets the items in the crate. He leans into the crate. He smells the blankets to see if Lion has been inside. It does not smell like dog. He straightens the blankets. Lays his own body there. He drifts off to sleep.

He *hears* the sound of the animal before he sees it. The breath is like a bull's, forceful and low. He lifts up, bumps his head on the ceiling of the crate. He hears the soughing of the muscular body and the quick pounding of feet. Simon pulls his head out. The dog is running toward him from the east, from the dilapidated greenhouse. He seems wild. Is he baring his teeth? Simon stands quickly. He thinks of rabies, of bugs in the brain. The sleep has made him disoriented. *Is he coming for me? Is he coming for me?*

Simon slowly backs up, forgetting the crate behind him. The backs of his knees hit it. He falls on his ass.

"No," he says. "No, no, no!"

He keeps his eyes on the dog, feels a pain in his left wrist. He crab-walks on all fours, tries to scuttle away, but he has sprained something. He has injured himself.

He lifts his hurt wrist. Holds it in his good hand. The dog moves in circles around him. The circle closes, the mouth, the jowls. Simon can see the spittle spewing from side to side.

"Please no, Lion," he says, but the dog is upon him. "Please no."

Simon attempts to protect his face. He squeezes his head behind his arms. He thinks he should stay covered. He thinks how stupid he is, how afraid he is. Why would he ever trust a dog like this?

He closes his eyes, waits for the bite. He waits and he waits and he waits. There is the sick smell of the dog's breath. Seconds pass as the dog sniffs him patiently, all over. There is the tickle of whiskers on his forehead. The spray of spit. Simon stays perfectly still, perfectly quiet, playing dead. He opens one eye, closes it, and then suddenly, a lick. Light and tentative. The end of it like a soft thistle. Tongue to cheek next. Then tongue to his tender hand. Simon looks out through his fingers. The dog sniffs again. Finds the center of Simon's palm and licks again. He must smell the ear, the hoof, Simon thinks. He sits up slowly, dust sticking to his wet hand. The dog freezes. He is there, his head as big as his own. They are face-to-face. Simon looks down. He thinks he has moved too suddenly.

"Please don't hurt me," he says as if the dog can understand.

There is another lick then, right across Simon's nose, totally intentional, a head bow, as if in worship, and then the dog's rump in the air. His shape is like a small slide. Simon works up the nerve to reach out, but when he moves to touch the dog, Lion barks and canters away.

CHAPTER THIRTY-THREE

JOCELYN

1

"So?" Maud says, just that. They are in Jocelyn's condo—dinner, a playdate for the kids. Conrad has planned it with Scott. A Sunday-night surprise for the wives. Jocelyn hates it.

"So, what?" Jocelyn says.

"Come on. Tell me. We've all heard."

"What have you heard?" Jocelyn asks, feeling completely defeated. When Maud says nothing, Jocelyn says, "God, I hate her."

Maud says, "I told you. Why don't you listen to me? Tennis makes everyone twelve again."

"Ha!" Jocelyn says, but her voice is without humor. "Did she say anything to you?"

"She knows better than to say anything to me, but she's insinuating. We all just laugh. I mean those of us who know you. Nobody believes her. It's too ridiculous."

Jocelyn finds herself reaching out and squeezing Maud's hand.

"You're too sensitive, Jocelyn. You can't let this shit get to you. You worry about *everything*."

"She hates me. I don't even know why she hates me. She's not going to stop saying stuff. She has it out for me."

"Who cares?"

Jocelyn doesn't speak for a moment. She feels tears coming to the surface and doesn't want to cry. She is so tired. She longs for sleep.

"Tennis was making me better, you know. I've just been under things. My mom dying, and Conrad is gone all the time, and it's just all so hard. It's so hard to be a really good mother. I want to be a really good mother, but I can't do anything right."

"Honey, it isn't true. Don't let her do that to you. If people *don't* talk about you, *then* you should worry. That's my motto."

Jocelyn sighs and Maud goes on. "Missy is just weird about Kate. She's been like this. I mean before you even started playing at the club. We used to make fun of her. I should have warned you. It's a girl crush."

Maud pauses, and Jocelyn feels uncomfortable, exposed.

"I'm not sleeping. I have to figure out a way to sleep."

"Let's have a shot," Maud says. "You need to loosen up. I have Ambien. I'll give you some. Don't even worry about it. You need to give yourself a break. You're too hard on yourself. Go get the tequila."

"Okay," Jocelyn says. "I'll get the tequila."

She gets two shot glasses, the salt shaker, and two lemon slices. She is pleased that Maud has defended her. They throw the shots back perfectly and slam the glasses down on the table like two sorority girls.

"One more," Maud says, and after that one, Jocelyn feels a buzz in her body, not just in her head. The tingle of tequila.

"The thing is, Jocelyn," Maud says. She is whispering, leaning into her more closely. "Whether you are fucking Kate or not . . ." She puts both hands up in a gesture of submission. "You should come back to drill. The fact that you don't hang out anymore, you don't come to tennis at all, makes you seem guilty. It doesn't look good. You've got to go. Let's go tomorrow—together. Trust me. I've been there, done that."

Jocelyn feels her face drop for a half a second. She isn't clear what Maud is confessing: Sex outside her marriage. Sex with Kate. Her face grows hot.

"Oh, my," Maud says. "Oh my! Are you doing it?" she whispers intensely. "I had no idea."

Maud pours a third shot, swigs it back, and sort of laughs.

Jocelyn doesn't want to go to drill, and she can't have this conversation.

She points at her own empty shot glass. Maud fills it and then fills her own again.

"Wow," Maud says. "Cheers, girl. You are a mystery. Let's get drunk. I think I'm sleeping over. We're all sleeping over."

Maud's family stays in the large guest suite, and in the morning through her hangover, Maud tells Jocelyn they will never speak of it again. They are standing side by side in front of Jocelyn's master bathroom mirror, putting on makeup, getting ready for drill.

"Just be careful," Maud says. "Have your fill and then end it, okay? I had my own little tryst after Austin was born. I mean, how long is a girl going to look good naked? I just kept thinking, 'Forty more years of just Scott? Really?'"

Maud laughs at her own joke. Jocelyn knows she is trying to lighten the air between them, but it isn't working.

"Don't be a child about it, Jocelyn. It's never worth giving up your family. I mean I don't know how deep in it you are, but it's not worth that. You've got everything. Other women would die to have our lives."

"Yep," Jocelyn says, thinking she's not really admitting anything, but knowing she's admitted it all.

"Conrad is great," Maud says. "Scott is great too, but make no mistake. They're men who get their way. They're men who don't like losing. Conrad would take custody of Lucy from you before you could even react. He's not letting you keep his daughter if he finds out you've cheated on him. Even if it's just to hurt you, he'll take her."

"*My* daughter," Jocelyn says. "Not his."

"Trust me," Maud says very solemnly.

Jocelyn's head is pounding. She has never even considered Conrad, and custody, and life without her child. She gets an Advil, gives one to Maud. She wants to say something. She wants to share a moment and explain more than just this. She wants to tell her friend about Gladys, about Uncle Al, about Mr. Baird, and Lucy's panties in a brown bag. They are too hungover though.

They have already spoken too many words. They walk out into the kitchen. Conrad and Scott are making omelets. The kids are taking turns on Lucy's small bike and scooter. They ride back and forth along the length of the balcony deck. *I learned to ride a bike when I was twenty years old. There wasn't anyone to teach me before then.*

She looks around at the large condo. It is a mess. It will take her all day to clean. She notices how much she hates the curtains. They are too dark for a house on the sea. Too dark for this space.

"Let's go," Maud says. "I left the Ambien in your bathroom mirror."

They go.

SHE CALLS THE MEN WHEN SHE GETS HOME FROM THE DRILL, AND THEY come with squeegees and scaffolding to conquer the windows.

"There are smears," she says, showing them. "In just that light," she says. "I need the view to be clear," she says. The men are baffled. "Can't you see?"

She begins her own work in the corner of the kitchen, blocking thoughts of drill. Kate ignored her. Missy made jokes. Make them go dark, she thinks, and stares at the floor.

The floor is an enemy to be conquered. There is never enough time. Her fingers and knuckles are wrinkled and dry. She likes the pain of it, the skin tight from the hot water and bleach. She works for two hours on the floor, changing the water constantly. And then she has to stop. She has to pick Lucy up from school. From Mr. Baird. She will not be late.

WHEN THEY GET BACK FROM SCHOOL, LUCY SITS AT THE WHITE MARBLE kitchen island.

"I'm hungry," she says.

"A snack," Jocelyn says and gets it. She is efficient about it— all business. Lucy rattles on and on about the fun she had with Maud's family. The bread crumbs from Lucy's Nutella sandwich settle on the counter and fall onto the freshly scrubbed floor. Jocelyn stares at the crumbs.

"Can they come again?" Lucy asks.

"Who?" Jocelyn asks.

Lucy sighs. "You aren't listening to me, Mama. You have to listen to me."

"I'm listening," she says, wetting a paper towel, lifting the crumbs into the trash. "How about some Netflix?"

Lucy is astounded. Television exists for her only as a special treat. "Yes," she says, excitedly. "*Octonauts*, Mama. I want *Octonauts*."

Jocelyn is pleased to have made her baby happy. She continues with the kitchen. The trash bag smells, even though it is almost empty. She sends one of the window cleaners to take it out. She empties cabinets, cleans the pantry, dumps all unhealthy food. The sun sets and in the evening light, she is surprised to see that there are still streaks on the kitchen floor. She decides to begin again. *Sun to sun*, she thinks, trying to retrieve something. *Sun to sun*, but she's forgotten it. She bends over a floorboard. Scrubs. Each time she looks back to see what she has accomplished, she finds that she is not so far along on the floor as she would expect. She has faith, continues, eradicates the dirt. Sits back to admire her work.

The men move from one room to the next. The smell of lavender and eucalyptus follows them. *A man's work is from sun to sun*, she hears now. Lucy giggles from time to time about something that's on the cartoon. Jocelyn moves to the next square of floor, but this time when she looks back, the spot she's just finished is somehow dirty again, and so she begins again. Time passes. Lucy whimpers about being hungry, about Simon or Maud's kids, but Jocelyn just tells her to find something new on the TV.

"I'll make you something in a minute."

By the time Conrad gets home, her hands are red and blistered. Her face is strained. He walks quickly to Lucy, kisses her cheek. *A man's work is sun to sun, but a mother's work is never done.* Mother or woman? she thinks. She can't remember.

"Is everything okay, my love?" he says to her, but she doesn't answer.

"Jocelyn?" he says.

She feels her face tighten.

"Can I help you, love? What's going on here? What's happening?"

The window cleaners are still milling around, dumping their buckets, wiping their squeegees.

Jocelyn sits holding the brush she's been using on the floor. The water dripping onto her thighs and the parquet floors.

"I'm going to do it well," she says. "I'm going to finish and make it nice again."

Conrad tells the men to leave. He tips them into silence. "We won't talk about any of this," he says into the telephone, speaking to their boss. The window company is a local Palisades business. The owner has kids at the same school. She is puzzled by what Conrad is saying.

"Papa is going to put Mama to bed," Conrad says to Lucy, but Jocelyn just vaguely hears. He lays her on her pillow.

"We're not doing this again, Jocelyn. I love you, but I can't. You've got to get it together."

HE DRIVES HER TO THERAPY. HE WANTS HER THERE FIVE DAYS A WEEK. HE seems confused when the therapist asks him to stay.

"Just for this session," Dr. Bruce says, with an air of subservience.

Conrad vents about Jocelyn. He tells the therapist to put her on medicine, that she needs something. Things aren't going well.

Jocelyn blinks at him, realizes just at that moment that her husband is sick of her, and why wouldn't he be? The things she carries are unbearable. She is sick of herself too.

On the second day, they sit—just she and the doctor this time, unable to connect. Jocelyn knows that she cannot disentangle herself from the past, no matter what Dr. Bruce says. No mater what Conrad offers her. It is in her. Even with the bounty that is in front of her, it is not possible to fix her. She cannot get empty, and she will be heavy and filled forever. And this is the lifelong smothering, a big body on a small one. A slow, steady killing of that original girl. By whom though? By someone? By something? *Acceptance*, she thinks. *I accept it.*

"Can you tell me anything that you are feeling, Jocelyn?" the doctor says as if she is afraid to break her. "Anything you are thinking? Right now is okay."

Jocelyn hesitates. She lets the words come. "I just think how strange it is," she says to Dr. Bruce.

"How strange what is?" Dr. Bruce asks.

"Me."

"What do you mean, Jocelyn? Why do you say that?"

"That I am still, no matter what, who that girl is too, but I can't get her out. I can't get her out, even with Lucy and Conrad."

"What girl?"

"The girl from before."

"From before what?" Dr. Bruce says.

Just before, Jocelyn thinks.

"Do you want to tell me about the girl?" Dr. Bruce asks.

"Not really."

"Is she you, Jocelyn? Or is she someone else?"

"Of course she's me," Jocelyn says, thinking how exasperating the doctor is. "I'm not crazy."

"Then tell me about her, please. I know you aren't crazy."

Jocelyn looks at her nails, clean and white. "I used to think if Gladys died, then I'd be her again. I'd be my good self, my un-soiled self. I always thought she'd be great. It's like I wanted her to stay hiding until just then. She'd be amazing and successful and untouched, and so I'd be amazing and successful and clean again."

"In what way?" Dr. Bruce asks softly.

"Well, in a lot of ways." Jocelyn pauses. Thinks. "I mean, she wouldn't be me, first of all. Me as I am now."

Jocelyn opens her water bottle. An indigo thing that she has purchased at her local spa. Twenty-eight dollars but it keeps the water cold.

"What do you see as wrong with you, Jocelyn? What's so bad about you?"

"I should have saved my sister," she says, suddenly. "I should have saved my brother. I should have done that."

"You were a child, Jocelyn," Dr. Bruce says. "You were a child."

"I'm not a child anymore," Jocelyn says. "I should have kept *this* life clean, but I couldn't. I didn't."

"What are you talking about? I don't understand."

Jocelyn doesn't answer. "I can't sleep anymore," she says. "At night, I sit on my balcony."

"I want to prescribe something for you, Jocelyn. I think it's a good time. Your husband agrees. What do you think? To pick up your mood."

"Last night, I was sitting out there, and the wind was blow-ing, and I was feeling good, and then out of nowhere, I thought about how he raped her at night, and then in the morning on the way to school there were ducklings. Just like that in the middle of the night, on my balcony, this far away, this many years later, in peace, it came to me. I can't be clean. I can't have anything that's pure. I ruin it."

"Ducklings?" Dr. Bruce asks.

"Ducklings. You know, like baby ducks."

"Yes. I know what they are."

"They were too small to get up on the curb. Black and gray with a little bit of yellowish brown on their chests." Jocelyn shivers. If she were a therapist she would find a place filled with light. She would make her office warm.

"Go on."

"He made us get out of the car. He told us to make a line beside the car, to block the oncoming traffic. It came to me last night. It's the girl. She won't let me sleep. Memories. But I can't figure why."

The therapist nods.

"Uncle Al lifted them. One little ball of feathery fur at a time onto the curb. The mother tried to bite him. I watched him. I've been thinking about him, about all of my mother's boyfriends, about my mother, each of us. The ways we make no sense. That's what I do when I can't sleep."

"What do you mean you make no sense?"

"I mean it's *all* inside of each of us, right? All of it."

"Well." Dr. Bruce pauses. "All of what exactly?"

She can't figure out how to say it. She knows the girl is there, beneath that other girl, but neither of them can get out.

She sits up startled.

"What is it Jocelyn?"

Could it be me? she wants to say. *Me on top of her?*

"What he did was wrong," Dr. Bruce says, swiftly.

"The dregs, the residue," Jocelyn says, not really hearing. "They're there. Even when everyone who knows you can't see them." She waves her hand around the room, hoping to signify something. "This," she says. "It's all for nothing."

"That's not true, Jocelyn. There's healing."

"I have to go and see Gladys's grave," she says, firmly.

"Okay," Dr. Bruce says, but Jocelyn can feel her resistance. "Let's talk about that."

Jocelyn stays silent. So many moments of silence in therapy. It never seems real. It isn't real. It's talking to a stranger about incomprehensible things. We are all alone in the world, no matter what we believe.

"What do you hope to accomplish?"

I have been dismantled by her, Jocelyn wants to say. *I want her to give me back to me. Relinquish me to me.*

"Closure," she says instead to the doctor—the smart doctor, who can never really know.

CHAPTER THIRTY-FOUR

JOCELYN

1

SHE GOES TO THE CABIN ON A DAY THAT SHE DOESN'T HAVE TO VOLUN-
teer in Lucy's class. She thinks she can feel Kate again, get better
again, here in the woods. She lies in the cool sheets of the iron
bed, head on a soft pillow, pretending Kate is beside her. She takes
one of Maud's Ambiens.

She dozes and sleeps and sleeps and sleeps. All the lost sleep
of the weeks before is found in the bed that she shared with her
lover.

When she finally wakes, her phone is alight with missed calls,
voice mails: Kate? But there is only the bland voice of a bored
school secretary, the panicked anger of her husband.

She surges, runs bleary eyed up the long series of steps, trying
not to slip. She cannot believe it. She has never done anything
like this.

I am not even a good mother, she thinks, when she reaches the top
of the stairs. *I can't even be a good mother.*

How could she have done this? How could she have taken something and then slept through picking her daughter up? She is just like Gladys. Her daughter is waiting. Waiting, always waiting.

Defeat is alive inside her.

2

CONRAD IS AT THE SCHOOL WHEN SHE GETS THERE. MR. BAIRD IS WAIT-ing with Lucy. Conrad is apologizing. Jocelyn just looks, studies, sees.

Mr. Baird says it's no problem. He stays this late anyway, he says. Things happen.

And, of course, it's no problem, Jocelyn thinks. Not for men like Mr. Baird. Not for the men waiting in her childhood. The brown bag. The panties. Gladys, late, more often than not. The teachers, the janitors who depended on her being alone. Jocelyn knows how it goes, how it goes and goes.

She reaches for her daughter's hand, nods at Mr. Baird. She wants to lead Lucy out of the classroom. Her daughter is pale and angry. She will not take her mother's hand. She will not touch her mother. Conrad shakes Mr. Baird's hand and the three of them walk out. Lucy holds on to Conrad, who scolds Jocelyn as they walk out to the parking lot.

"I have to work," he says, harshly. "Got that?"

"I've got it," she says, as if she were a toddler, just learning the language. There is no fight inside her.

"How can you forget your own daughter at school? What the hell is going on with you?"

What the hell is going on with me? she thinks, but she says nothing.

He quiets his voice just a bit. "Ever since your mother, we're back to this shit. You're up half the night. You're working your way around the house with a rag and a bucket like a maid. If you can't deal with your responsibilities, get a fucking nanny."

She says nothing and he goes on.

"Do I begrudge you anything? Do I? Do I?"

"No," she says.

She walks beside her husband and her child. They seem a part of each other and yet separate from her. She is just a robot follow-ing instructions. Mr. Baird, saying *No problem*, is at the fore of her mind. *I'll watch her*, the camp counselor said. *Of course, you don't have to come on the trip. We've got plenty of volunteers*, the pastor at their church said. Free babysitting is what Gladys thought. Always happy to be rid of them.

"Go get some meds," Conrad says, interrupting her memo-ries. "I don't give a shit about how you feel about drugs. We aren't doing this again. I'm telling you. I called *everywhere*. I called Maud. I called Theresa. I called the club. I called my mother, for God's sake. I thought you might be dead. Where were you?"

She looks at her husband. She considers telling him about the pill. She will not take medicine. If she has learned anything today, she has learned that.

"I was shopping," she says, because Conrad comes from the kind of woman who shops. "My phone was off. I haven't been able to sleep. I turned it off last night. I forgot to turn it back on. I was just taking a little rest in my car in the mall parking lot, waiting for pickup time."

"You have a six-year-old!" His voice is sharp and angled. "You cannot forget. You need to get your ass in gear. Go *do* something. You aren't even playing tennis anymore," he says. "I thought you were doing well for a while."

"I was," she says.

They keep walking across the lush green courtyard of the beautiful school. She feels very small on this great campus.

"I have to go home," she says. "I think I have to see Gladys. I think that will make me better."

Conrad stops walking. He looks at her, his face goes com-pletely white. "Gladys is dead, Jocelyn. Your mother is dead."

"I know," she says. "I know. I didn't mean it like that."

The blood returns to his cheeks, and she realizes he has thought her completely and finally mad.

"Her grave," she says. "I have to see the grave, and I want to see the old apartment, and maybe the bridge. I think that's what's wrong with me. I was talking to my therapist. I need closure."

He opens up the back door of Jocelyn's car and seatbelts Lucy into her booster. Lucy is crying now: "I want Papa to come home. I don't want you to go to work, Papa. Please."

"It's okay," he says to Lucy gently. "Papa will be home very, very soon." He kisses her. She snuffs a bit, trying to stifle her tears. He shuts the door, turns to Jocelyn.

"Get some plane reservations for the two of you. Get yourself to Cincinnati and get right back here. I told you to go before. I told you to go to the funeral. You need to listen to me, Jocelyn."

She wonders if he will kiss her goodbye, but he just opens her car door for her.

She sits down. He leans in. No kiss, just the continuing lecture. "My mother is expecting us at the club at six tonight. Get yourself in order before then. Be on time."

SHE WATCHES IN THE REARVIEW MIRROR AND LISTENS FOR CLUES—SUBTLE and insidious. Unseen, but present.

"What did you and Mr. Baird do, while you were waiting?" Jocelyn asks, trying to be casual.

"Mr. Baird says we get to go to the zoo next week."

"He does?"

"Mr. Baird says I'm a really good artist. We had Art Trek today."

"Does he?" Jocelyn asks.

"Mr. Baird is my favorite teacher."

"Lucy?" Jocelyn says, trying to sound as if she has no agenda. "You know if Mr. Baird ever does anything that makes you feel uncomfortable, you will tell Mama, won't you?

Lucy is confused. "Like what?"

"Like anything you don't like," Jocelyn says. "Like anything at all."

"He moves us down from Starfish sometimes. Our clip down, I mean. Into rough waters. If you get shipwrecked, it's a phone call home."

A smile comes to Jocelyn's lips. She tells herself to stay focused. When Lucy sees the smile, she continues.

"Sometimes, he gives us money, Mama. Money from his pockets."

"Really?" Jocelyn asks, looking in the mirror. The pitch of her voice goes up just a half step. Lucy gets quiet. Jocelyn has given her suspicion away. Lucy can feel the air change. She has noted it.

"What do you mean he gives you money?" she asks.

"Nothing, Mama. Nothing."

———

IF THE MOMENT COULD HAVE BEEN SEEN FROM THE OUTSIDE BY SOMEONE else, it would have looked like this:

Her child, herself. One single thing that remained. The same. What remains? Potential? No. Pain.

A hand on the child's neck. Mr. Baird gives us money. I'm not supposed to tell you, Mama. But she didn't say that. Did she?

He told me not to tell. Change in his pockets. Lots of change. He lets us keep it. The pastor did that.

Commerce. Business. She, the only one in the world to understand that it never, ever ends. Like water making its way through earth, creating canyons, holes, gullies, over many generations.

White fingers in soft child's hair. Her. William's soft as eyelashes. Does she remember? The only one left of the family of fuckups, of the family of flawed. Not the only one though after all—Lucy.

It is there in the blood, embedded. Bed. Her mother has warned her. Like the tip of a welt.

Beloved. The most beloved. Lucy is my beloved. I will not. I will not what? A bloom cut and captured.

I almost saved you, she wants to say, but it is *in* you. It is on its way. Almost here, and I can't let it have you. There is nothing worse.

A light extinguished. An end. It is impossible to leave her behind if it is to be clean. Pure. The tip of a welt. Final. Don't leave a single thing.

CHAPTER THIRTY-FIVE

SIMON

1

HIS COLLEAGUE, GRACE, TELLS HIM TO KNEEL AND TO PUT OUT HIS hands to be smelled whenever he visits the dog, and he does just that. Each time Simon lays out the bag and the water and the snack, he kneels, opens his palms, and the dog nuzzles him. *Still shy, but there*, Simon thinks. *Definitely there.* "Good boy!" he says, because he has seen that on television.

Simon pours the food out. Lion hovers. He fills the water. He goes to his usual spot and the dog follows him. He touches the dog's forehead and talks to him. He tells him his worries. He sits on the ground, and Lion sits too.

"Go, Lion," he says. "Go, have your supper." But the dog does not go to the food today. The dog waits with him. Rests a head between crossed paws. Doesn't eat.

"What are you doing, Lion?" he asks. "Aren't you going to eat?"

The dog sits as settled as he sat the first time Simon saw him—a statue on the side of the road then, a prone statue beside Simon now. His paws are huge. He sits and waits next to Simon, but Simon doesn't know what the dog is waiting for. He wants to understand but does not.

"Okay, then," he says, like an impatient governess. "I must go back to work. I have to leave. You eat. I want you to be well. You do not want to worry me."

Simon stands to go, begins to walk back to his car. The dog walks too.

"No," Simon says, pointing his finger at the dog. The dog gets low. "No. It is dangerous. Do not follow me onto the road," he says.

He turns back to the highway shoulder again, back toward where his car is parked. He walks. The dog follows.

Simon sighs with exasperation. "No. Stay," Simon says firmly.

Simon walks more quickly now. He hurries, clicks the remote, unlocks the door, and hops in. He starts the car. Looks in his sideview mirror and his rearview. He pulls into a line of traffic. He does not know what to do. He can see the dog in his rearview mirror. Sitting there, next to where the car was parked minutes before. Looking after him. He is too close to the road.

You have been left before, Simon thinks. He feels something hollow and dull in his chest. *This is not any different.*

"I will be back," he says, but of course, the dog cannot hear.

AT THE NEXT EXIT, HE GETS OFF TO CIRCLE BACK. HE IS WORRIED. WHAT if someone runs over the dog? The light he sits at to reenter the freeway is slow. It goes on and on. He prays as he enters back onto the freeway. He can tell now that he needs the dog. The dog has come to him for a reason. *Why?* he wonders. *Why did I not let him in?* He beeps his horn at the driver in front of him. Traffic is so slow. It is unbearable. Relentless. He has such a short way to go. Maybe he should walk. "Go!" he screams inside the car's interior. He has the awful idea that he will find the dog dead.

It takes him twenty minutes to enter onto the highway. It is like a parking lot. He keeps his eyes on the road ahead, and finally he can see the outline of the dog, sitting in exactly the place that

Simon left him. A heavy breath of relief leaves his body. He says a small prayer. When he opens his eyes again, he notices a VW Beetle parked, a woman, blonde and fat, standing beside it. She is standing on the side of the road where Lion is. Simon can tell, even from this bit of distance, that she is trying to coax the dog into her car. She is six feet away from the dog at least. The door to the Beetle is open.

Simon panics. He tries to go faster, but the traffic, the fucking traffic. He beeps his horn, wanting to alert the lady. He waves his hand out of his window, shouts, but the man in the car in front of him misunderstands and lifts his middle finger.

He sits for a few more minutes, watching the woman waving at the dog, signaling for Lion to come to her. Finally, he decides to drive onto the shoulder.

"Do not go with her, Lion!" he shouts. A mantra, over and over.

He drives dangerously, passing two cars, then four cars, then ten cars, until he has finally arrived, one car behind the woman's blue Volkswagen Beetle.

Simon puts the car in park, does not bother to turn it off, and leaps out of the car.

"He's mine," he says to the woman. "He's mine." He can hear the urgency in his own voice.

"Oh," she says. Her voice is calm and slow. The polar opposite of his. There is the round cushion of something Southern in it. "Oh, my land. I'm so glad. He was not going to come with me, and well . . ." She looks at all the cars on the 10 freeway. "It's so dangerous here."

"Yes," Simon says, smiling. "Yes." He is out of breath. "I will get him."

For a moment, he worries that the dog will not come to him, that the woman will see him for the liar that he is. He opens the car door. The BMW shines in the afternoon sun.

"Come on, Lion," he says. "Let's go home."

The dog sidles over, covering half the space between them.

He hesitates for just a moment. He looks behind him at the dilapidated greenhouse and then back at Simon cautiously, as if making a decision. He stays close to the ground, a bit fearful, but still agile as a predator. He makes his way to the open car door, stops.

"Are you sure he's yours?" the woman asks, watching the dog's tentative movements. Her brow is furrowed. "He seems a little scared. You aren't one of those dog fighters, are you? I've heard about these dogs . . . what people do."

"Get in," he says to the dog. Desperation is hot and obvious in his voice.

Lion hops in.

The Good Samaritan smiles. The dog is willing. She sees that. He waves goodbye to the woman and gets into the driver's side. The stink of the dog is surprising. It is like Fritos and old garbage. He feels alive as he slams the car door. All that is him is pulsing. He looks down at his forearm, which seems transparent. It is as if the blood that keeps him alive can be seen through his skin. He has done something—enacted change. He has gotten the dog. He has saved him. A life finally. One life saved.

CHAPTER THIRTY-SIX

JOCELYN

1

SHE LEANS INTO CONRAD'S BACK, FEELING THE HEAT OF HIM. THEY ARE able to get along, now that she has accepted the way things are. She is weightless, driven. Nothing can get in her way. She loves him. She longs for him. She doesn't understand why she is leaving him any more than she understands the men who abused her, a mother who let them, Ycidra and William dying. She has given in to not understanding. She will go with it.

Dr. Bruce says she will be fine. Dr. Bruce says if she takes the medicine, if she waits out the depression, the deferring, the past, it will all become manageable. Dr. Bruce doesn't realize that it *is* her. She is the same flawed girl, no matter how hard she has tried to be different. She is rebuilt but rebuilt out of all the same pieces. It is harder and harder to keep from merging. Scenes from the past happening right now. Ycidra, fresh from the morgue, slid from a drawer, a kiss on her forehead, not realizing she'd be cold. She takes the bottle from Dr. Bruce, but never puts the pills in her body.

"Hey love," Conrad says, turning his sleepy self toward her. "How are you still so beautiful?"

She smiles at him but feels as if she might cry. "It's your eyes," she says. "We are old now. You can't see very well."

"No," he says. "You *are* beautiful. I'm glad you're working so hard."

A silence enters the room for her, a dark web of something heavy. Conrad doesn't seem to notice.

"Thanks," she says.

"So, how long will you be gone? Are you sure you still feel like going?"

She answers. "Just a couple of days. I'll go to the grave. I'll show Lucy my old neighborhood maybe, or the bridge. She always asks about the river. That's something pretty in the city."

"Why don't you two come with me instead, and then we can all go to Cincinnati later? Baton Rouge is beautiful this time of year."

He is holding her now. She feels him kiss the top of her head. The kiss is chaste like Ycidra's hand after a beating, like Ycidra's hand when she was too high to get anything else to work, a smearing, as if she were trying to rub something on her. She feels tempted. She should go, but it is not the time for weakness. *Act*, she says to herself. *For once in your life, act!*

"We'll come next time," she says. "The weather's meant to be beautiful and clear in Ohio. You know how rare that is."

"I do," he says.

"Mama?" They both hear Lucy's sweet little voice, and they smile at each other. They are in love with the girl they've made. "Mama? Can I wake up now?"

"Of course you can, my sweetheart. Have you slept enough?"

It is 5:25. Lucy has always been an early riser. She is happy to meet the day.

"Yes."

"Good," Jocelyn says.

"Papa?"

"Yes, my love."

"I was just checking to see if you were here," she says.

"I'm here, my love. I'm here today. Are we going to have fun?"

"Will you bring me some pancakes?" Lucy asks.

"I will," he says.

Jocelyn lets herself smile. She surveys this space. She lets herself feel this family that is almost perfect. *I am the only thing that is not right here. It isn't going to change.*

Conrad kisses her on the mouth.

"Yick," she says. "I haven't brushed my teeth."

"Later, when you have, we'll make out." He smiles.

"You're relentless," she says and sits up in bed.

"Do you want coffee?" he asks.

"Yes," she says. "Please."

She looks at him as if for the last time. He is such a good husband. A good father.

"You okay, my love?" he asks. "You seem far away. You're not getting down, are you?"

There is just the smidge of irritation in his voice. She wants to please him.

"No," she says. "I'm just sorry we're leaving. We're going to miss you."

"We'll have fun when we all get back. You guys hurry, and I'll hurry too."

"Yes," she says, knowing she is lying. "We'll race right back to you."

She sits too long in front of her vanity. It is hard to get started.

"Mama?" Lucy says. "Wanna see something?"

"Yes, my love."

She has a Winnie-the-Pooh blanket around her shoulders.

"I am making the wind," Lucy says, leaping from the bed to the floor and then running in front of Jocelyn's large picture window. "I am making a storm with my cape. See it, Mama? See how the waves get bigger outside when I do it?"

"I do," Jocelyn says. Movement, she thinks. Children are movement.

"Mama?"

"Yes, my love."

"Are you still a mermaid? I mean if you went outside into the sea and you wanted to, could you become one again?"

Jocelyn is surprised that her daughter remembers the story. She has not brought it up since the first telling. She doesn't know why she is surprised. Lucy remembers and questions everything—the Easter bunny, Santa, the little leprechauns on Saint Patrick's Day, the fairy that will eventually steal her tiny milk teeth. But it has been so long since they have talked about mermaids, about the scars—the fisherman and his net.

"Yes," she says. "I just don't have my tail anymore."

"Well," Lucy says, running past her again. "Margery has a tail. You can buy them. Can I get one of those tails? If I had one of those tails, I could swim anywhere. We could get you one of those tails too."

"We'll ask Papa," Jocelyn says, which is what she always says when she wants to put an answer off.

She stares out the window at the sea. The waves do seem

rougher than minutes before. She is happy to be caught up in Lucy's imagination. Her power.

"Look at me, Mama. I'm making them bigger. Why aren't you looking?"

She turns from the window to see her little girl.

CHAPTER THIRTY-SEVEN

SIMON

1

HE TAKES THE DOG TO THE VET, WHO TREATS LION FOR PARASITES AND gets him up to date on his vaccines. After, it takes the groomer two hours to wash the dog. Simon buys toys and beds and blankets. The groomer goes on and on—what a find, what a temperament, a good bloodline. You'd better put an ad in the classifieds.

Simon lies, says he has. The dog has a golden ribbon around its neck as they leave, and seems suddenly full of himself, as if he's always been the thing he is right now—clean, beautiful, and rare.

They are home in minutes, and an hour after they get to the condo, the dog is asleep on Simon's white couch. There is water spilled on his kitchen floor. Toys are easy to stumble over.

Like a new father, Simon sits and stares at the dog, watches its eyes flutter in a dream. The legs move, running, running. He watches the chest rise and fall, making certain the dog is alive. There is a steady whimpering. Simon wonders what the dog dreams of, but knows it isn't good.

As he did when Claudette was just a little girl, he moves close to the dog, he whispers, he says: *It's okay, my little one. I'm here. Nothing can hurt you, because Papa is right here.*

AT FIVE THE DOORBELL RINGS AND THE DOG BARKS AND THEN MAKES A deep vibrating, growling sound. Simon opens the door, holds Lion by the collar, and before he can tell her to be careful, Lucy is in the foyer, squealing, all shrill joy, and reaching for the dog with delight. The dog wiggles its rear when he sees the girl, as if they already know one another.

"Come in," he says. "I've got a dog."

"I can see that," Jocelyn says.

"I hope I didn't bother you. I just thought I'd text you. I thought Lucy would like him."

"A dog, Mama!" Lucy says. "Simon has a dog."

"He looks mean," Simon says. "But pay no attention. He is just a big baby. He has taken over my white couch. My bed too. Don't put your face close to his until he gets used to you. I don't want him startled."

Lucy looks angry. "Don't say he looks mean. You've hurt his feelings." She kisses the dog's forehead, utterly ignoring the warning Simon's given just seconds before. The dog gives Lucy his paw.

He notices immediately that Jocelyn is subdued. She smiles at the dog, pats its head, but isn't really present. She is like a ghost, he thinks, or like those women who have taken one too many pills. He realizes that he hasn't seen her in a while. He has been so caught up in his own life. Has she lost weight?

"We came to say goodbye," she says, abruptly. "We're going to Cincinnati tomorrow. I'm going to see my mother's grave."

"Oh," Simon says, and he reaches to touch her. "I'm sorry. I feel as if I haven't been here for you. It will be hard," he says. "But better, once you do it."

She does not look at him. Her eyes remain on her daughter.

Lucy has Lion's collar now. She is leading him around the living room, telling him to heel, to sit, to stay, as if he were a show dog. When he does what she tells him, she kisses him on his fore-head. "Don't you have any treats?" she asks. "Dogs need treats."

"No. He has had enough spoiling for today. Next time. When you come back from your trip, you can give him treats."

"Okay," Lucy says. "Okay."

"Do not stay away too long," he says. "I will miss you too much. Lion will miss you, Lucy. I can tell that he loves you already."

He clasps his hands together, looks at Jocelyn, Lucy, the dog. Lucy is placing pretend blue ribbons around Lion's neck. He sits still, earning them.

"Can we get a dog?" Lucy asks, suddenly.

"Maybe when we get back," Jocelyn says. "When we get back."

Simon can see that Jocelyn is not herself. There is sadness, deep and dark as ink, in her today. It scares him.

"What is it?" he whispers, low, so Lucy can't hear. But Jocelyn just walks over to his french doors to look out at the sea.

He follows quickly behind her. "Do you want to talk? You and I can talk," he says, trying again.

"I'm good," she says. "Really. I'm glad we got to see you before we left."

They stay fifteen more minutes before Jocelyn says it is time to leave.

It seems so fast to him. He feels urgent. Abruptly he says, "I have seen my daughter again." He thinks the subject might shock her into staying. "She is having a baby."

Jocelyn looks up at him. "How wonderful," she says. "A baby is always a blessing."

Upon leaving, Jocelyn holds him tight in a hug, and then Lucy leaps up into his arms.

"Can Lion be my dog too?" she asks. "He told me he wants me to be his sister."

"He is your brother, then," Simon says. *Which makes you my daughter in a way*, he wants to say, but he doesn't say it aloud. He sets his beautiful Lucy down.

"I will miss you both," he says, trying to remind them of their value. "Please call as soon as you get there. Tell me you are safe and sound."

"We will," Jocelyn says.

He thinks he should say something else but doesn't. He can see the tears starting in her eyes.

CHAPTER THIRTY-EIGHT

JOCELYN

1

SHE HAS PACKED CAREFULLY. SHE HAS REMEMBERED THE NECESSARY things. The plane ride goes well. No turbulence. She uses the time to feel her life. Lucy colors in an Alice in Wonderland coloring book that keeps her occupied. The White Rabbit is not white. It is pink eyed and colorful. Later she plays with her figurines, entranced by her imagined world.

Jocelyn keeps her eyes on her daughter, tries to feel her without putting her hands on her. She traces the straight little nose, the tiny fingers, the lips. She has never loved as deeply as she has loved this child. The pilot announces their descent.

"Hold Mama's hand," Jocelyn says. "I'm scared."

"Are we here?" her daughter asks. "Cincinnati?"

"Kentucky," Jocelyn says. "In just a few minutes and then across the bridge. But yes."

She kisses her daughter's forehead. "You are the best traveler, Lamb."

"Let's call Papa when we get on the ground," Lucy says, unmoved by Jocelyn's compliment.

"Yes," Jocelyn says. "Let's."

———

THEY RENT A LUXURY CAR AT THE AIRPORT. THERE IS A CONVERTIBLE TOP. It takes thirty minutes from CVG, but the bridge waits for her—a patient friend, inevitable. She remembers so much of her child life as they drive the rental car through Covington. It is a little bit cool. There will be a light ribbon of fog on the water. She sees her small self, her sister, her brother. She sees the debt she owes for all the things she has denied and looked away from. No happy ending, no allowances made. There has always been this lurking. She is what she has always been. She is the suffocation. There is no escape.

She hears Lucy chattering on the phone with her father, but it is not enough to save her, to clean her. Conrad's warm back, holding on to him. It just won't do.

The voice is there. Louder in her home city than before. The tiny ticking treble of it. There is Gladys as there always is. A bunk bed slat. The wood board against Ycidra's forehead. The rooms in Winton Terrace, the air saturated with begging. *Please, Please.*

She pushes harder against the gas pedal, trying to press the memories away. The car surges through Kentucky, the top of the state, the base of Ohio. She has forgotten what woods are, what green is, having lived so long in what is essentially desert. *Blood will out*, Gladys says, speaking to her. *Trash will stay trash.*

As the four lanes of traffic merge onto the bridge, there is a bit of a backup, but the traffic here is nothing like the traffic in Los Angeles. At the entrance to the bridge, she sees a group of tourists walking. She sees benches, a homeless camp, a small tent in the park. There are two young people asleep outside it, their bodies leaning into each other. Heroin, she knows, the red, red hands and feet of Ycidra. There are people rubbernecking.

She looks ahead at the car in front of her. An arm shoots out of the car window and dumps ice from a cup onto the road. She slowly rolls her car forward, sees a dog sleeping, just at the bottom of a city parking sign. A heavy chain around its neck. Too heavy for such a small living thing. *Lion, Simon*, Jocelyn thinks, and then looks away.

She tries to follow the overhead signs into the city. It's been a long time though. She tells Lucy to hurry up with her phone. She doesn't want to miss her exit.

"Mama needs the GPS," she hears her daughter say, and then, "Yes, Papa. Of course, we miss you."

Jocelyn reaches to take the phone from her daughter. She loses sight of the road in front of her for just an instant, and when she turns back, the car ahead of her has stopped. She slams on the brakes to avoid hitting it. Her daughter sits forward, looking. A picture unfolding. The long body of a young woman in jeans, leaning into the car in front of them. A prostitute, Jocelyn knows. Quite pretty, she thinks. The hair is too shiny, too well done. A wig, Jocelyn realizes. Shoulders a bit broad, a swimmer's body? A woman? Jocelyn wonders suddenly. Not a woman, a voice inside her says.

The car in front of them moves away. The negotiation is over. No takers. Jocelyn watches as the prostitute walks slowly and carefully in front of their rental car—narrow hips swaying, lots of confidence. A horn behind Jocelyn sounds. The red heels don't quicken. The shoes are huge. What size could they be? What would they go to in men's sizes?

The head finally turns when more horns chime in. The man (no woman) looks back, catches Jocelyn's eye. She knows me, Jocelyn thinks. She knows what it is to be both—to realize that the person who isn't you, *is* you. Another horn sounds, and another. Jocelyn keeps looking, watches as the prostitute carefully and confidently lifts a middle finger. Jocelyn laughs, feels the sharp ping of pity and respect. The red nails are like fire.

Blood will out, Gladys's voice says again, and it is, she knows, a relentless lesson. *I couldn't become anything else*, she whispers. *I couldn't lift me out.*

SMALE PARK IS NEW. IT IS ON THE EDGE OF THE OHIO RIVER. A PLAQUE on the river walk says that it was built with money left to the city by a successful P&G businessman. It is part of the gentrification of downtown, of Over the Rhine, or the OTR as the modern signs call it. She had hoped the bridge and the park would be a bit more crowded. She had hoped to get lost in a crowd. She and Lucy dip their toes into the splash pad. There is the squeal of her daughter. A sound she loves. She is aware of time passing. Aware of losing her nerve. She cannot wait forever, although a part of her asks why not. She reminds herself that she is always weak, always uncertain. She is stern with herself, knowing that when she has a clear mind, there is only one choice.

Her daughter has the loveliest hair, sunlight lives inside it. At each turn of her tiny, perfect body, it seems to dance and glow.

"Let's go on the carousel again, Mama," Lucy says.

"Okay," Jocelyn says. They've gone five times.

It must be a perfect day. Anything her daughter wants. A trade: what Lucy wants, and then finally what Jocelyn wants. "How about we go for a walk after this? And then up to the bridge."

She watches Lucy look. She has told her daughter the plan. She has explained the ultimate jump—like the club, she says. We are mermaids. She has waited until they are alone and away.

"It's super high," her daughter says. "Do you think we can do it?"

"We're super brave," Jocelyn says, trying to seem assured. "It's how we'll earn our tails."

She can feel the sweat dripping down her back as they walk away from the carousel to the car. She will retrieve the carrier—the Ergo—the warm padded cotton of it, the safety clips. She has held her child in it since the day she was born—body to body, skin to skin. They will go to the car and drive to the Covington side of the Roebling Suspension Bridge. She has looked it up online, and foot traffic is easier from there. She must fall headfirst. Make certain of the outcome. Her phone rings. It is Simon again. Simon. Four missed calls. She has texted that they are well, but there must be something inside him that senses it isn't true.

"Let's swing," Lucy says. "Before we go to the bridge. We haven't tried these swings."

"Yes, my lambchop. Let's. Let's swing."

When they've finished, Jocelyn leaves the phone there. Again a buzzing, real or imagined, but still, they walk to the car.

When they are almost to the rental, she looks back at the water. Lucy looks too.

"This is the Ohio River, Lucy. It's different than where we live with Papa. In the Palisades, it's the sea. I never saw the sea until I was a grown woman. When I saw the ocean for the first time, I was happy, because I knew there were so many things in the world still to see. So much that I could still know. You can't imagine how much I love it."

"Do you love it more than me?" Lucy asks. Everything is always a competition.

"I don't love anything more than you," Jocelyn says simply.

"Not even Papa?"

Jocelyn can feel her voice catch. The answer is always the same.

She squeezes her daughter's hand tightly. Pulls her closer. "I'd sell Papa down the river in a heartbeat for you."

"What river?" Lucy asks, playing her part.

And this time Jocelyn points at it. "The Ohio, my love."

She stands with her daughter, wondering if she is making a mistake. This time in front of the rental car's back door.

"Let me help you with your seat belt, sweetheart," she says.

"I don't need help," Lucy says. "I can do my seat belt my own self."

"I'd like to help," Jocelyn says.

She wants to pull the belt slowly and safely across her child. She wants to touch her knees, her little arms. She wants to push the sun-filled hair behind her ears. Tap the straight little nose that only Jocelyn knows she has inherited from her sister, Ycidra.

"No way," Lucy says. "I'm big. Go away, Mama."

"I love you Lucy," Jocelyn says, settling for opening the door for her child.

And with a brightness that is unusual for the very serious, unaffected child, Lucy says, "I love you too, Mama. I love you too."

THE BRIDGE WHEN THEY GET BACK TO IT IS STILL NOT CROWDED. THERE IS a barrier when they first begin to walk, which makes Jocelyn panic. She hasn't thought of this. Online, the bridge looked open. As a child, there was nothing there. Nothing but the sound that the bridge made, and this memory tackles her, because it is here now, as it was then. The cars humming over it. Her sister's voice. *Listen, Jo-Jo. The bridge sings.*

As they walk along though, the barrier disappears. There is just a railing, waist high, no longer a cage. There is a perfect view, a perfect drop into the river below.

She bends down, looks into her daughter's dark brown eyes.

"You are the best daughter anyone could ever have. Do you know that?"

Lucy looks at the river. "I'm a little scared, Mama."

"Don't be scared, sweetie. It's an adventure, remember? Like I told you. Just like at the pool."

"It's bigger than the pool and there's no board."

"You're right," Jocelyn says, sensing that disagreement won't work. "We're mermaids, though, remember? Remember Mama's back, the marks. I'm going to hold you. You'll be in the carrier."

The child says nothing.

"Have I ever dropped you?"

"No, Mama."

"We love it at the pool, right?"

"Yes, Mama."

"I could never ever hurt you, Lucy. As soon as we hit the water, we'll have tails."

The child peers over the edge. She is sizing it up, deciding. "Just hold me tight, okay?" she says at last. "Will the air be like cotton balls?"

"Absolutely," Jocelyn says.

When she picks up her daughter she holds her hard and firm against her chest. She presses her face into her breasts, remembering how she fed her, how she was able to do every single thing for her, except this one thing.

"Don't look," Jocelyn says. "Don't look down when we go, okay?"

"Okay," Lucy says. "I won't look. I won't look."

Lucy snuggles into her. Jocelyn wants to feel every part of her girl, smell her, crush her even, press her body back inside her own, place her back inside her belly. She smells the hair that reeks of baby shampoo and sweat. She lifts the cotton back of the Ergo, wrapping her daughter in it. She lifts the straps, one over each shoulder. She clicks the clasps closed behind her own neck, making sure all of it is tight.

"Hold on to me now, Lucy. You hold Mama as tightly as you can. Even though you're in the carrier, I want you to hold on to me, so I can get onto the rail. And when I get my balance, I'll put my arms around you again."

The child does as she is told. Jocelyn can feel the little heart beating. She can sense the child's fear. She lifts herself onto the edge of the railing slowly, drapes one leg over, and then another, slowly, slowly. She grips the top rail tightly, finally finds her balance, teetering a bit. She remembers climbing fences as a child—the blinding metal, hot in the summertime, the urge to slip forward as much as back once she reached the top.

Lucy begins whispering. A small sound. Jocelyn cannot understand the words, doesn't try to. A mantra, like a confession, quiet as a prayer. Jocelyn wishes she could sit for a while but knows there are cameras, does not want to torture her daughter. She is aware that she has very little time. She wants to hold her child in these last moments, feel the river breeze that she grew up with, but there is movement in her peripheral vision. Someone coming.

She holds tight to Lucy with one arm, tight to the top rail with the other hand. She will have to jump away from the railing. She will have to balance on the edge for a few minutes and then jump out far enough. She doesn't want to bump her head on the bridge wall.

"Miss?" she hears, a male voice, invading. It is a few feet away now, but still far enough. She does not look toward the voice, keeps her eyes on the water.

"Ready?" she says to Lucy. "Don't open your eyes."

"Miss?" she hears again, more insistently. A slow walk toward her. Afraid to startle. There is the edge of confusion in the voice. Hesitation. *I can be stronger than he*, she thinks. *This time I will be.*

"I'm afraid, Mama," Lucy says. "I'm afraid."

A pause then. A stutter in Jocelyn's intentions. A need to explain. "Don't be afraid, baby. I've got you." She tightens her grip around her daughter. "Miss?" she hears again. "We're mermaids. Remember? Mama and the fisherman and his net. I've got you."

The whispering begins again from Lucy's little mouth, so fast. Sounds running together, desperate. A bit louder now. Words merging. "Please, Mama. Please. Don't jump, Mama. Please!"

The little hands are in the fabric of her shirt and are gently plucking, but it is a child's T-shirt now in Jocelyn's mind, and she feels the dried blood against her own shoulders, pulling away from her skin.

"It's okay," Jocelyn says to her daughter. "It's okay." *Don't listen,* she tells herself. *Don't listen. Do what you must.*

"Please don't, Mama!" Lucy says again. And Jocelyn wishes she could cover her own ears, but she can't let go of the rail, and she can't let go of her daughter. Not yet, not at all, and the voice will not relent. And it is Ycidra. And it is William. And it is herself. *Please, Mama. Please, Mama. Don't!* And the tears prick. And her own heart is like a weight in her chest.

"Miss?"

"Don't," Jocelyn says. Just one word to him, because he is close enough for her to see his eyes now. The eyes that are made up to be smoky and the wave of the fake hair—the curl. They called it feathered, a Farrah Fawcett hairstyle, but not Farrah Fawcett—a poster on Ycidra's wall. A hairstyle they could not accomplish. Farrah Fawcett was blonde. She was blonde, Jocelyn says to herself, and that sort of rights her. The blending of the past, and the now, and a man who is also a woman, and the thin waist, but the broad shoulders: *I know any black girl,* she remembers saying, joking with her sister. *No matter how white she is. You can tell he's a man by his feet,* her brother said. *The Metro.* William, at the bar, braiding someone's hair. A man's. *Isn't she beautiful?* he asked her. She was solidly confused. There are so many, many of us. If only I could not see.

"Miss?" she hears again, and she knows she has to jump. She can feel the heat of the man's body. Will she be able to? Maybe she shouldn't? Will it be like the phone, the pajamas, the doubt? Forty years ago, she could have stopped it. You shouldn't have been put in the position, she hears Dr. Bruce saying. Act now, she says to herself. Act now!

"Miss?" she hears again. A step toward her, a finger light on the small of her back. And in just that moment, she lets go of the rail, and she is not sure if she has done it, or if the man has pushed her, and she feels the drop and the panic and a tick of regret for having done it, and then the surprising painful pull and stop, the stretch of the fabric and the press of her daughter's body against her chest, so tight that she thinks her ribs might break, a hand in her own hair suddenly, pain, close to the scalp and holding, and a swinging—the clutch of fingers, a strong grip around the Ergo's straps, knuckles in her back. A man's grip. A woman couldn't do it.

She holds tight to her daughter, not wanting her to tip out of the carrier, to go down to the water below without her. The screams of her daughter are so loud. And then the voice that is this man's voice, shouting, begging. "Help!" Panic. "Somebody please! Help me!"

IT TAKES MANY HANDS AND ARMS AND MEN TO LIFT THEM BACK OVER THE railing. They are dropped, the three of them, onto the safe side of the bridge like a pile of laundry. The man who has saved the two of them is on his back breathing heavily. His makeup is smudged. He is gripping and rubbing the hands that kept them in this life. A heel from his red shoe has broken off and looks wicked against the stone walkway.

Jocelyn is aware of people around her, trying to get Lucy off her chest, trying to release her from the Ergo. She kicks at them, shouts for them to get away. Lucy is crying—a continuous wail. They all stand around her staring. Fear in their eyes more than anything else. One of the women is on her cell phone, calling, Jocelyn knows, 911. Her daughter presses her face against Jocelyn's chest. Jocelyn pulls the little hood of the Ergo over her daughter's head, giving her privacy.

"I'm sorry, Mama," she says. Little gasps of breath interrupt the words. "I don't want to be a mermaid. Please don't make me. I want my papa."

Jocelyn stills her own body against the ground. She holds her daughter, soothing her as she cries. *I have made my daughter afraid of me*, she thinks. *I have done what I said I wouldn't do.* Gladys. *I have been like Gladys.*

"It's okay, honey," she says and pats the small back. "Shh. Shh. Shh." In rhythm. "It's okay."

She is bouncing Lucy now, as she did when she was a baby on her chest. Nothing else is on her mind but her child and her own failure.

"It's okay," she says. She strokes the golden-brown hair. "We won't go," she says. "It's okay. Mama is so sorry."

SHE TURNS HER HEAD TO THE SIDE, AND THE MAN WHO HAS HOOKED them, snagged them back into the now, his hands under the strap, tight around her hair, clenched, has started crying. Horrible rushing tears. His face is dirty, his smoky eyes are smeared, his wig has fallen off somewhere, and all that remains is a stocking cap. She thinks for a second that this is a shame she has brought to him. She has made him ugly. She has not meant to do this. She is sorry.

"I couldn't let you go," he says to her in a loud whisper that only she can hear above the crowd of gossipy voices. "You weren't going to make me see you falling for the rest of my life."

He stares at her, breathing quickly. He is angry at her, she realizes. Spittle flies in the small space between them. "There was no fucking way," he says again sharply. "I was not going to let you do that to me."

"I want my papa," Lucy says, interrupting the man. "Make that man stop talking, Mama. Make him stop talking to us."

Jocelyn hears the sirens in the distance. She knows they are for her. When they ask her whom to call, where home is, she is surprised when she says Simon.

HOURS LATER, CONRAD AND SIMON COME IN SIMON'S PLANE. CONRAD IS raging. He threatens her. *You will never go near my daughter.* He says that to her, as if it were true: *my* daughter. Only when they've been in the air for almost an hour, only when Lucy begs her father to let her go to Jocelyn, does he relent, allowing the girl to climb up onto Jocelyn's lap, onto the fine leather seat, to be held. Lucy falls asleep almost immediately. Jocelyn watches the small chest move up and down, the smallest snore. She kisses the cheeks, sings a quiet song. She doesn't care about her husband. She doesn't look at him. She looks out the window. She contemplates telling him to fuck off. She imagines tearing his eyes out, beating him down. *No one will take my child from me*, she says inside.

And all the things she has lived through, everything that she has survived, comes to her now. Lucy is as old as I was, she realizes. I was she, in front of the black phone in my yellow pajamas, calling who? Ah, my little lamb, she says to her younger self. There was no one to call for help.

Simon reaches for her. He just touches and then holds the hem of her shirt. He knows not to invade her body. She sees his beautiful brown hand. His urge to pull him to her.

They take her directly to the "treatment facility." It's a psychiatric hospital, although no one calls it that, and no one except Simon and Conrad's family knows she is there: Malibu Gardens.

They bathe her, sedate her, and then tuck her in. Conrad leaves with Lucy almost immediately, but Simon stays, making sure she is all right.

When they put her in her bed, there is no hospital gown, no nurse in a uniform. A helper is provided, warm pajamas, a cup of pills. There is a view of the ocean. There are grounds. They mean to make the place feel like home.

"He can't take away my daughter," Jocelyn says to Simon, because it is all that matters.

"Rest," he says. "I will stay with you. Don't worry. We will work it out."

CHAPTER THIRTY-NINE

SIMON

1

HE LEAVES HER SLEEPING AT MIDNIGHT. THE NURSE TELLS HER THEY WILL call him as soon as she wakes.

"As soon as she wakes," he says, reiterating. "I am coming any time. I do not want her to be alone."

He drives through Las Virgenes Canyon, ending at the ocean. He makes a left onto PCH, feeling his way home. When he gets to the condo, he goes directly to her unit. He knocks on the door, not caring about waking Lucy. He knows what is important.

Conrad answers the door immediately, seems confused by the visit at this late hour, but Simon knows he's been up—the dark circles, the drawn face, the speed with which he's opened the door.

"May I come in?" he asks quietly. Conrad opens the door wider.

They sit, as Conrad suggests, on the balcony, in order to not make noise. His mother is there, he explains, and Lucy is sleeping finally.

"She had a difficult time falling asleep," he says, looking out at the ocean. "She is used to being with Jocelyn."

They sit in silence, and then Conrad offers drinks. A cognac—warmed in a steamed glass.

"Thank you for the plane," he says.

"It's the least I could do," Simon answers.

"I couldn't leave her there. When we were younger we went there once, to confront her mother. She threw up in a bag on the drive. She was so afraid. I couldn't leave her in that city."

Simon thinks of Cincinnati, the green of Jocelyn's hometown. Just as she said. Nothing much but the river. Nothing much but the beautiful bridge. He was not afraid this time. Not on takeoff and not on landing. She was his project. She was the only thing.

He takes a deep breath. "I will tell you a story and then I will leave. I would like very much if you would not interrupt. It is the least you can do."

"Okay," Conrad says, drinking his drink.

And in the dark night, above the dark, rumbling sea, Simon tells the story of being unable to protect his wife, his daughter, about the realization of helplessness, of powerlessness, about his acceptance of it all—how small one can be, how quickly one can be reduced to almost nothing.

"You are their protector," he says. "I know you are afraid. You think you are angry, but you are scared. You can save both of them. Don't be like me. A child must have its mother. A woman is the foundation of the family."

Conrad's head lowers, the crying starts. It is a huffing sound, like the chugging of a train.

It goes on and on.

"Lucy cannot thrive without Jocelyn," Simon says. "If you love your daughter, you will protect her mother."

THEY ARRANGE FOR A NANNY AND NURSE TWENTY-FOUR HOURS A DAY when Jocelyn comes home. There is a confidentiality agreement, because that is what important families do. There is an outpatient facility in Santa Monica—twenty hours a week for therapy. It is like a part-time job for Jocelyn.

The days pass, and Jocelyn gets better. The medicine helps. The nanny is required to watch her take it. Simon and she and Lucy and the ever-present nanny spend their time together walking Lion, getting ice cream, playing at the park. Simon has taken a leave of absence, awaiting the birth of his grandchild, so all of them have more time together. Conrad joins them on some of their outings. He is tentative with his wife and sometimes even bitter. When he is intolerant, or tries to pull his power, Simon tells him to be patient. He reminds Conrad of his fear, he recalls certain parts of his own story. *You have seen nothing*, he says. He listens to Conrad's still-present resentment, and then he reminds Conrad of his own net worth.

"You don't want to make this a custody battle," he says, when Conrad implies that he might take Lucy. "It will be long and expensive. I am a very wealthy man."

Conrad stares at him as if they are strangers, and then laughs. Two worthy warriors in an uncertain alliance, always moments from a kill.

CHAPTER FORTY

JOCELYN

1

JOCELYN SLEEPS IN HER DAUGHTER'S ROOM. SHE DOES NOT KNOW HOW TO be with her husband, but mothering is something *inside* like her lungs or her heart; it has not left her. Her days are less antagonistic now, the images are softer, the merging less painful. The medicine takes the edge off.

As they build a Lego house, she tells her daughter about Ycidra, the good parts of her sister.

"I want a sister," Lucy says. "Can you get me a sister? I'll take care of her, Mama. You just have to get her."

When they walk along the path at Will Rogers beach, Jocelyn does not resist when a song, taught to her by her brother, compels her to sing: "Poor Jenny. Bright as a penny."

Lucy giggles at the silly verses. A cartwheel then, a leap in the air, a flit off to the water.

The past is not the past, Jocelyn thinks. She is sure of this. It is the same as today and different, a hand that tips forward and pulls back. Like a river to the sea, two separate bodies of water, and yet indivisible, constant.

Don't think about it, she tells herself. *Look at the surfers in front of you, at your daughter pulling off her silver sequined shoes.*

"Sing, Mama!" Lucy shouts, placing the shoes in the sand beside her. "The satins and furs part, Mama. Again, Mama."

Jocelyn's heart lurches, remembering the *Again, Mama* of the diving board, remembering the bridge and Lucy's fear. A tick of regret. *That is all I will allow myself to think about. I will not wonder if my daughter will forget. I wished, I did, for a second, to live.*

She feels her anxiety heighten at the thought. Her new Santa Monica psychiatrist says to take one step at a time, to not let her mind spin. She practices now. There, right there, is the blue of the sea, the blue of the sky, her husband's blue eyes, searching. He cannot see what they are to each other anymore. She cannot either, but she senses that she should not let go of him. She did not let go of Lucy on the bridge. Not once.

She scolds herself. So hard to undo what one is. She draws herself back. Try again.

What is just here? See what's right now. Look: There is my bossy girl. A wave, larger than expected, the skinny legs, pedaling backward, fast. Jocelyn watches as her daughter's silver shoes get swept away as the wave recedes.

"Mama!" Lucy shrieks, pointing after them. "Mama. Get my shoes!"

Jocelyn is already after them though. She does not need to be told.

We are here. Still. Now.

CHAPTER FORTY-ONE

CLAUDETTE

1

ON THE NIGHT THAT HER SON, PHILIP, IS BORN, SHE FINALLY HAS THE
nerve to ask him. He is there, at the hospital as fathers are, even
when they aren't really fathers.

The baby is almost purple, mottled looking, eight pounds,
ten ounces, against the odds. His skin is soft like overripe fruit.
Having a baby makes her brave.

"Why?" she asks, feeling only a little uncertain. "That's the
part I can't understand. Why would you give me away? I could
never give my child away. I'd rather die together."

She looks at her tiny boy. "Was it because of the war? Did you
know my parents were coming to the States?"

His face turns almost gray. She has not seen him look this
way before. Not in any of the brief meetings they've had. She feels
afraid of him suddenly. Feels the fact that he is, after all, a stranger.
She pulls Philip into her. She waits. She wants to know her story.

CHAPTER FORTY-TWO

SIMON

1

HE KNOWS NOW, BECAUSE HE HAS LIVED THROUGH THE DEEPEST LOSS, through the worst of humankind, that he cannot explain to his daughter that the thing that Abrahm did was not a rescue. Her American self—and that is what she is, what he sees before him—cannot fathom the truth.

He cannot tell her that there were thousands of Tutsi children, just like her, who needed to be saved, and almost none of them were saved. Almost none of them were mixed into Hutu families. Instead these children were cut and starved. Where was all the mama kindness? Where the mother love? A woman is not a woman in war. A man is not a man. She can never understand.

If he tells her the truth, he will have to explain that taking her from him was an act of hatred, a hatred that was coddled and nurtured over many generations. It simmered next to the skin and ended with Abrahm's final wish to harm him.

He wanted me to see. He wanted me to wonder. He wanted me alive and Vestine dead. Your mother could not live without you. He skipped me, so I could see her suffer, knowing someone would come for her and for me after. Even now, Simon can see his wife running. Running from him. Everyone dead so fast. Speed and efficiency, the American president said, as if he were discussing the space program.

He clears his throat. He has organized the story. He has predicted the question. He has lifted some of its mythology from an Internet story that is presently being circulated: "The Saviors of the Rwandan Genocide." The theme: *We will never forget.*

I would forget, he wants to say to her, say to the writer of the Internet article. *If I could forget, I would.*

The baby sleeps against her. The room is sterile and cold. The baby breathing there, a chirping sound from its tiny lips, allows him to go on. And so he speaks:

"Abrahm's brother was a famous soccer player. You do not know this, but soccer is like a religion in Kigali."

The lie comes more easily than he has expected.

"There was the opportunity to leave. The conversation. Well, to save you. They had had a child, a daughter, she died. From malaria. It is not uncommon in Africa. The switching of identity cards was not a difficult thing."

He pauses. The last lie not really making sense, but he figures she will believe what she wants. Most people do.

He waits a beat, wanting the rhythm of the story to be just right. As if the details were coming to him from old memories.

"He could not save your mother. Or me. Only a white man could save me. Or God."

He laughs. He pauses. He prays she will not ask. "I will tell you that story a different day."

As he continues, he can see her relaxing into it, finding the fairy tale. What good would it do to speak of her dying mother? The way it felt to have her child body drawn out of his arms. How it was to wake and find his wife raped. The screams of other women in the swamps day after day after day. His mother and her limbs cut off. It is hardest on women in war. Men are just killed.

"He came to us. Made the offer. We were lifelong best friends.

A favor, but you had to go that day. We had no time to think about it." He can feel his voice breaking. He has to force himself. *Look at the baby. Look at your grandson.*

"Wow," she says, a slight smile on her face. "That must have been dangerous for my father." And, as if it were an afterthought, "And for you."

"Yes," is all Simon can make himself say.

"I can't believe it," she says. "It's almost heroic. Like a movie."

And in her face, there is gratitude and pride, and he can see her as she must have looked when she was Abrahm's little girl, and he can also see how much she loves Abrahm, and he is both envious and understanding, because he has loved Abrahm too. And he is grateful, in the way that he has learned to be grateful, for the smallest crumbs, for a day without tears, for the Twa disappearing from his living room from time to time.

He knows that it is all dirt off the sole of a boot, but he will take it, because his friend and her child are still alive, and his long-lost daughter is alive, and they have all found him, and there is tomorrow, and tomorrow, and tomorrow.

"Yes," he says. "Very heroic," but then he starts laughing.

In her face, a tinge of indignation. "What is it?" she asks. A small blush runs across her cheek. Anger? They are uneasy with each other.

"Nothing," he says. *I am crazy. I am trying. I am always just barely surviving,* he wants to say. But instead he says, "Just a silly joke me and your father used to tell. I cannot translate it into English."

She lifts the baby, looks at it lovingly. She is trusting him a bit more.

"Do you remember any of Africa?" he asks her, meaning, *Do you remember any of your mother?*

"No," she says. "My parents never wanted to talk about it, so I don't even have their memories."

"I understand why they wouldn't," he says. And he does understand, and in that moment, there is common ground again between him and Abrahm.

"Can you do me a favor?" she asks, out of the blue. A dimple, one he has forgotten about, presents itself on her cheek.

"Yes," he says. "Anything."

"Can you get me a cannoli?"

"A what?" he asks.

"It's a dessert," she says. "I'm dying for it. I'm usually not very hungry, but I don't know. Maybe it's the baby. The hormones. You can get yourself one too. You'll like it. Do you like sweets?" she asks.

"Yes," he says.

"Mike's Pastry," she says. "It's just a few blocks away. Some people like Modern, but I prefer Mike's. It's cash only. Do you have any cash?"

And she is chattering and blathering on as she did when she was a small child, only now in English, and about flavors and sweets, Florentine and traditional, powdered sugar or not, but there is some of the same rhythm in her speech, and his heart pounds when he thinks: We are, at our essence, always the same. We are! We are! The same inside as we were before, and this thought heartens him.

My child, he reminds himself. *My grandchild*, he thinks, looking at the tiny baby in her arms. He does not allow himself to think of Vestine. *I am the one left. No. We are the ones left.* And this time, he finds the joy.

As HE MAKES HIS WAY BACK FROM THE PASTRY SHOP, HE FEELS CERTAIN HE has made the right decision. The lie is right. The truth is wrong. Our story will begin right now. He has expanded his family. He has gathered them, as Abrahm and he once gathered banana leaves. The almost loss of Jocelyn and Lucy has made him clear about so many things, about what can be done, about what can't, the weight and value of people, another human being's fragility. He knows that there is not a way to tell the true story, so he cannot tell it.

The box in his hand is full. The smell of the pastries is sweet. He has bought an extra one for Lion, who waits for him at the Royal Sonesta, asleep in the hotel bed. *A dog in my bed? How can I call myself African?*

He has not been silent this time. He has told a story. A story that will allow his daughter's life, his grandson's life, to go. Lucy and Jocelyn are safe. *Oh, what a large family I have!* He presses the Walk button. He walks.

ACKNOWLEDGMENTS

I AM MOST GRATEFUL TO JOHN BERAN, MY HUSBAND, MY WRITING PART-ner, and my very best friend. We have almost reached that perfect middle where I have been in this world, in love with him, longer than I have been in the world without him. All this time spent together, and our wonderful marriage, makes me a very lucky woman.

I am deeply indebted to my editor, Amber Oliver, for her flex-ibility, understanding, and vision. Thank you for taking a chance on a debut writer. I appreciate the hard work that she and every-one else at Harper Perennial did to make this book exist in the world.

My writing life is less lonely because of the writers and friends that have supported me, especially Dana Marterella for never, ever, being judgmental, and for talking me and this book down from the ledge more than a time or two; Theresa Heim for sharing her own work with me, and for being a careful reader of all my work from the very beginning; Chieh Chieng and Lance Uyeda for their belief in my writing when my own confidence waned. Thank you to Jill Smith, who taught me the kindness of strangers. Our abiding friendship started with a starving dog on the side of the road. Thanks to Yoshiun Wong for sticking with me, on and off, the tennis court. Thank you to Michelle Latiolais for introducing me to all sorts of unique fiction.

All my love to my family, especially my sister, Tracey Montilla, who has always picked up the phone for me, has always had the answers to most of my questions, and, most importantly, has always taken care of me as only big sisters can; my mother, Anneliese Jaensch, who taught me to value books and stories, using her own stories to teach me about my Oma and Opa, the war, and where I come from. Thank you to my father, Charles Page, who has always known I could do it and is not averse to claiming genetic responsibility for my talent. Also, much love to my husband's parents, Marilyn and David Beran—the best in-laws in the world.

Like many mothers, my biggest blessings are my two fabulous daughters, who keep me young, and happy, and inspired. Thank you to my eldest, La La, who teaches me what brave is, and what kind is, and who was absolutely meant to be mine. Kisses to my youngest, Izzy Bee, who is smart and serious and sweet. I hope she will forgive me for putting Goo Bob Beran in the book.

Almost last, but definitely not least, this book is immeasurably better because of my brilliant, generous, half-therapist, half-agent, and whole friend, Laura Usselman, who has shepherded this book from the start. She has gently pressed me to keep improving the book without making me give up my intentions for it. She is my ultimate reader and absolutely crucial to my process.

Although my brother, Ricky, is not in this world anymore, I am grateful and honored to have been his little sister. Each happy space is tainted by the absence of him—even this one. But the Kurt Weill in these pages is us, and something he taught me, and I love it, and miss hearing him play it, and of course, I also miss him.

About the author

About the book

Insights,
Interviews
& More . . .

Meet Robin Page

by John Beran

ROBIN PAGE WAS raised in Cincinnati, Ohio, and has degrees from UCLA and University of California, Irvine's MFA program. She is married, has two daughters, and lives in Los Angeles. She has powerfully mined her experience as a transplanted midwesterner, a woman of color, and a mother in these pages. ❧

Q&A WITH ROBIN PAGE

1. What was your writing process like for Small Silent Things?

Because this story has three separate narrators, I had to find a way to organize them. I had separate, compartmentalized passes early on: one for the story, then another for the theme of resilience, and then one for the theme of damage. I always use index cards and put lists on my wall to remind me of what my intentions are for the characters. I also listen to music, especially when I get stuck. It can bring me to a character's emotional state, and it gets me in the mood to write. I have a musical history that relates to my childhood, my family background, my neighborhood, and my characters do too. A song can bring me back to a moment in time, and I remember *that* party, *that* car ride, *those* friends, because of the music. I listen to a different set of songs and genres for each character.

2. What real life experiences did you draw from in order to write this book?

I am a mother of a daughter under ten, and I also have an older daughter. Love and exhaustion are ever present emotions in my life. A mother is protective, caring, worried, afraid, thrilled, overwhelmed, invested, frustrated, angry, happy, helpless, and a million other emotions in relation to her children, AND a human being that carries her own burdens. This is problematic and amazing. Jocelyn allows me to explore some of the emotional complexities of that role, while Simon and Claudette allow me to explore family. What is a family? How do we identify ourselves? What is the impact of family secrets? What is the importance or insignificance of biology? Can we create our own families? Can we release our biology? My older daughter is adopted, and so these questions intrigue me.

I'd also say the loss of my brother to AIDS, and the grief that I carry because of that, informs the novel. Jocelyn's story is not a parallel to mine, but the seeds of the things I've experienced ▶

allow me to begin creating her, and then she takes on a life of her own. In this same way playing ladies tennis helps me to create Jocelyn's social life. Tennis in the real world has everything in it—racism, classism, sexism, bias against difference, friendship, infidelity, health, competition, so it's a very fertile world to explore in fiction.

3. How did you decide on the two central characters, Jocelyn and Simon? And why do you think they needed each other in their lives?

I was very intentional about making Simon and Jocelyn very different from each other. Simon is perceived as an African American in the US, even though he is not that at all having lived his childhood and much of his adult life in Rwanda. He is not what he appears to be. A facade obscures his true past and true self. It's the same with Jocelyn. She is African American, but not exactly. She is a wealthy black woman in an upper-class neighborhood, but not exactly. All of the facades Jocelyn presents hide her true origins, her past abuse and poverty, her present grief, anxiety, and fear. The facade is armor, but the truth will find its way out. Of course, neither character is just their history, but the suppression of their histories is problematic for them, and ultimately one of the things they share.

4. You talk a bit here about serious topics such as mental health, trauma, HIV, among others. Why did you decide to write about these topics?

The older I get, the more I am surprised if someone I know is *not* having mental health issues. Mental health, trauma, HIV, abuse, are all things that get hidden, swept under the rug. Once you put a lid on them it is inevitable that they will explode and boil over in destructive ways. I did not seek help for my grief after my brother died. I just pushed forward. Many, many years later, when *I wasn't ex*pecting it, I had to deal with it, and other issues, or I was going to be flattened. Enduring doesn't work, and yet, we, as black women in particular, are taught to "take" what life gives us, to endure, to be resilient, and the consequence of this is a lack of practice in relation to acting (especially in our own defense). We also have this expectation of children—they are young, they'll get over whatever is done to them. I do not believe that, and it's important to me that we are serious about pain and its impact, so that we don't repeat damaging behavior. As a community we have to make it okay to seek mental health help. We have to acknowledge and respect another person's experience and support rather than shame them.

5. What do you want readers to take away from this book?

Most importantly, I'd like the reader to be in touch on an emotional level with Jocelyn and Simon and to feel empathy where they may not have felt it before. Is there anything in Jocelyn's story that will make the reader see a person with AIDS differently? Is there anything in Jocelyn's story that allows the reader to be more tolerant of someone who has survived abuse or is suffering with mental health issues? Is there a warning for us in Simon's Rwanda? The fiction I love makes me question the real world. I can enter and exit fictional experiences in a safer way than I can enter and exit real life, but nevertheless it informs my views. I'd like readers to walk away from this book seeing, even if just slightly, the real world a bit differently than before. ∽

A Behind the Book Essay on *Small Silent Things*

I'VE PLAYED TENNIS for many years and have watched a number of marriages fall apart around a fantasy relationship with the tennis pro. I wanted to write a literary "affair book" that really considers what might bring someone to adultery, and what the aftereffects were as well. Is it trauma? Is it middle age? Is it a need for something other than what a spouse can give? It was essential to me that the lovers have equal power (outwardly anyway), as opposed, for example, to a professor who has an affair with her student. I also wanted Jocelyn to have an essentially good marriage, one that was sexually passionate, so the answers to why she would choose something else would be less obvious. I had listened to Esther Perel quite a bit while writing, and her idea that "the most intoxicating 'other' that people discover in an affair is not a new partner; it's a new self" is very true for Jocelyn. Jocelyn needs anonymity, a place to hide, a place to look toward, so she doesn't have to look back. I'm also interested in the fluidity of sexuality, especially in women, so it made sense that it would be a lesbian affair.

My brother, like Jocelyn's, died of AIDS, and it altered my life permanently.

I am disturbed by the fact that women and children in our culture tend to be described as resilient. To be a "steel magnolia" (especially for black women), is considered to be a good thing. As I was writing, I wanted to challenge that. What really happens when women aren't taught to act against something, but instead are taught to endure? What happens when we keep silent when we should speak? Can friendship, especially between trauma survivors, change the future?

As a mother of a young child, I am always struggling with trying to protect my daughters, and so Jocelyn felt like someone I could write. As far as Simon's story goes, I have been interested in the Rwandan genocide for a long time, but more generally interested in wars between neighbors *and even friends*. Our political times are more divisive than ever, and I think we have to be aware of how dangerous it is for the "powers that be" to turn us against one another based on race, gender, sexuality, age, economics, or demographics. What happened in Rwanda can inform us of what could happen in our own country. I wanted Simon to be carrying all the things that had happened to him (and the same with Jocelyn and Claudette). I wanted to emphasize how the deep loss of his daughter and family has stayed with him over the years.

Some of the book's ideas about race come from my own life. I'm always trying to figure out what it is to be black, to be a woman, to be a mother, to be straight, especially in our unique American culture. Jocelyn's character was a way for me to question those terms. Simon is also trying to understand who he is—a longtime resident of America but without an American history. He cannot be the same person of color that Jocelyn is, and Jocelyn is not the same as Claudette, and so on. Claudette's story is an exploration of identity as well. Who is our family? How do we see ourselves when what we think is true about our genetics, isn't true?

I love to read, so I read a number of books while I was writing. Some of them were "affair" books like Ingeborg Day's *Nine and a Half Weeks*, which in novel form is absolutely different than the ▶

film. Others were about sexual abuse like Kathryn Harrison's *The Kiss*, and Alexandria Marzano-Lesnevich's *The Fact of a Body*. In relation to Rwanda, I mostly read books by Jean Hatzfeld, and, of course, Paul Gourevitch's *We Wish to Inform You That Tomorrow We Will be Killed with Our Families*. I tried to focus on the internal perspective of the survivors and perpetrators — the people. Hatzfeld's work has both the perpetrators' points of view and the victims' points of view. For me, it's essential to see the point of view of the perpetrator in order to not repeat the victimization. The fact that Simon and Abrahm are lifelong friends complicates our understanding of what it is to be enemies in a genocide.

Finally, as far as the setting for the book goes, I presently live in a small community that is very different, but very near, to the Palisades, so that coastal neighborhood was an easy choice for Jocelyn. I lived in Cambridge, Massachusetts, for two summers, and I thought it would work well for the academic Claudette. The book took me two to three years to write and I'm glad that it exists in the world for people to read. ∾